Chee Hong Young holds a doctorate in Chemical Engineering. He began his working career as a university lecturer and later spent twenty-four years in the petrochemical industry, where he started as an engineer and progressed to managing the development of multimillion dollar engineering projects.

In the process of juggling family commitments and working in highly dynamic and demanding environments, he could directly observe the effectiveness of applying the teachings of the Buddha in those contexts.

For Dearest Beautiful Cloud, Precious Jade and
Vigorous Courage.

Chee Hong Young

An Approach to Living and Joyful Growth

Austin Macauley
PUBLISHERS LTD.

A CIP catalogue record for this title is available from the British Library.

ISBN 9781785548475 (Paperback)
ISBN 9781785548482 (Hardback)
ISBN 9781785548499 (E-Book)

www.austinmacauley.com

First Published (2016)
Austin Macauley Publishers Ltd.
25 Canada Square
Canary Wharf
London
E14 5LQ

I bow with deepest gratitude to:

The Three Treasures (the Buddha, the *Dharma* and the *Sangha*) that are my refuges and the greatest blessings to the world.

My *Dharma* teachers, the accomplished translators and the scholars who have given me the highest gift of the *Dharma*.

My family, friends and fellow practitioners who have given me love, guidance, sustenance and support.

Contents

Preface

I had always wondered what my role in this life really is, and was unsure what this person called "me" is supposed to be doing in this world. It was when I studied the teachings of the Buddha, and started practising meditation while I was an undergraduate student, that I finally found a clearly marked out path of practice, which provided the meaningful answers.

After graduate studies and obtaining a doctorate in Chemical Engineering, I taught at a university for two years, before working for a multinational engineering company where I stayed for twenty-four years. I started my career there as an engineer, and ended with managing the development of multimillion dollar petrochemical and refining projects, where together with the emphasis on safety, controls compliance, and quality, the predominant focus was on timely and cost effective completion. Meanwhile, my family had grown with the addition of two lovely children.

In the process of juggling family commitments and working in highly dynamic and demanding environments, I could directly see first hand, the effectiveness of applying the teachings of the Buddha in those contexts. Having seen and experienced many missteps in my personal life and career, I had thought to offer my learnings here in the hope that they will be of use to another.

Introduction

To cursory onlookers, Buddhism may be perceived as the religion which teaches meditation, practised by monks in saffron robes. It appears to be perhaps escapist or negative in outlook. But if we draw the curtains and let in some light, it will become apparent that we have been carrying a misunderstanding of the teachings of the Buddha. If we delve a little bit deeper, we will see even more starkly the profundity of his teachings, and their relevance to this day and age.

What I have come to understand about Buddhism is that it provides a path of joyful exploration and discovery. The Buddha taught the path to awakening; how to get there and what we will need to have to get there. He left us detailed maps showing the different routes we can take, depending on our strengths and inclinations. There is the steep climb of intense meditation and self-relinquishment, if we have the stamina and strong determination, and there is also the more gradually sloping path of the cumulative cultivation of virtue, concentration and wisdom, if we prefer to pace ourselves.

Most of us may not have lofty aims like attaining the enlightenment of the Buddha for the benefit of all beings. We have our own fairly comfortable, sometimes worrisome, sometimes fun existence. Whatever our way of life, whatever our interests, we may have found that we are somewhat receptive to the teachings of the Buddha. Perhaps we have come to know about it as the path to freedom from distress, in the liberation of Nirvana. Perhaps we are receptive to the emphasis on kindness and compassion, or to the teachings on non-grasping and no-self, as opposed to the egoistic and individualistic culture around us. We may have felt that the teachings of the Buddha seemed to resonate with our own inner thoughts about what living a life of non-harming, or a meaningful life of developing our full potential, could be like.

The Buddha taught all who came to him: wanderers or seekers of truth, those who came to disparage him but ended up taking refuge in him, whole communities, courtesans, kings, farmers, fisherfolk, householders — in other words, all the different strata of society of his time. The Buddha, in reaching out to the community at large, formulated his teachings so all can derive benefit from it.

The practice of the *Dharma* (the Buddha's teachings) is positively transformative. When you sincerely practice the *Dharma*, your view of yourself and of the world will no longer be the same. You will be a much improved version of "yourself"; the new "you" will be steadier, wiser, happier, friendlier and more compassionate. You will be a more effective person; a better husband or wife, a better parent, a better brother or sister, a better friend, a better co-worker and a better member of humankind. You certainly will no longer be easily hoodwinked by the many distractions, or the encumbering superstitions that incessantly swirl like a dark haze around you.

This path of practice is a self trod path. We need to embark on the training and do it ourselves, for "the Buddhas only point the way". Treading the path is a commitment that calls for sincerity, discipline and perseverance. For those who have taken refuge in the Three Treasures (the Buddha, the *Dharma* and the *Sangha* — the community of those undertaking the training), practising the *Dharma* becomes

iv

affirmative and empowering. It leads to a transformation in ourselves, which is clearly apparent, and which affects our close ones and the community around us, in a very positive way.

In this book, the reader will find an interpretation of the Buddha's teachings that would have been helpful to be known upfront, in the development of an understanding of the *Dharma*. However, there may be other methods of practice or teachings of the Buddha, which at a certain stage of our practice, may be better suited to us. There will also be teachers who we, perhaps by karmic affinity, will meet on our way and at critical junctures in our practice, who will help with our awakening.

The practice of the *Dharma* will set us on the path to greater well-being. We will be led to explore our innermost thoughts and feelings, and gain a deep understanding of ourselves and others. We employ proven practices that restore the emotional balance within us. Living a lifestyle in accord with the *Dharma* helps us cultivate a positive mind-set, clear discernment, and gives us the strategies to better manage the many challenges arising from our work, family, and life relationships. This results in a firmly grounded sense of happiness. As we grow in the practice, this relatively coarse happiness will further develop into an equanimous state of mind. It then becomes a cooled and calmed happiness, a smoothed joyfulness that arises from the nature of deepening insight. If we do not grow in happiness and peacefulness with the practice of the *Dharma*, then for certain what is being practiced is not the *Dharma*.

The world in which we are now living is as it is, and we need not judge it. What we can directly experience right now, at this very moment, are ourselves. We know what it feels like to be happy, to suffer pain, to be calm or agitated, be loving or hateful, to feel restless, or to worry. No one needs tell us all this; we feel it intimately and we know these feelings directly. The Buddha tells us that how we feel and think, our tendencies, habits, and our perception of the phenomenal world, are all mind-made. We can, through cultivating our mind, change our destiny.

Quoting from the *Dhammapada* (a collection of verses spoken by the Buddha):

"Mind precedes all mental events.
They are led by mind, made by mind.
If one speaks or acts with a pure mind,
Happiness follows him like a shadow that never leaves."

The Buddha's *Dharma* is about the attainment of true ease, happiness, and freedom; by way of knowing the nature of things. It also leads us to fully develop our potential for compassion and wisdom. In so doing, we will be enlightening ourselves and will be of benefit to all beings. The path is neither difficult, nor is it easy. We do not need to saddle ourselves with these views. There is just the practice and the unfolding of goodness, joy, and inspired beauty from within us.

As one sees the profundity of the *Dharma*, so one sees the need to deepen one's understanding. As one sees the benefits it gives, so one feels deep gratitude and sees the need to share it, to alleviate the pain and suffering in this world. As one sees the clarity, directness, and beauty of the *Dharma*, so one wants to practice and demonstrate it, to bring happiness to all beings.

The Buddha's expression of his full enlightenment in the *Dharma* has been transmitted to us through the many schools and traditions. Though the *Dharma* has taken on the various guises of the different Buddhist traditions, it has but one aim; to lead us to the highest freedom. The sea has one taste, the taste of salt, so the Buddha says of his teaching; that it has the taste of freedom, of emancipation.

The number of approaches to the teaching of the *Dharma* and the way it can be made relevant to a particular culture, depend on the creativity and the skilful means employed by the enlightened masters. The Buddha sanctioned for the *Dharma* to be taught in the local vernacular, so it would be widely disseminated, available to all and not just to the cloistered few.

The emphasis in this book is on conveying to the reader the beauty of the *Dharma,* and how it can be an inspiration on the path to awakening. This is the sublime spirit of the *Dharma*, which points directly to that which is beyond mundane experience. It can imbue us with the certainty and the inspired vision necessary for us, the practitioner, to forge ahead.

I hope this book will benefit the reader, and aid him or her in the understanding, and in the practice, of the most excellent *Dharma*.

I bow with deep gratitude to the enlightened masters who have consoled us with their compassion and wisdom, and with deep humility to all beings. May all be well and happy! May all attain to the highest peace!

Explanatory notes:

* The pronouns "he" and "she" have been interchangeably to mean "she or he". This is only for brevity. No gender bias is intended.

** Unless the context of the sentence calls for the use of Pali, Sanskrit has been used throughout. So the Sanskrit "*Dharma*" rather than the Pali "*Dhamma*" is used to refer to the Buddha's teachings. An exception to this is the use of the Pali "*Sangha*" rather than the Sanskrit "*Samgha*", to denote the community of the followers of the Buddha, as it has seen much wider usage.

Chapter 1: A Framework for Understanding the *Dharma*

The Historical Buddha and His Legacy

The Way to Highest Bliss and Utter Release

The Four Noble Truths

The Noble Eightfold Path

Anitya – Impermanence

Anatman – The Doctrine of No-Self

Dependent-Origination

The Middle Way

Voidness and Emptiness

The *Arhat* and the *Bodhisattva*

Developing the Perfections

The discovery of fire gave humankind security and sustenance. There is a method to making a fire. The tinder has to be dry, the flint stone and iron have to be struck right, and the first flames have to be continually fanned and nurtured with the measured addition of kindling. If the method is wrong, or if the material had not been prepared well, there will be no flame and no fire.

Similarly, the Buddha has given us a method of training, which leads to utmost freedom and ease. It can guide us to the realisation of our full innate potential. This is the path for complete release from the unease and suffering, which arise from our clinging to false views of ourselves and the world around us. The groundwork for understanding the teachings of the Buddha (the *Dharma*), has to be correctly laid. The early insights into our conditioned state of being, which will arise from our practice of the *Dharma,* have to be further nurtured and developed with vigour and perseverance.

Just as there are other ways to start a fire, the Buddha had also adapted his methods to suit the different dispositions and circumstances of his disciples. It is when we have felt the warmth of a fire, seen its usefulness and perhaps been in awe of its raging power that we will naturally want to treat it with care and respect. Similarly, after we have practiced the *Dharma* and enjoyed its benefits, we will treasure it even more.

The Buddha's teachings are not dogmas which cannot be questioned, or which have to be accepted without critique. They do not have to be accepted on blind faith, or be taken as the ultimate truth. The Buddha taught his *Dharma* by way of invitation, to be known and directly experienced by ourselves. Thorough investigation and the direct experience of the *Dharma* are needed to establish a firmly grounded faith in it.

The Historical Buddha and His Legacy

We may say it was no accident that the Buddha was born in the northern Indian subcontinent, in about 480 BCE, some two thousand five hundred years ago. In that time of the Buddha, the extant late Vedic culture was supportive of seekers and wandering mendicants searching for spiritual truth. They were able to survive on alms from the villagers or townsfolk, and could retreat to the countryside or surrounding forests to conduct their spiritual practices. Disciples would gather around revered teachers, and debate with those aligned to other beliefs or practices. It seemed to be a land and a time which were rich with spiritual endeavour; a time when the disciples were readied, and that was when the Buddha made his entrance.

The historical Buddha was born as a prince of the Gautama clan, in the kingdom of the Shakyas, in what is now the part of southern Nepal bordering India. His name at birth was Siddhartha, and his parents were the King Suddhodana and Queen Maya. The young prince Siddhartha was shielded from witnessing the suffering of old age, disease and death while he was growing up within the palace. It was later, on his trips outside the palace walls, that he first set eyes on the decrepit, the diseased, and the decaying dead. Confronted with the realisation that suffering is prevalent and universal, he was deeply disturbed. He then understood that life and its trappings are transitory, and resolved to search for a cure from suffering and the pain of old age, sickness and death, which seemed to be an unavoidable fate. In his quest for enlightenment, the Buddha-to-be gave up everything. He relinquished his birthright to kingship, left his family and newborn son, and took on the homeless wandering life of a seeker of truth.

The Buddha-to-be sought out many renowned teachers in his quest, learned from them and surpassed them, but he was not satisfied even with having attained the highest meditative states. He realised that those teachings only led to mundane attainments. What he was taught did not lead to direct knowledge or to enlightenment. So he left his teachers to further his quest:

"Still in search, of what is wholesome, seeking the supreme state of sublime peace ..." [1]

The Buddha-to-be tried the way of severe meditative and bodily austerities, and endured suffering to near death, but found that these practices did not result in the knowing of any truths which could free him from all vexations, or give him total ease and freedom from suffering. He wondered if he was on the right path, by way of practising the severe austerities.

He then recalled a childhood incident, when he had naturally entered a deep meditative absorption in the cool shade of a rose apple tree. When this memory came to his mind, he realised that the correct path of practice, the path to enlightenment, lay with developing the concentration of mind that is firm, joyful and pure, and directing it to penetrative knowing. He also realised he needed to sustain the body to support his efforts.

The Buddha-to-be accepted an offering of milk and rice to regain his strength. Seeing this, the five ascetics who had been attending to him, in the hope that they would derive benefit from his attainments, left him. They thought he had succumbed to pleasure, and had given up his quest.

The Buddha-to-be then sat in the shade of a fig tree and resolved to the attainment of perfect knowledge. He uttered his firm resolve:

"I will not rise from my seat until I have obtained my utmost aim." [1]

The world rejoiced, but Mara (the personification of spiritual death, the Evil One), was fearful. Mara assailed the Buddha-to-be with his troop of demons. His three sons; Confusion, Gaiety and Pride, and his three daughters; Lust, Delight and Thirst, attempted to dissuade, distract, seduce and terrify him. The Buddha-to-be was unshaken. Mara was vanquished and fled with his army.

At the end of his forty-nine days of meditation, the Buddha-to-be unravelled the cycle of becoming, acquired the transcendent knowledge and powers of a Buddha, and attained full and perfect enlightenment. The poetic rendering of the Buddha's triumphant conquest of the hordes of Mara, is beautifully and movingly described in the Buddha-*carita* (Life of the Buddha), ascribed to the great Indian philosopher-poet Asvaghosa (circa CE 100).

On attaining enlightenment, the Buddha knew thus:

"My deliverance is unshakeable; this is my last birth; now there is no renewal of being...This Dhamma that I have attained is profound, hard to see and hard to understand, peaceful and sublime, unattainable by mere reasoning, subtle, to be experienced by the wise." [1]

He is now "The Buddha"; which translates as "The Awakened One" or "The Enlightened One".

The Buddha relished the state of liberation for a full seven days, and then out of compassion for the world, roused himself to liberate those who were open to receiving his *Dharma*. It is in the Buddhist tradition that the momentous event of a Buddha's enlightenment was the result of his practice and development of the Perfections, over eons (Skt: *kalpas*) of life cycles. In gaining enlightenment, the Buddha rediscovered the *Dharma,* and joined the lineage of the Enlightened Ones.

After the Buddha was enlightened, he thought to reveal his teachings firstly to his former teachers, as they had trained minds capable of understanding, but they had passed away. It was to the group of five ascetics, who attended on him when he was practicing the severe austerities, that he first expounded his teachings. On seeing his presence and demeanour, when the Buddha met them again, these five ascetics could not help but treat him with deference and respect. He told them he had attained to the deathless; that he can teach them the *Dharma* through which they, too, can have the direct knowledge of reality, and be similarly enlightened.

The Buddha set the wheel of his *Dharma* in motion with his first discourse on the "Four Noble Truths", followed by another discourse a few days later on the "Doctrine of No-self". By the end of these two discourses, his first five disciples attained *Arhat*-ship. An *Arhat* is a Noble One, one who is perfected and enlightened, who is totally freed from greed, aversion, and delusion.

The Buddha went on to spread his *Dharma* in Northern India. He taught kings and commoners, men and women, over a period of forty-five years. Through his teachings, they gained varying degrees of awakening; from the attainment to "stream-entry" (with no regression to states of woe, and destined for final Nirvana), up to the attainment of *Arhat*-ship.

The Buddha is also known as the "Compassionate One". He personally attended to ailing monks, and urged his followers to wait upon the sick and to care for each other. When the Buddha's passing to final Nirvana was drawing near, Cunda, the smith, provided him with his last meal, which caused him great pain and sickness. Even though in pain, the Buddha was concerned Cunda might be remorseful. He sent his attendant disciple, the Venerable Ananda, to dispel the remorse in Cunda; to tell him that his offering of alms food just before the Buddha's attainment of final Nirvana was a good deed, which will result in blessings.[2]

Just before the Buddha entered the sublime meditative absorptions prior to his passing, he addressed the monks for the last time, asking them if they have any doubts regarding his teaching. The monks remained silent. There were none who had any doubts. Soon after, the Buddha uttered his famous last words:

"Now, monks, I declare to you: all conditioned things are of a nature to decay – strive on untiringly." [3]

The Buddha then entered into the sublime absorptions, and at eighty years of age, passed into final Nirvana.

A few months after the Buddha's passing, a First Council of five hundred *Arhat*s was called by the Elder Mahakassapa, during which the *Arhat* Upali recited the monastic observances and code of ethical conduct (the *Vinaya*), and the *Arhat* Ananda, the Buddha's personal attendant who was known for his phenomenal memory, recited the utterances and teachings of the Buddha (the *Sutras*).

In the third century BCE, the emperor Asoka convened another council to finalise the oral teachings of the Buddha. Missionaries from this period disseminated this codification of the Buddha's teachings to the neighbouring Asian countries. Asoka's son, the Venerable Mahinda, brought these teachings to the present day Sri Lanka, where it was transcribed, in the first century BCE, some four hundred and fifty years after the Buddha's passing, into the Pali Canon. This Buddhist tradition in Sri Lanka came to be known as the Theravada (Doctrine of the Elders) School. In the Theravada, the spiritual path culminates in the attainment of *Arhat*-ship.

In India, the early Buddhist tradition, by the first century BCE, had developed into many schools of Buddhist thought, including an emerging Mahayana (the Great Vehicle) School. The Mahayana started out not as a separate sect or school, but as a movement focused on the practices of the *Bodhisattva* (enlightenment being). The *Bodhisattva* of the Mahayana dedicates his training to the attainment of the supreme enlightenment of Buddhahood, for the benefit of all beings. The Mahayana especially emphasized the twin ideals of perfected compassion and wisdom.

As the teachings of the Buddha spread beyond the Indian subcontinent, in each of the regions where it took root, it was coloured with the local graces and culture of that region. This process of local assimilation was to carry on with the flowering of many schools and sects, as the *Dharma* was transplanted even further afield, along the trade routes (e.g. the overland silk routes) to the Far East and beyond.

The Buddha penetrated into, and transcended the workings of conditioned phenomena upon gaining enlightenment. The teachings of the Buddha derive from what we may refer to as transcendent wisdom, which is beyond mundane intellectual philosophising. It is not about him being introduced to a revelation from a divine creator, or having thought up a new philosophical system which does little to directly address our human condition.

To the clan of the Kalamas from the town of Kesaputta, who were confused by the many teachings from visiting teachers who had taught there, the Buddha gave this advice:

"Come, Kalamas, do not go by oral tradition, by lineage of teaching, by hearsay, by a collection of scriptures, by logical reasoning, by inferential reasoning, by reasoned contemplation, by acceptance of a view after pondering it, by the seeming competence (of a speaker), or because you

think: 'The ascetic is our guru.' But when you know for yourselves: 'These things are wholesome; these things are blameless; these things are praised by the wise; these things, if accepted and undertaken, lead to welfare and happiness,' then you should live in accordance with them."
(4)

The Buddha teaches us not to attach to self-serving dogmas; that there is no need to hold rigidly on to our prejudices and beliefs. It is up to us to do our own assessments of his teachings, to put forth the effort to submit the *Dharma* to our direct personal experience and test. We may have taken up certain practices, based on our initial favourable disposition towards a particular teacher or teaching. Perhaps we strongly believe in its efficacy, or it may have appealed to a deeply felt need to have a belief that can give us hope. We are warned in the *sutra*, not to place our trust in any teacher or teachings easily. We need to reject that which we clearly discern to be unwholesome, or detrimental to our well-being. We apply this advice of the Buddha throughout our path of practice of the *Dharma* and decide where we will be heading.

The *Dharma* is therefore not to be accepted on blind faith, or with unquestioning belief. If anything, we are to subject our self-conceived notions of reality to intense scrutiny, and to abandon any self-created delusions. This incisive scrutiny is directly carried out in the practice of Buddhist meditation. The practitioner learns to still and focus his mind, and develops the clear discernment to allow him to look into, and beyond himself; to cut though the veneers of collected delusions and defilements in his mind. The practice of Buddhist meditation allows the mind of the disciple to grow in clarity, and be pliable enough to assimilate those insights which arise from his probing deep into the nature of mind.

It is not surprising that the Buddha's teachings, which have come down to us from over two and a half millennia ago, have taken on many hues and styles. It will have been dyed many colours by the many cultures which have adopted it, and passed it on. It is also not surprising that there are many local beliefs and cultural predispositions, which have found their way into the teaching and the practice of the *Dharma*. These may seem completely alien, or perhaps even unacceptable, to someone else from another culture. We have to bear in mind that there are many aspects and levels to spiritual practice, in addition to the many accretions of local customs, in the popularized form of the *Dharma*.

It is therefore critically important that we do not pass judgement on how the *Dharma* is practiced in another culture, or how it appears to be contradictory to our sensibilities.

The *Dharma* is to be lived. We have to develop a familiarity with it. The process of being acclimatised to a foreign *Dharma* will require us to discern what is helpful, and what can be a hindrance; taking into account our cultural sensitivities. Just as the earlier Pali texts of the *suttas* (Skt: *sutras*) incorporated the use of language in the context of the Vedic culture of that time, so too, for example, the Ch'an (or Zen as it later came to be known in Japan) Buddhist texts in China, used the linguistic forms and norms with the then prevailing indigenous Taoist and Confucian influences. We can appreciate the many outer forms of the *Dharma*, but this is not enough. We need to further substantiate the profound truths it embodies, with our own insightful practice.

We do not need to be enmeshed in issues and views which do not concern our practice. The Buddha dissuades us from entertaining these unbeneficial views, and from becoming entangled in them. He had this teaching for the monk Malunkyaputta, who felt strongly that he needed to have answers to what the Buddha would call speculative views;

whether the world is eternal, or whether the Buddha exists after death, and so on. He had threatened to leave his training if the Buddha did not state his position on these questions. [5]

In his admonition to Malunkyaputta, the Buddha said firstly, he had not given any promise to take any position on these speculative views as a precondition to accepting Malunkyaputta as his disciple. He then gave the simile of a man who was wounded by a poisoned arrow. A surgeon was brought to the wounded man to treat his wound. If the wounded man would not allow the surgeon to pull out the poisoned arrow until he was told whether the man who wounded him was a Brahmin or a trader, whether that man was tall or short, the kind of feathers used on the arrow shaft and so on, then the wounded man would die before he gets the answers. The Buddha said that he had left undeclared what was unbeneficial, and that which he had declared, lead to direct knowledge, to enlightenment.

There are a great number of things we really do not need to know. Even if we think we have come to know about them, they will just be superficial knowledge which are not based on our own experience. We cannot therefore assimilate them fully. Those things will not benefit our development or well-being. They will remain as foreign matter, embedded amongst all the other clutter in our mind — not of any real use.

The Way to Highest Bliss and Utter Release

The Buddha did not resort to tenuous philosophical arguments to teach. He used the experience of suffering, which is the common ground we can all identify with. He relates the highest bliss and freedom of Nirvana to the cessation of the unease and suffering, which we directly experience.

We do know unease and suffering. We cannot deny this experience which affects us individually: in different ways, to different extents, and at different times. Every person we know of, will have experienced some kind of distress or suffering sometime. Even when life feels positively thrilling, there is always some unease about.

Pain or suffering is always lurking in the background, and flares up every so often. Someone we love passes away, and we grieve deeply. We feel hurt when a relationship fails. We feel physical and mental pain when we are sick and bedridden. We feel tortured when we cannot escape a situation where we feel bound and constrained. We are discontented when another gets praised. We feel dejected when we are falsely blamed. Anger consumes us when we feel short-changed. We suffer when we could not get enough of something we crave, and so on.

Perhaps for most of the time, we may be in a state of unsatisfactory uneasiness, not really happy with what we are thinking or doing. We experience listlessness and disillusionment, or are just muddled and lost, amidst all the rushing about. At the end of all this confusion, there is the suffering of old age, disease, and death, which seems inevitable. Regardless of whether we have a supportive community, or loved ones to help soothe our pain, we are still the ones directly experiencing and bearing with the pain.

We do have the freedom to choose what we want to do with ourselves in this brief lifetime. If we are in fairly favourable circumstances, and seemingly are living the good life, we may be tempted to stay with the status quo. However, nothing ever stays as it is. If we are not prepared for aging, disease and death, or have not seen into the nature of change, dissolution and decay, then our world will, at some stage, be turned upside down. If we accept that we are fated to be in the condition we are in, or that our condition is due to divine intervention, then we will likely resign ourselves to be enduring our unsatisfactory circumstances. We may even take it to be a test of our allegiance to a divine power and accept whatever an uncertain "fate" brings, or resign ourselves to a future that the higher power is deemed to have allotted to us. Some of us may have a desire to seek a higher cause or the meaning for our existence, but may be unsure how to go about doing so.

If we want a way out of our predicament, and feel it is worthwhile to put effort into having lasting happiness, to find meaning in our lives, and to resolve the issue of life and death, then there are ready answers in the teachings of the Buddha. Therein is the cure, if we take heed of the prescription from the master physician. We will learn that true lasting happiness is within our reach, and that suffering is not inevitable.

The Buddha did not claim to be a divinity or divinely inspired, but in our practice of his *Dharma*, we will experience states of unbounded bliss, and be uplifted to states of consciousness beyond the mundane, which we can call "divine". These are the states of consciousness which we can directly experience in deep meditation; when loving-kindness, compassion, sympathetic joy and equanimity are highly developed. The Buddha did not determine the working of miracles or other trappings of divinity to be useful. These attainments, though of a high order, are still mundane attainments. The Buddha teaches that we are capable of even more; that we can shatter our bondage to the unsatisfactoriness of mundane existence, and that we can attain to the "deathless", to what he had attained.

In the following segments, we review the core teachings of the Buddha.

The Four Noble Truths

In the first discourse after his enlightenment, the Buddha gave a teaching on what he named the "Four Noble Truths".[6] The Four Noble Truths is the most comprehensive formulation of the *Dharma,* in the following four statements below:

The First Noble Truth: *The five aggregates* [7] *subject to clinging are duhkha.*

Duhkha is a Sanskrit word meaning unsatisfactoriness, pain, suffering or distress.

The five aggregates refer to the five constituents of form, feeling, perception, volitional activity, and consciousness, which make up the individual. They are the categories into which the whole psycho-physical person can be broken down. The aggregate of "consciousness" is treated as a sensory process. It is the cognitive faculty which senses the mental objects (e.g. ideas and thoughts). The whole of phenomenal existence can also be classified in terms of these five aggregates. In Sanskrit, they are the five "*skandhas*".

The Second Noble Truth: *Duhkha arises from craving.*

The Third Noble Truth: *The relinquishing of craving leads to a cessation of duhkha.*

The Fourth Noble Truth: *The Noble Eightfold Path is the path to the cessation of duhkha.*

When explaining the First Noble Truth, by saying that the five aggregates subject to clinging are *duhkha*, the Buddha is implicitly saying the five aggregates are in themselves, inherently unsatisfactory; that they are of the nature of unsatisfactoriness. The five aggregates or *skandhas* are unsatisfactory because by nature of being impermanent, they are subject to change. They transition from one changeable state to another. We cannot rely on something that is changeable, to give us lasting satisfaction.

The aggregate of form includes our body, all material form and their physical qualities. They can deteriorate, degenerate and decay to dust. The other mental aggregates of feelings, perceptions, volitional activities and consciousness, are also unsatisfactory in that they give rise to feelings, thoughts, emotions and experiences which are impermanent and continually changing: which in one moment may rise to high peaks and in the next moment, plumb to the lowest depths.

In our daily living, the five aggregates which are "us", functionally interact with the surrounding environment. They provide the physical form, and the mental cognitive processes which respond to stimuli and ideas, and build conceptual knowledge. Together, they allow for our going about living and experiencing life. We do not deny their existence in the here and now. In this process of cognition, our experiences are habitually evaluated and interpreted relative to an independent and unchanging "self". This is the "I", or the "me", as the experiencer. If we are to understand how these five aggregates relate to the conventional reality we call "me" and "I", we will need to probe deeply into their real nature. When we start doing so, we will begin to realise that the five aggregates are actually in constant flux and do not have any essence, or any separate selfhood. In this sense, we may say they have no fixed identities, and are therefore not self-existing realities.

If we are foolish enough to cling on to the five aggregates, which are inherently unsatisfactory, it is entirely predictable that our experience of life will be unsatisfactory. There is nothing wrong with having delightful feelings, but it will be painful if we try to hold on to them and want them to last, when by nature they are ephemeral and ever changing. We may be having a good time, but ultimately there will be change. What are good times now, do make a turn to be not that good anymore. This is not a matter of being optimistic or pessimistic about the future. We are part of the cosmic nature; driven by the laws of transitory change affecting all phenomena, and this includes both our physical and mental aggregates. That is just how it is. However, we need not be bound with suffering in this state of things.

In the Second Noble Truth, the Buddha explains that the unsatisfactoriness of *duhkha* arises from craving. Craving is the desire which we have for delightful experiences: our wanting to have or possess, to be or become something other than what we think we are, wanting to be rid of something we think we have, wanting this and that, to no end. If we understand the Second Noble Truth, we will not be swayed by the unjustifiable biases arising from our discriminatory mind. We will understand that we have been suffering the pain of birth, living and death; the pain of being apart from, or of coming together, because we cling to the notion of permanency in the world when there is only transitoriness. We have continually misplaced our trust, our thoughts, hopes, and feelings, in things that will change, deteriorate and break apart.

It then follows, as the Third Noble Truth puts it; if we can relinquish craving, we will be free from suffering. This is easier said than done. We may have some intellectual understanding about this and may agree it makes sense. However, to fully understand the Four Noble Truths, we will have to fully understand the truth of *duhkha*. It requires that we know how it arises, how it has been affecting us, why we let it affect us, or is it affecting us in the way we think it does.

The key questions are: What is the nature of suffering? Who or what is actually affected by suffering? Do we really know craving? How does craving arise? Is it at all possible to relinquish and be free from craving? Do we become less "human" if we relinquish craving? Our cursory view of the Four Noble Truths seems to be insufficient. It appears that we will need a much deeper understanding, and we will also need a clear way to go about developing that understanding. In the Fourth Noble Truth, the Buddha laid out this path to full understanding of the cause of pain and suffering, and the full emancipation from them. He named it, "The Noble Eightfold Path".

Let us look at the whole picture of what the Buddha is teaching us in the Four Noble Truths. The whole spiritual quest for enlightenment is laid out in the simplest form, in the Four Noble Truths. Herein, the Buddha addresses the unsatisfactoriness and pain of *duhkha* that arise from our clinging to the five *skandhas* (the First Noble Truth). He teaches that *duhkha* arises from craving (the Second Noble Truth). The Buddha next says that the relinquishing of craving leads to a cessation of *duhkha* (the Third Noble Truth), and the path to the cessation of *duhkha*, is the Noble Eightfold Path (the Fourth Noble Truth).

We can therefore conclude that the Noble Eightfold Path is a path of the development of insight, and the relinquishment of craving. When we can sustain the relinquishment of craving, clinging will not arise. When clinging does not arise, there will be the cessation of *duhkha*; the ending of unsatisfactoriness or suffering. We will then be enlightened.

To the extent that we really know the Four Noble Truths, we learn to experience life to the fullest, to enjoy the beautiful, and inspirational things around us, to be free from vexations, to develop our potential for wisdom and compassion to the fullest, without burdening ourselves with endless cravings or indulgences which cannot satisfy.

The Noble Eightfold Path

The Noble Eightfold Path is the path of training, which leads to the complete freedom from unsatisfactoriness and suffering; to Nirvana. [8] The eight elements of the Path are:

Right View or Right Understanding:

This refers to knowing the doctrinal basis of the *Dharma* as the methodology on how to go about the practice. The *Dharma* is not about having to accept a belief in a metaphysical system or attaching to our own self-created notions of the world. We direct our self-development with Right View. For example, we would not want to jump straight into trying to solve a problem without first understanding what the problem is about, or without knowing the intricacies of the issues around the problem.

In the *Kalama Sutta* [4], the Buddha laid down the guiding principles on how to differentiate the true from the misleading teachings. He cautions us not to easily adopt those teachings which have not shown their worthiness. It is as if the Buddha is telling us to look left, then right, and take care, when we cross a road in the way of our onward path. It is critical that we do not sacrifice our innate potential for growth and development, for want of careful discernment. We should not place our trust in an untrustworthy method of practice, or a false belief system. When we discern with Right View and adopt the true *Dharma* for our practice, we can cross the road safely and go on our way. If we are blindly led into false beliefs, we may end up in further bondage, instead of being free from them.

It is with Right View, that the disciple gains the knowledge of the purpose and the nature of the spiritual path. As he grows in understanding the *Dharma*, he further establishes himself in the joyful certainty of his faith in the *Dharma*.

Right View clarifies the path of training that he undertakes to realise the highest bliss of full enlightenment.

In the *Kaccanagotta Sutta* , [9] the Buddha points out that Right View involves not seeing the world dualistically as either existing or non-existing, not clinging, not attaching to the idea of a "self", or of a "self" which suffers, arises and passes away, not being attached to extreme views that "everything exists" or "everything doesn't exist", but instead, understanding the causal conditioning of dependent-origination (refer to the following section) as the process for the conditioned arising and conditioned cessation of all phenomena.

If we have been going about our lives in a rather superficial manner, and feel we need to go about making some changes, we will want to understand why we feel so. Let us look at an example where we may have been caught up with pandering to our egotistical urge of wanting to appear successful or wealthy in the eyes of others. We may have been spending unnecessarily on expensive clothing, cars, and other trappings of wealth, so we can parade them to the envy of others. However, we may have begun to grow weary of doing so; of living our life for others. We may have come to realise that doing so has not given us any lasting satisfaction, and we begin to seek for something better.

We thereby have made a turn, and have started on Right View because we have begun to see that we had a wrong view of what happiness is about. Happiness is certainly not about living our life for the sake of the envy of others, or to seek their applause. It is clear that if we do not have Right View or Right Understanding, there will be no change for the better. If we continue with wrong views, we will be in the rut of unhappiness, continually caught in hankering for that which cannot satisfy.

Right Aspiration:

The disciple finds direction and purpose with the Right View, and with Right Aspiration, he is inspired and energised with vigour to tread the path of morality, concentration, and wisdom. He aspires to develop mindfulness, discernment, goodwill, compassion, and renunciation. He gathers inspiration and support for his practice from the spiritual community (the *Sangha*), and from seeing the genuine results from his practice of the *Dharma.*

Continuing with the example given earlier, after having gotten some sense as to what we have been doing wrong, and wanting now to move in the right direction, we energise that vision with Right Aspiration. We begin to take the steps to propel our being towards living a fulfilling life. This may begin with a resolution to put more effort into activities which will deepen our appreciation of life: for example in cultivating healthy and loving relationships, rather than to be spending time and money on creating illusory images of ourselves for consumption by others.

The disciple further develops the ethical roots with Right Speech, Right Action and Right Livelihood.

Right Speech:

The disciple is mindful of how he communicates, and he communicates in a manner which is in accordance with the path of virtue and wisdom. He therefore abstains from speaking falsely, divisively, harshly or frivolously. He refrains from speaking crudely, confusingly or communicating mindlessly; knowing his speech can cause pain, or disrupt an ongoing happy relationship. His communication then becomes clear and pleasing, contributing to harmony, and if he needs to be firm, he does it skilfully and with consideration.

As non-monastics, we will have to, in the course of our work and householder duties, be involved in much social interaction which involves talking. However, it is instructive to bear in mind the admonition the Buddha gave to his monk disciples, when he found them assembled together and discussing politics and the kingship of the kings of Magadha and Kosala:

"It is not right, bhikkhus that you...should talk on such a topic. When you have gathered together, bhikkhus, you should do one of two things: either engage in talk on Dhamma, or maintain noble silence." [10]

Right Action:

Right Action refers to the actions that affirm the disciple's commitment to the *Dharma*; not to cause harm or suffering to himself or others. He abstains from doing unskilful deeds and cultivates the skilful, with a mind dwelling in loving-kindness (a caring friendliness), compassion (the motivation to bear the pain of others, and wanting them to be free from suffering) and guided by Right View. He further helps others grow in the happiness and peacefulness of the *Dharma*.

We would have seen many examples of the lives of friends and acquaintances, which have turned out badly due to the wrong views they had. It may be the neglect of their work, overindulgence in sense pleasures, addiction to the excitement and greed in a gambling habit, intoxication to escape from the suffering that they are in, chase of the fantasy of making it rich with little effort, plain laziness of not willing to expend effort, abrogation of their responsibility to upkeep themselves and family, and so on. There are also those who ended up badly due to the bad company they keep, or from having untrustworthy friends.

Life sometimes, does deal out sets of very poor cards to us. Though we may have had some part to play with us getting those cards, there really may not be much we can do about it, other than to accept the state we are in. We have to move on, and with Right View and Right Action, we create the conditions for a better future. Guided by Right View, regardless of our station in life, we tread in the direction which leads to the betterment of ourselves and those around us. As we grow in understanding the *Dharma*, our energies are channelled into actions which bring beneficial outcomes and we will be truly happy for such rightly directed actions.

Right Livelihood:

The disciple earns his livelihood in a manner that supports his practice. He lives by fair means and does not cause pain or suffering to others. As a non-monastic, he may have the responsibilities to provide for his family, help raise his children, support his parents in their old age and contribute to the community.

With understanding the Four Noble Truths and the Buddha's teaching on non-clinging, the disciple will be able to handle these responsibilities without being misguided by indulgent craving or self-interest. He will not be unduly affected by, and will handle better, the troubles at work and at home, and will bear his social responsibilities well. His life will be simple because he has not allowed greed, enmity, or delusionary views to complicate the way he lives.

The next three elements of Right Effort, Right Mindfulness and Right Concentration on the Noble Eightfold Path point the disciple to the refinement of consciousness.

Right Effort:

This refers to the disciple's efforts in the cultivation of skilful and virtuous mental states. Right Effort is about the implementation of Right View in concrete actions; into actively going about self-cultivation with skill, vigour, and perseverance. The disciple cultivates emotional stability, friendliness and compassion. He lays down the burden of neurotic self-referencing, and learns to act and interact in all situations with skilful ease.

Right Mindfulness:

Mindfulness is the gentle non-judgemental awareness in experiencing the present moment. The disciple cultivates this awareness and mental clarity, which is without attachment or discrimination, and bears in mind the ethical teachings of the Buddha. Mindfulness sustains his positive and joyful states of mind as he goes about his daily interactions. With mindfulness, and a good measure of discernment, he conducts himself in accord with the *Dharma*.

Mindfulness is at the core of the *Dharma* because it is through mindfulness that the process of insightful knowing starts. Mindfulness enables us to be aware of how our thoughts and feelings are affected by the situations we are exposed to. It supports our conscious development of the skilful states of mind, and harmonizes our thoughts and emotions as we engage our understanding of the *Dharma* in our daily living.

Right Concentration:

The disciple develops joyfulness, calm, and focused attention. Through the practice of meditation, he attains to higher states of the meditative absorptions, and gains the insights which help with his awakening.

The Noble Eightfold Path is not a sequential training in the cultivation of the elements of the path. It is not meant for us to fully develop one element of the path (e.g. Right View), before we start working on the next element (e.g. Right Aspiration). The development of each element on the path supports the development of the other elements, in interdependent mutual enrichment. As we go about developing all aspects of the Noble Eightfold Path, we will continually grow in our understanding of the *Dharma*. We then also grow in happiness and dwell in the unruffled restfulness of a mind at ease.

Though we speak of a path we follow, as we develop on the path, it is internalised into the way we conduct ourselves. We then become the path, as the path becomes more a natural expression of ourselves. This path will start out with us having to negotiate rocky, muddy, and slippery slopes, but we keep our eyes on the horizon, for the path is well sign-posted. As we walk the path, it starts to get easier, not because the path is better paved, or because the incline is less steep, but because we have shed our heavy boots and left our overladen rucksacks behind. We are travelling light and are continually uplifted by the beautiful scenery unfolding before us. We can smell the fragrance of the overhanging blooms and are moved to sing with the chirping birds. Further on, we now and then have little glimpses of the end in sight. As we walk on, we experience the joy in seeing the beautiful panorama unfold before us, and of having the certainty of reaching our goal. We even begin to feel that we are not walking anymore. Anyway, is there anywhere we have to be going?

As we tread the Noble Eightfold Path, we find that what had started out as "the way of doing" has become the "doing of the way"; the way to awakening.

Anitya - Impermanence

The Buddha also expressed and communicated his realization in terms of the "three marks of being". These refer to the marks of impermanence (*anitya*), unease or pain (*duhkha*) and no-self (*anatman*), which characterise all phenomena. It is from understanding these truths that a realistic and satisfying paradigm for the interpretation of our existential experiences can have a realistic basis. We can then develop a preliminary framework for understanding the phenomenal world around us. We have to also note, however, that this framework of understanding is also impermanent, and is subject to revision. It is a provisional framework, against which we test and clarify our initial understanding. This is the preliminary phase in our self-cultivation — getting a foothold on the Right Understanding or the Right View of the Noble Eightfold Path.

Let us explore the characteristic of *anitya*. *Anitya* is a Sanskrit word that is usually translated as "impermanence", but it is much more than that. *Anitya* is the process of continual and ceaseless becoming, which entails ceaseless dissolution at the same time. There can only be renewal if there is decay and dissolution. There can only be flowers if there is manure. There can only be life if there is death. Every phenomenon is subject to *anitya*.

The word "change" does not fully describe *anitya*. When we say something has changed, it can mean it has changed into something completely different, which bears completely no relation to the earlier state before the change occurred. The "change" in *anitya,* however, includes the causal dependence in the process of conditioned arising. This is the dependent-origination at work in *anitya*, which we will discuss later in this chapter.

Anitya appears to be a characteristic we can easily point to and say, "Hey, that is *anitya*," or "That is impermanence."

However, we have to remind ourselves that the *anitya* we are trying to understand, is actually a complex, multifaceted and multi-linked process, in which the conditioned arising, conditioned becoming and conditioned ceasing, is in a cosmic web, in continual cycle.

If we dwell in the past, we will view the present moment as the continual renewing of the past, i.e. the past as being continually created from the present. If we dwell in the future, in the sense that our mind is preoccupied with thoughts or worries about the future, we will see the present moment as the moment of the future that is dying into the past. In both situations, we lose touch with living in the immediacy of the present moment.

The present moment is time in transience. It is already a past moment, in the next moment. The present is a moment in the present, only in the context of a past and future. The concept of a discrete "present moment", in the context of the above discussion, therefore does not exist as an absolute reality. It is *anitya*. Our present existence; the conditioned world of phenomena which is a continual process of conditioned becoming, is *anitya*. It is therefore also not real in absolute terms. Even so, it is in the present moment that we can create a new future.

There is beauty in the impermanence of *anitya*. It allows for transformation and growth. It allows for the good to take root and grow, and for the negative to die away and be uprooted. So *anitya* is beautiful, especially when we see ourselves transform and grow to become more loving, more caring, and more responsible for our well-being and the well-being of others in our larger community. We often hear from others, "You haven't changed at all!" after not meeting them for a number of years. This is usually meant to be a compliment. They are trying to say we have been keeping well, and perhaps we are looking just as good as when they last saw us. However, we would also wish we had truly changed; that we had overcome our hindrances and had grown happier, steadier, wiser, and more compassionate. We would wish *anitya* has been working well for us.

When we observe *anitya*, we will see it occurring universally. Incessant change occurs in our body, in the physical world around us, in our thoughts and our feelings, in the world of mental constructs, and even in our conscious cognition of who we think we are. We can clearly observe that the material things breakdown, break apart and decay. Our thoughts arise and perish. Our feelings change in that we are happy one moment then sad the next, loving one moment, then angry the next. We come to realise they are intangible; they depend on past and prevailing conditions, and they are not "us". We do not own them, and we cannot control them. It seems like they just pop up and go when they want. Our preferences, likes and dislikes sway, and our tendencies and habits do change. They are all *anitya*.

The practice of the *Dharma* is transformative. In a sense, if we do not see ourselves as separate from *anitya*, there is really nothing we need to change. There is only the process of continual transformation. There is no need to segregate out the discrete changes, or to try and allocate specific time instances to them, to define when the change has taken place. As we have seen earlier, within the universality of the process of *anitya*, the dimension of time may be regarded as merely a conceptual designation.

We only need to move forward with our practice from this moment. There is no need for us to lean back to change anything. There is no need to push the burden of the past along with us. We let ourselves grow naturally into change when we cultivate the Right View and Right Aspiration of the Noble Eightfold Path. This means we accept real transformation, are prepared to put down all baggage from the past and not weigh ourselves down. We leave all the unnecessary burdens behind and move on ahead into new possibilities. If we can experience this deeply, we will see the past which is to be left behind as inconsequential and unreal because there is actually nothing left behind. There is only this continual unfolding of new beginnings from the present moment.

What then, about those beautiful memories and uplifting experiences that we treasure? Do we also leave those behind? Are those good moments not something we will want to cherish? Here we have to be clear about what we mean by cherishing a wonderful past moment. When we go about this activity of cherishing a memory, we are actually inducing our mind to recollect past thoughts and feelings associated with that pleasant memory, which we bring to our mind as a mental object.

There are two ways of considering this. If we are cherishing a memory by way of allowing its recollected beauty to further inspire us to goodness, and to give rise to positive states of mind, then it has some value. However, if we are wanting to relive that memory by spinning out thoughts and feelings about it, or if we are longing for that past experience, then we are clinging to that memory. This clinging will bring on feelings of loss and regret, which unsettles us, and which drains us emotionally.

Anatman – the Doctrine of No-Self

The Buddha taught the characteristic of no-self or *anatman*, in his second discourse after his enlightenment. He explains that we do not have mastery over the five aggregates. They are ever changing and impermanent. We can say of each of the five aggregates (*skandhas*),

"This is not mine, this I am not, this is not myself." [11]

There is no unchanging or any inherently existing separate self, no permanent or separately existing witness, in our experiencing of phenomena. The so-called person is but a coming together of the five aggregates (i.e. form, feelings, perceptions, volitional activities and consciousness). There is nothing in these aggregates that we can point to, and identify as our "self". This so-called "self", is itself in continuous change. Thus, it has no identifiable "selfhood", and is subject, as with all phenomena, to *anitya* and to the process of conditioned becoming or dependent-origination (*pratitya-samutpada*). There is also no substantiable "self" or any "thing" which can be said to possess the *anitya* characteristic.

In the *Aniccasanna Sutta* (teaching on the perception of impermanence), the Buddha taught that the development of insight into impermanence is the key factor in helping the disciple overcome craving for sense pleasures, or craving for extinction. It uproots the deluded belief in a separately existing "self". He likens this to when a bunch of mangoes is cut at the stalk. All the mangoes which hang from the stalk are thereby similarly cut away from the tree. Similarly, with the development of insight into impermanence, the disciple's attachment to a separately existing "self" is also severed. [12] The understanding of *anatman* (no-self) rests on an understanding of *anitya* (impermanence).

The physical or mental objects of the conventional world of phenomena do not really belong to us. We cannot lay any claim to our thoughts, feelings, habits and dispositions, or our cognitive consciousness. All these are not of us and we are not of them. They are *anatman*. They do not exist by, or in themselves, nor do they have any own-being. They are not definable in terms of any ultimate realities.

Our attachments may be to physical phenomena, to our mental constructions, ideas, or unfounded beliefs. The five aggregates are all of the nature of *anatman*. When we begin to understand *anitya* and *anatman*, we begin to realise the futility of being attached to the transient and unreal things in the world. We come to understand that if we cling on to them, thinking they can belong to us, we will be sorely disappointed. We will suffer for it. This suffering and pain, we bring upon ourselves. It is of our own doing. This is *duhkha*, the unsatisfactoriness, the unease, pain or anguish, which results from clinging to that which is subject to *anitya,* or is *anatman*. This is as stated in the First Noble Truth.

The anitya and *anatman* teachings make the Buddha's *Dharma* unique among all the other major religions. The teachings of *anitya* and *anatman* unleash the consciousness of the disciple from being tied to belief systems that are anchored in eternalism or nihilism, in predestined outcomes, or in the subjugation of personal will. The Buddha's *Dharma* frees him from being tied to these epistemological structures of his own creation. When we begin to understand *anitya* and *anatman*, we will have received the twin blessings from the Buddha which endow us with the means for awakening to the true nature of phenomenal existence; to be truly free.

In the *Culashanada Sutta* [13], the Buddha taught that craving is the conditioning origin for clinging of the four kinds: clinging to sensual pleasures, clinging to views, clinging to rules and observances (or the belief that rites and rituals can predetermine an outcome), and clinging to the belief in a permanent and separate "self". The Buddha stressed that if clinging to the belief in a "self" is not understood, or is not taught together with the other three types of clinging, then the teaching is deficient. In the teaching of dependent-origination (which we will be looking at in the next segment), it is craving that conditions the arising of clinging.

One enters the non-regressive path to enlightenment when clinging to the belief in an inherent and separate "self", doubt about the Buddha and his attainments, doubt about whether the *Dharma* will really be of benefit, or whether it will lead to enlightenment, uncertainty as to one's own capabilities to pursue the path of training, and clinging to the mistaken belief in the efficacy of rites and rituals, are all abandoned.

Dependent-Origination

The Buddha expressed the insight from his enlightenment in the teachings he gave on the Four Noble Truths, impermanence, unsatisfactoriness, and no-self. These core teachings are further elaborated by the Buddha in the teaching of dependent-origination (*pratitya-samutpada*). He demonstrates how our existential experiences can be understood in terms of the processes of the universal conditioned causality of the dependent-origination.

The dependent-origination is usually presented as a cycle of twelve links. It characterises human existence, being and becoming, as a continuous cycle of physical and mental processes, which arise and disband, as conditioned by prior causes. Dependent-origination means there is nothing eternal. There is only the continued renewal and becoming, subject to causal conditioning. It also means there is nothing which is completely annihilated, as there is continual change and coming into being.

Dependent-origination provides the "whys" and the "hows" to help with our deeper understanding of *anitya* and *anatman* (impermanence and no-self). In this way, the dependent-origination conveys the conditioned arising and disbanding of all states of being, and negates both the doctrines of eternalism and nihilism.

Let us look in some more detail at each of the twelve links (as given below) in the formulation of dependent-origination.

1) Ignorance (Avidya)

The first link in the traditional presentation of dependent-origination is ignorance, or *avidya*. *Avidya* is the state of darkness; the state of unknowing. The person who is blinded by ignorance is likened to being in a drunken state. He is lost and grasping in the dark; buffeted by the winds of uncertainty and mistaken views of the phenomenal world. Without the Right View of the Noble Eightfold Path, he flounders in the state of spiritual ignorance of the *Dharma*.

Ignorance is pervasive, and is very deeply embedded in our consciousness. It conditions the mental events very early on, when consciousness begins to stir with the arising of the subsequent link of volitional activity.

2) Volitional Activity (Samskarah)

Under the dark cloud of ignorance, the person, as he fumbles about, keeps generating wilful or volitional activity, which oftentimes will be unskilful and lamentable.

Samskarah refers to the volitional activities which are the precursors to the compounded mental formations of consciousness. The willed activity of *samskarah* generate mental imprints and condition the arising of the next link of consciousness.

3) Consciousness (*Vijnana*)

The sixfold consciousnessess (i.e. the eye, ear, nose, tongue, body and mind consciousnesses) arise as conditioned by the volitional activity which grew out of ignorance. They are the mind processes which receive, investigate and register the sensed information from the objects around us. They manage the process of sensory perception and condition how we perceive the phenomenal world.

4) Mentality and Materiality (*Nama-Rupa*)

Consciousness conditions mentality-materiality.

Mentality refers to the three aggregates of feeling, perception and volitional activity. The aggregate of consciousness, which is already the conditioning cause for mentality-materiality, is therefore not repeated here. These mental factors generate the experience of cognitive recognition and mental construction.

Materiality is made up of the four great elements (of solidity, fluidity, heat and mobility) and the forms derived therefrom. These physical qualities provide the physical medium for the process of cognition.

5) The Six Bases (*Sadayatana*)

These are the five physical sense organs: the eye as the sense organ for seeing, ear for hearing, nose for smelling, tongue for tasting, the body for touch or pressure, and the mind base which senses mind objects (e.g. ideas or concepts). They provide the sensory inputs for the being to sense and cognize himself, and the external world.

The process of sensing and interpreting phenomena carried out by the six bases is conditioned by mentality-materiality, which apprehends the sensory inputs from the six bases. The thread of conditioning in the cycle that began with ignorance thus finds its way into the operating mode of our sensory processes. The latent deluded consciousness is then ready for interaction with phenomena, ready for contact.

6) Contact or Impression (*Sparsa*)

Dependent on and conditioned by the six bases, contact arises. Contact (or impression), is the mental factor which arises from the impingement of stimuli on the sense bases. These six kinds of sense impressions affect the five kinds of sense consciousness and the mind consciousness. The object is now apprehended by consciousness in the process of cognition.

7) Feeling (*Vedana*)

From contact, there arises feeling as the object is experienced. There are six kinds of feelings with respect to their origin from six different types of conditioning impressions. Feelings can be pleasant, painful or neutral. Our feelings affect the way our mind further develops ideas about the contacted object.

8) Craving (*Trsna*)

There are six kinds of cravings with respect to the objects of craving, i.e. the sensory objects of form, sounds, smells, taste, bodily tactile sensations and mind objects. If the feeling is pleasant, there arises the craving to extend the experience of the feeling. If the feeling is unpleasant, there arises craving to end the unpleasant feeling. There are also the cravings for existence (the craving to be established as an existing entity with characteristics) and for not-becoming (the craving to be annihilated, to escape pain or suffering).

The craving referred to here, is the deep-seated habitual mode of response rooted in ignorance. In the unaware and the unawakened, craving follows on from when feeling is experienced. The challenge for the practitioner is therefore to experience the interactions with phenomena which give rise to feelings, but not to further crave them. This means we can enjoy the pleasant feelings, but being mindful of the Second Noble Truth (which states that suffering arises from craving), we stop there and not let ourselves be overcome by craving. Similarly, we can experience the unpleasant feelings, but refrain from the craving to give vent to anger, etc. We do this by employing mindfulness and by cultivating the wisdom of seeing into emptiness.

We apply the mindful intervention, which will allow us to break out from the cycle of dependent-origination, in the moment of our experiencing of phenomena. The fertile ground for our practice of the *Dharma* is in the here and now, in the present moment. It happens in this link of craving. We are mindful of the arising of craving which if unchecked, further conditions the arising of clinging.

9) Clinging (*Upadana*)

Craving becomes a problem when we let it further morph into clinging: into greed, addiction, unbridled desire, and strong attachment.

Clinging is of four types: clinging to sense desire, false views (unfounded beliefs or dogma), belief in the efficacy of rites and rituals, and clinging to the belief in an inherently existing self. Opinions, views and superstitions can also be objects for clinging.

10) Becoming (*Bhava*)

Dependent on clinging, there arises becoming.

In becoming, the desirous attachments to sensory experience, or mental and physical objects, are acted upon. Clinging now manifests as karmic action in becoming. These karmic actions condition the arising of the false "self" or the "I" ego in the next link of birth.

11) Birth (*Jati*)

From becoming, the "I" ego becomes fully established. This false "I" ego continually takes "birth" in every cycle of the dependent-origination, in the course of our interactions with the phenomenal world. The seed for this false "self" is there right at the very beginning with the deluded consciousness. It is continually fed with sense impressions from the six bases and identifies itself with the five aggregates. Whenever the processes of craving, and clinging occur, they condition the arising (birth) of the "I" ego.

12) Suffering - As in decay and death (*Jara-Marana*), pain, grief and despair.

The processes in the dependent-origination occur moment-to-moment, in an unending cycle in which the state of suffering continually comes to be. The certainty for anything that comes into being, is dissolution, or decay and death. The unease and suffering that comes with decay and death is the inevitable outcome for one caught in the unending cycle of dependent-origination. When the particular cognitive process ends, the consciousness of the false "self" decays away. The state of unknowing (i.e. ignorance) again conditions another tryst with phenomena as the wheel of dependent-origination takes another spin.

There is not just one "self", but a succession of the many different "selves" arising from the moment-to-moment factors which condition its becoming. We may be experiencing the "self" which is seeking sense gratification one moment, and when that "self" dies away, depending on conditions, it may be followed in the next moment by the "self" which feels a deep concern for others.

The turning of the wheel of dependent-origination can be described as follows: In the state of ignorance, our volitional activities condition the consciousnesses which cognize sense objects. Contact of the sense objects with our sense organs and consciousnesses, give rise to feelings. When we experience a pleasant feeling, there is craving for the delightful feeling. We then develop clinging to the object of our craving. If the feeling is unpleasant, we crave for it to end. We direct our aversion or disdain towards what we deem to be the source of our unpleasant feeling.

This clinging conditions the coming into being of the "self" or "I" ego. In this way, the process of conditioned becoming gives rise to the delusion of the "self" which arises in the realm of experience. When the causal conditions supporting the functioning of the "I" ego disappears, the false "I" ego decays, and the cycle repeats itself as long as there is ignorance. This process illustrates how the dependent-origination can be correlated to our conditioned states of consciousness in our daily life, moment-to-moment.

It is as if we have been infected with a malicious virus which has programmed the specific responses into the way our consciousness handles sensory data inputs. The virus constantly employs the "me and mine only" override on our entire mind processes. The objective of the virus program seems to be the allocation of everything into its sphere of control, to ensure its continued existence at all costs. The infestation starts with the arising of every thought and feeling in our mind. By the time we develop preferences and emotional responses, our defences will have already been overrun. The virus program's ultimate objective of gaining absolute control over our mind, however, can never be met because it is the nature of things to change and be changeable. The virus program does not realise it is pursuing an impossible task. However, while the virus program will not be able to meet its objective, the psycho-physical being that is host to the virus, suffers high fever and pain from the infection.

The virus infestation represents our state of ignorance which conditions our responses to the interactions we have with phenomenal existence. We suffer the unsatisfactoriness of living with the infestation. However, the virus can be wiped away if an antivirus program can be uploaded. It is when the virus is purged from our operating system that we can be rid of the pervasive false "self", which breeds the "me and mine only" mentality.

The dependent-origination clearly demonstrates the process by which spiritual ignorance percolates through our deepest consciousness, to taint the arising of all aspects of our experiencing of phenomena. Understanding the dependent-origination is the key to knowing the workings of mundane existence. We will thereby be empowered to free ourselves from the bonds of ignorance.

The path of emancipation entails breaking out of this mode of conditioned existence, by way of the practice of the Noble Eightfold Path. It is our ignorant mind that creates false notions and preferences. These wrong views lead to craving and attachments which lock us into living the life of deluded egoistic reactivity. We can take leave of this bondage to the cyclic existence of dependent-origination. We can break free into the path of spiritual growth. This is the conditioned development of virtue and wisdom in the transcendent dependent-arising, which we will cover in the next chapter.

The dependent-origination illustrates the continuity in our experiencing of phenomenal existence in terms of processes which do not require any "essence" as a continuing agent which transmigrates from moment to moment, not to speak of transmigration to a new life upon death. It also provides a way of understanding the interplay of the processes of conditioned becoming and ceasing-to-be, without requiring any recourse to the belief in predetermined fate or a divine creator. The forward cycle of dependent-origination (i.e.

from ignorance to suffering) is, in the words of the Buddha, *"the origin of this whole mass of suffering."*

From this teaching of dependent-origination, we develop an initial conceptual understanding of the conditioning factors which drive the interactions in life as we live it. It describes the continual coming-to-be and the dissolution of conjoined physical and mental factors, as a succession of the processes of conditioned arising of states of consciousness, mental factors and form, which are shaped by ignorance. The teaching of dependent-origination presents the tantalizing possibility to recreate our total being, in the moment-to-moment unfolding of the guided experiencing of ourselves. We have the choice for renewal and transformative change in every moment. When we realise how ignorance conditions our clinging to phenomenal experience, and results in unease and suffering, we rethink our strategy for living. We can consciously direct our efforts to not be caught in the endless cycle of trying to indulgently satiate ourselves with ephemeral sensory experiences that do not last.

The traditional presentation of the dependent-origination takes it as occurring over a sequence of three (past, present and future) lives. In this traditional approach, the volitional activity *(samskarah)* of the past life (i.e. the two links of: ignorance → volitional formations in the past life) conditions the arising of the consciousness in the current life (i.e. the eight links of: consciousness → mentality and materiality → six bases → contact → feeling → craving → clinging → becoming in the current life). The future life (i.e. the two links of: birth → suffering of decay and death) begins with another physical birth, which leads to the suffering of decay and death. The focus of this traditional presentation is on how the past, present and future lifespans of the "person" fits in with this core principle of the conditioned process of dependent-origination. Implicit in this traditional formulation of dependent-origination is the

47

concept of rebirth, in which the five aggregates undergo dissolution upon death, and a new being is dependently originated in "rebirth".

It is imperative to understand that rebirth, in the Buddhist context, is not a reinstatement of the past "self" or "soul" into a new physical being, in the new life. There is no transmigration of any spirit, or essence, in rebirth. The Buddha's teaching of no-self (*anatman*) makes it very clear that rebirth is a conditioned coming-to-be process, rather than a re-becoming. There is therefore continuity in the process of rebirth, but the "being" which is reborn, is neither identical with, nor wholly separate from, the being of the previous life. We have to drop all notions of any "thing" being carried over from one life to the next, as that will be attachment to a characteristic or a reality, however minute, which can exist in itself.

We may say that the traditional presentation of dependent-origination over three (past, present and future) lifetimes is a "broad brush" presentation of the processes of dependent-origination, as contrasted with the moment-to-moment presentation, which we can call "fine brushwork". The processes of dependent-origination therefore actually operate in "fine brushwork" fashion, within the "broad brush" span of the past, present and future lives.

Karma is willed action through word, deed or thought. It is not predestined fate. The cultivation of virtue and ethical conduct serve to condition the "good" karma, which in turn support the arising of positive states of being. Karma operates like as a medium of conduit, for the conditioning activity which affects the coming-to-be and the ceasing-to-be of phenomena. It is therefore linked up with the conditioning processes, which have been explained in the dependent-origination. We may not have the cultural or religious background which will let us be naturally comfortable with the ideas of karmic retribution and rebirth in a next life. If so, the "broad brushwork" presentation of dependent-origination over the past, present, and future lifespans, may not mean much, or be directly useful for us.

The Buddha had anticipated that we may be in the predicament of being accepting of his teachings, but do not subscribe to the belief in rebirth. He thereby also taught (in the *Kalama Sutta*[4]) that even if there is no rebirth, his *Dharma* will still be of benefit to our well-being; i.e. we will not be disadvantaged if we accept the practice of the *Dharma,* regardless of whether rebirth occurs in the way we think it does, or not. The process of rebirth is however, very much woven into the fabric of the *Dharma*. In the Pali *suttas* (Skt: *sutras*), the Buddha taught that the recollection of past births is knowledge which can be gained from the cultivation of the unblemished and imperturbable mind established in *dhyana* (the deep meditative absorptions). [14] The knowledge of his past births, and that of other beings, is traditionally presented as a feature of the Buddha's enlightenment "experience". [15]

Rebirth is the conditioned coming-to-be of a being in the new life by way of dependent-origination. It will have *anitya* and *anatman* at its core. We may provisionally take it on faith that the rebirth process, which occurs moment-to-moment, also works for the traditional lifespan-to-lifespan "broad-brush" dependent-origination. This can serve as a provisional view, even though we may not have directly had any experiential awareness of rebirth.

In the *Kalama Sutta*, we are taught by the Buddha to eschew undeterminable beliefs if we do not find them helpful, or if they do not benefit our practice. If we happen to be not at all comfortable with the concept of rebirth, then on the Buddha's own advice, we will not want to further let the many views about rebirth (if we have issues with them) distract us from our development in the practice of the *Dharma*.

There is no need to hold on to any view as to how the past to present life transitions occur. The Buddha did teach that the attachment to a "self", will give rise to views on what we are in the past, what we will be in the future, where we have come from, and where we will go. These views are not fit for attention, and he calls them *"the thicket of views ... the fetter of views."* He warns us not to become entangled in them. They do not lead to freedom from suffering. It is more fruitful to shift our focus back to our *Dharma* practice, rather than to indulge in such speculative views.

The Buddha did declare that enlightenment comes from fully understanding the dependent-origination. This formulation of universal conditioned causality gives us much needed rest from our tendency to otherwise be involved in endless speculations about the nature of the arising and ceasing of phenomenal events. We can then direct our development of the Right View of the Noble Eightfold Path, based on our deepening insight into this natural process of dependent-origination.

The Buddha emphasized that the whole sequence of universal conditioned causality, which is instigated by ignorance, comes to an end when ignorance is completely uprooted. With the cessation of ignorance, there is cessation of the next link of volitional activities which are conditioned by ignorance, and so on. When ignorance is uprooted, the sequential forward turn of the wheel of the mundane *pratitya-samutpada* then ceases. The suffering of decay and death, pain and despair, will be transcended. The whole process of conditioned arising that is the dependent-origination will be unravelled; leading to the cessation of *"this whole mass of suffering"*. [16]

It is the moment-to-moment ("fine brushwork") experience of dependent-origination, which provides the key for the disciple to deeply penetrate into the understanding of the *Dharma* of no-self (*anatman*), the Four Noble Truths, and emptiness. It is this moment-to-moment mindfulness of the process of impermanence (*anitya*), in the here and now, occurring in the present moment that we directly experience phenomenal existence. This is what is directly relevant to our practice of the *Dharma*.

The Middle Way

"This being, that becomes, from the arising of this, that arises; this not becoming, that does not become; from the ceasing of this, that ceases."

This verse, as adapted from the *Culasakuludayi Sutta* [17], succinctly enshrines the teaching of conditioned causality, upon which rests the sublime teaching of dependent-origination and emptiness.

Nothing exists independently. There is no permanent "selfhood" or "self" in anything. By being dependently originated, all things are therefore empty; empty of a permanent and separate "self".

Our views or beliefs are also subject to the process of dependent-origination. They are formed from our ideas, interpretation of past experiences, preferences, cultural bias and even our use of language. These views are thus conditioned and are changeable. Having a view of things (including holding to a view of Buddhism), is like having developed an attachment to a mental construct. Knowing this, we can discard our outdated views and beliefs, as we grow in understanding. We need not be attached to any view.

Buddhism rejects the existence of a permanent self, or any kind of essence which exists forever. The other extreme, the annihilation of a person after death, or the severance of any continuity upon death, is also rejected. The Buddha instead taught that no-self, impermanence and dependent-origination, are the processes which govern the phenomenal world. No direction or control by any supreme being is required. We can redirect the process of dependent-origination by our own actions. We can nurture the arising of positive mental states and wisdom, and create a new future for ourselves.

In his discourse to the ascetic Kassapa, the Buddha said that the view "*suffering is created by oneself*" amounts to eternalism, and the view "*suffering is created by another*" amounts to nihilism. These are extreme views. The Buddha then taught Kassapa the dependent-origination to explain the the origin and cessation of suffering.[18]

The Buddha teaches us to view any of the constituents of the aggregates of form, feeling, perception, volitional activities or consciousness whatsoever, in any period of time; be it of the past, present or future, whether they are manifested as gross or subtle, internal or external to us, inferior or superior, near or far removed from us, with the correct view as,

"This is not mine, this I am not, this is not myself."[19]

The notion of a permanent unchanging self, the notion of an independent selfhood or any acknowledgement of the reality of a self, is a deluded view, a false view. It is clinging to eternal identity (eternalism) or to non-identity (nihilism), and we have to outgrow and be rid of these delusionary views, however subtle they may be. The Buddha taught this Middle Way.

Voidness and Emptiness

When we begin to develop an understanding of phenomenal existence in terms of the teachings of *anitya, duhkha, anatman*, and the dependent-origination of *pratitya-samutpada*, we begin to see into its empty nature. Emptiness or voidness is how we can describe the true active nature of the phenomenal world. We cultivate the empty mind; a mind which sees the universality of emptiness in phenomena.

Emptiness is applicable thoroughly and universally. There are no entities that are ultimately self-existing, or which have distinct unchanging attributes. All things are empty; empty of any selfhood; empty of any distinguishing marks. Ultimately, they are illusory, and are empty of any mind-concocted references, or notional distinctions. From this ground of emptiness, there are therefore also no absolute designations or conceptualizations that can be generated, or which are ultimately real.

As we develop a mind attuned to emptiness, we lessen our attachments to the habitual manifestation of the "I-centric" type of thinking and behaviour. When such thoughts or feelings relating to the discrimination into "me" or "mine" arise, we can step back, not be caught in our habitual reactions and responses, and let it pass.

If we are to be aware of the arising of the habitual mind, we will need to sharpen our sensitivity by cultivating mindfulness. We will then more easily discern how the habitual mind can influence our thoughts and feelings; to give rise to a potentially unskilful response, and we can choose to let it pass. We let it go, and in this way, we practise dwelling in emptiness. The practice of mindfulness is therefore not complete without the supporting factor of discernment in the *Dharma*. Mindfulness gives us the present moment awareness of a mental state as it arises, and our discernment in the *Dharma* lets us see its empty nature. We are then not swayed by it.

The teaching of emptiness is not to be taken lightly. It is a profound teaching, which invokes much transformative power, so it needs to be delved into with care. It can uproot not only our grasp on to an illusory selfhood, but also our hold on the conventional reality of the phenomenal world around us. We may not be ready to delve deeply into emptiness, if we have not prepared ourselves with a strong grounding in compassion and loving-kindness.

In the *Dhammadinna Sutta* [20], the lay follower Dhammadinna and a gathering of lay followers, approached the Buddha to request for teachings that will lead to long lasting well-being and happiness. When the Buddha advised them to contemplate his discourses, which are deep in meaning, which deal with emptiness, they protested that they have to untiringly attend to the needs of family, have business dealings, and have to put on appearances appropriate to their stations in life. As lay disciples, they felt it would be difficult, while being caught up in these mundane activities, to dwell on the Buddha's profound discourses which deal with emptiness. The Buddha accommodated their request; he taught them to further cultivate faith in the Three Treasures (i.e. the Buddha, *Dharma* and *Sangha*), and to develop the virtues which lead to concentration. Dhammadinna declared they have been living in concordance with the Dharma, and the Buddha confirmed their attainment of stream-entry. We are, in this *sutta*, told that the contemplation on emptiness may not be easy for those having many distractions in their way, and that even householders can, with faith and the practice of the *Dharma* of virtue and concentration, attain to the supramundane path to liberation.

Our mundane perception of phenomena is based on the discriminating mind, which differentiates and isolates. When we view the phenomenal world, we are actually viewing our own mind-created mental images, and we relate to these mental images as if they are real. We see things as being independent in themselves, or as having discrete individual existences, without appreciating their interconnectedness. We are focused on their distinguishing characteristics in stark contrast to everything else, and lose sight of their causal interdependence with the cosmos, in the web of dependent-origination.

We tend to take the objects we can perceive through our senses (i.e. sensed by our eye, ear, nose, tongue, tactile sense and mind consciousness) to be separately existing "out there"; separate from ourselves. We also latch on to these sensed objects as having attributes of permanency because by doing so, we feel secure and our existence is affirmed. We feel secure because we can define a unique sense of belonging in a world of particulars; in a world we can substantiate within the limitations of our discriminating mind. This gives us the (false) sense of an existing "I", in a permanently existing world. These false notions of a separate inherently existing self and permanence, are dispelled when we abide in emptiness.

This emptiness, being an emptiness of discrimination, is also a sameness of all things. There is interpenetrating sameness in emptiness, and there is not one side, or any sides, to emptiness. Lest we create some notion of reality in, or of emptiness, we have to also realize that this emptiness is also empty. Ultimately, the phenomenal world, the conditioned and the unconditioned, are all empty. This is also not something we should understand conceptually.

It should already be apparent from the preceding discussion that the emptiness we have been referring to, is neither a "zero" nor a nihilistic "nothingness". This is not an emptiness which is devoid of the Buddha's teaching of *anitya, duhkha, anatman*, the Four Noble Truths, or the Noble Eightfold Path. The emptiness is empty of the five aggregates not in the sense that the five aggregates do not exist in the world; for that will be falling into nihilism. The emptiness referred to here, is an emptiness of our own self-created notions about them. This implies being empty of our attachment to, and empty of our notional ideas or biased conceptualizations about phenomena, or even about the *Dharma*. It is important for us not to mistake what are the extreme views of eternalism or nihilism, couched subtly in language. The taints of eternalism and nihilism are mistaken views which are to be abandoned, to be let go of, together with all the other taints of greed, hatred and delusion, for full emptiness to manifest.

We do not need to hold on to any metaphysical view of reality. Nagarjuna (late second century CE) the great Mahayana Buddhist teacher, in his philosophical treatise *Mulamadhyamakakarika* (The Philosophy of the Middle Way), warns us about the attachment to views. Even taking a view on emptiness; in trying to give it a meaning, or in trying to give it a characteristic "nature", amounts to a reification of an already misconstrued metaphysical concept.

We do need clarification on how to go about our practice on the Noble Eightfold Path, and to identify the mistaken views, which we will need to relinquish, which can otherwise adversely affect our practice.

Nagarjuna states:

"The Victorious Ones have taught

That emptiness is the relinquishing of all views.

Those who have a view of emptiness,

That one has accomplished nothing."

The "ultimate" emptiness is a relinquishing of all views: ultimately, even views about emptiness are to be relinquished. Nagarjuna pronounced that there is nothing which exists independently and that dependent-origination is the existential reality:

"Whatever is dependently originated,

That is emptiness.

That, being a dependent designation,

Is itself the middle way.

Something that is not dependently originated,

Such a thing does not exist.

Therefore a thing that is not empty

Does not exist."[21]

Nagarjuna clearly is telling us that the emptiness, which is dependent-origination, is the middle way which does not stray into eternalism or nihilism. In the continual moment-to-moment process of dependent-origination or dependent-arising, there is no eternal essence. There is continual conditioned becoming, so there is no annihilation.

In the *Diamond Sutra*, the Buddha says:

"Selfless are all dharmas (here referring to the elements of phenomenal existence), they have not the character of living beings, they are without a living soul, without personality." [22]

To develop a working understanding of emptiness, and in employing the teaching of emptiness to penetrate into the *Dharma*, we do not view the development of compassion as a separate or unrelated activity. Our understanding of emptiness is deficient if it is not supported by the development of compassion. In a deficient understanding of emptiness, "no-self" or "no-selfhood" may be interpreted to merely imply "no-other". This skewed understanding of emptiness will be deficient of compassion, warmth, and the concern for others. The wisdom of *prajna* and compassion both have to be manifest, in the complete understanding of emptiness.

In straightforward terms, this is the Buddhist perspective of life. It is a perspective based on our own undeniable experience, and we can relate to it from having directly observed how the events of our life have unfolded.

However, the phenomenal world is enticing, holding much promise of enjoyment and fulfilment, such that we get easily seduced. Again and again, we get caught in the endless cycle of craving, grasping, clinging and becoming, and suffer the consequences. So we tend to go through life scratching at every itch, but still we get no real relief, and subject ourselves to unending stress and suffering. When we begin to see things as they really are, and not hanker after wearisome distractions, we will have fewer itches. Life will entail less of running after distractions, towards which we develop attachments. We will then enjoy more of the simplicity of not having to cater to the unnecessary.

We will not be squandering time and effort on ruinous relationships, nor seek unnecessary gains to be spent on temporary experiences which are of little benefit, and which may even bring harm and destruction in their wake. We will be able to put more effort into building true loving relationships, investing our energies for the betterment of ourselves and the community, and be truly happy and fulfilled. We can then aspire to be at total ease in any environment, and operate always with wisdom and compassion.

Our continual progress on the path needs the Right Understanding or Right View to be firmly grounded in the practice of mindfulness. It requires that we develop a discerning awareness of the present moment, relinquish the hindrances to growth, and to train the mind by the cultivation of virtue and meditation. All this is done on the supporting bedrock of ethical conduct and with a deeply felt respect and appreciation for the *Dharma*. In short, we walk the Noble Eightfold Path and cultivate the universal empty mind of a *Bodhisattva*.

The *Arhat* and the *Bodhisattva*

The focus on the path of the *Bodhisattva,* is what gave the Mahayana its unique form. The *Arhat*, in the Buddha's time, was an enlightened being who required no further learning, had destroyed the fetters of being and had done all that is needed to be done. [23]

Later in the development of Buddhism, in the Mahayana teachings, the *Arhat* came to be regarded (by the Mahayana) as a disciple who, though already enlightened, has the potential to take up the aspiration to further realise the supreme enlightenment of a Buddha. The Mahayana took this to be the highest spiritual endeavour one can ever undertake.

However, we are likely not in a position to be comparing the different levels of enlightened consciousness, or make any claim for the superiority of one school of practice over another. If we have chosen a path of practice and derive inspiration and benefit from that practice, then it is the right one for us. What is real to us is our practice and there is no need to dwell on speculative views which distract us from our practice. There are many doors for entry into the *Dharma* treasure and we need to walk the path ourselves. There is no superior or better teaching than that which we are using for our practice, which unfolds in profundity, and gives us joy and rich insights, as we sincerely practise. It may be tempting to think that the method of practice which we are currently using is uniquely superior, but dwelling on this temptation to discriminate, only distracts us from our practice of the *Dharma*.

The Buddha referred to himself as a *Bodhisattva* before he was enlightened. A *Bodhisattva* is one who is aspires to the goal of Supreme Enlightenment; one who is absorbed with the will to enlightenment for the benefit of all beings. In him, the *Bodhicitta* (the mind to enlightenment) has arisen. This arising of the mind to enlightenment is a most significant turning point for the disciple on the path, and will be felt deeply as a reorientation of his being. This is when his insightful understanding of the *Dharma* unfolds the heart-mind of compassion in him. He awakens to his spiritual lineage, and starts on the spiritual career of a *Bodhisattva*. He then directly draws inspiration for his practice from the Buddhas, the mighty transcendent *Bodhisattva*s, and the awakened sages of the spiritual community he is now "reborn" into.

We may say that with the arising of the *Bodhicitta*, the Right Aspiration of the Noble Eightfold Path is firmly established in the disciple. His heart-mind is open to the *Dharma* of transformative change. He finds fulfilment and solace in the care of the Three Treasures, and is invigorated by the clear joy of treading the Noble Eightfold Path.

At the onset of his career, in the Mahayana tradition, the *Bodhisattva* makes his Great Vows:

- To deliver all beings from distress.
- To destroy all harmful passions.
- To penetrate into the *Dharma* Treasury and teach others.
- To attain the supreme enlightenment of Buddhahood and lead all beings to Buddhahood.

The *Bodhisattva* develops an actively compassionate nature and a universal outlook. He has, as his support, the transcendent wisdom which sees into emptiness. It is with wisdom that his compassionate aspect is fully activated. He does great acts of compassion, but does not feel he has attained any merit. He sacrifices himself, but to him, there is no one who is sacrificed. He moves in the phenomenal world of cyclic existence with ease and assurance. Though immersed in the world, he is not of it.

The compassion of the *Bodhisattva* knows no bounds. Such is the greatness of his compassion that in the fulfilment of his vows to bring all beings to enlightenment, he postpones his due entitlement to enter Nirvana, and subjects himself to recurring rebirths in the samsaric world. Though the *Bodhisattva* works tirelessly with great compassion to liberate all beings, he is not burdened by it.

Developing the Perfections

In the Mahayana tradition, the *Bodhisattva* is on the path of developing the six (or with the later addition of an additional four; the ten) Perfections, which similarly cover the development of virtue, concentration and wisdom (*sila, samadhi* and *prajna*). This path of the Mahayana is put in terms of the practices a *Bodhisattva* needs to perfect, in order to attain the full enlightenment of a Buddha. In the *Prajnaparamita* (Perfection of Wisdom) texts, the practice of the Perfections is described as having the *Bodhisattva* "*armed with the great armour*". The path of the *Bodhisattva* is well described by Shantideva (circa 8th century CE) in his *Bodhicaryavatara* [24] (The Practice of the *Bodhisattva*).

The Six Perfections or *Paramitas* are:

- Perfection of Giving or Generosity

The *Bodhisattva* gives selflessly, with no discriminating of himself as the giver, of the recipient, or of the gift. True giving, in the language of the *Prajnaparamita*, has no giver, no recipient, and no gift. It is the full expression of giving, which is devoid of any separateness of the persons involved, and also devoid of any discriminating thoughts.

- Perfection of Morality

Ethical conduct affects others with whom we share our presence, i.e. the people we interact with. It begins with ourselves, so the basis of the perfection of morality starts with us guarding our mind, and being mindfully aware of the mental states, so that skilful and ethical actions follow.

- Perfection of Forbearance

The perfection of forbearance means being in a state of equanimity, which is patient and tolerant of vicissitudes, or that which can upset. This forbearance is supported by the *Bodhisattva*'s understanding of emptiness. The *Bodhisattva* has to develop a large capacity for endurance; to be like a big tree, which gives shade to all creatures, and is tolerant of inclement weather. Even if it is carved into, or has parts hauled off for firewood, it doesn't mind at all.

- Perfection of Vigour

This perfection of vigour is the perfection of the activated resolve to enlightenment. It is the energetic striving in the practice of the *Dharma* to establish roots of goodness, and to uproot the defilements. The *Bodhisattva*'s vigour is not dampened when he is faced with obstacles.

- Perfection of Meditation

The perfection of meditation is the development of the mastery of the meditative absorptions, and the development of the incisive nature of the mind in penetrative seeing into the nature of things; seeing emptiness.

- Perfection of Wisdom

Wisdom here is the *prajna* wisdom. It is the seeing and knowing things as they really are. It represents the collective insights which have transformed the *Bodhisattva* as he grows in his practice, and is also the means for him to transcend conditioned existence.

A later compilation expanded this list of the six Perfections to a total of ten Perfections. The Ten Perfections then correlate with the ten stages on the path of development for the *Bodhisattva*. The additional four Perfections are the Perfection of Skillful Means, Perfection of Vow or Aspiration, Perfection of Spiritual Power, and the Perfection of Knowledge.

In the *Arhat* ideal of the Theravada tradition, there are four stages of supramundane attainments. The first of these is the stream enterer who eradicates the first three of the five lower fetters of: the view of a permanent self; sceptical doubt about the Buddha, the *Dharma* and the *Sangha*; and deluded belief in the efficacy of rites and rituals. The stream-enterer has entered the stream of the non-regressive path to Nirvana, and traditionally is assured of attaining the enlightenment to *Arhat*-ship within seven births.

The once-returner is additionally further detached from (though not yet fully eradicating) sensual desire and ill will. He takes one more human birth before attaining Nirvana. The non-returner has completely eradicated all of the five lower fetters. He takes birth in the heavenly realm and attains to Nirvana there.

The *Arhat* will have further completely eradicated the higher fetters of attachment to the realms of form and the formless, as well as conceit, restlessness and ignorance. He attains to enlightenment, to Nirvana, in his lifetime. In the Theravada, the stream-enterer, the once-returner, the non-returner and the *Arhat* are the Noble Ones of the *Sangha* to whom we go for refuge. The Buddha is also addressed as an *Arhat*, a Holy, or Noble One.

In the Mahayana tradition, the *Bodhisattva*, in developing the Perfections, has ten progressive stages on his spiritual path. The path of the *Bodhisattva*, at the sixth stage is designated to be on par with the *Arhat* of the Theravada. For the *Bodhisattva*, this is the non-regressive stage to Buddhahood. In the quest for the complete enlightenment of Buddhahood, the *Bodhisattva* undergoes a further four stages of training prior to becoming a full-fledged Buddha; endowed with all the attainments of a Buddha. These stages of training are expounded, for example, in the *Prajnaparamita* texts of the Perfection of Wisdom *Sutras* [25] and the *Avatamsaka Sutra* [26].

The Theravada, the Mahayana, or the many different schools of Buddhism will each have their different approaches in style and perspectives, on the path of self-cultivation. However, they do not differ in having as their core doctrines, the teachings of *anitya, duhkha, anatman* (impermanence, unsatisfactoriness, no-self), the Four Noble Truths, emptiness and the *pratitya-samutpada* (dependent-origination). They all emphasize the threefold system of the development of *sila* (morality — by way of keeping the precepts and developing virtue), *samadhi* (concentration — by way of developing the meditative absorptions and clarity of mind) and *prajna* (transcendent wisdom — by way of developing the penetrative insight that sees the true nature of phenomenal existence). Whichever path we choose to tread for our spiritual development, will depend upon our circumstances and what it is that inspires us.

The fruit of full emancipation is ours for the taking; whether we (figuratively) use a sickle, an axe, or our bare hands to harvest. It depends on what is at hand, what we are comfortable with using, and what we find is most effective for us. There is no just one way to go about it. We should also bear in mind that in the earlier stages of the path, when we are tending to the growing sapling (of understanding the *Dharma*), we may prefer to use a hoe to loosen the soil, and a shear for pruning its branches. It may be a while yet before we get to harvest the fruit of full emancipation.

If we put our heart and mind into the practice of the *Dharma*, the differentiations in the outer forms of the *Dharma* will lose their opacity, and will ultimately be resolved in the true experience of transcendent awakening. Whichever path we chose to tread, we always remain ever grateful for the many options skilfully made available to us by the enlightened masters.

We feel deep gratitude for all that is taught to us, and for all teachings, which have been made available to all beings, which lead to their well-being and complete freedom from distress, in whatever form those teachings may take.

Chapter 2: Freedom to Develop and Grow

Going Beyond the Intellect

Direct Engagement and True Detachment

Why We Need to Do Good

The Path of Transcendent Dependent-Arising

The Individual Choice of Practice

Does following the Buddha's teachings make life more constraining, or perhaps even more complicated than it already is? It does not. In fact, the practice of the *Dharma* frees us from the unnecessary self-imposed constraints arising from our biases and clinging to unsubstantiated beliefs.

As we illuminate the darkness in our mind with the light of the *Dharma*, the encumbering negative emotions of restlessness, worry, greed and hate are cleared. Our habitual mind, which is caged with neurotic self-referencing and entangled in all the resulting self-created problems, can then bask in the inspired clarity of the *Dharma* and be free to know its true nature. In this process of awakening, we begin to learn to live in the ease and comfort of the wisdom that sees the true nature of things.

It is time to leave the remnants of our predatory instincts for self-preservation behind. We may say that the fate of humankind rests on us being able to develop the compassion and wisdom necessary to address the growing number and severity of the challenges facing our closely interlinked global community. There can never be any justification for driving personal agendas that sow hate and discord. This is even more so, when there is urgent need for cohesion and tolerance; to resolve the grave and complex issues which threaten the survival of life on our planet.

Going Beyond the Intellect

The material for an intellectual understanding of the three marks of being (*anitya, duhkha* and *anatman*, or impermanence, suffering and no-self), the Four Noble Truths and emptiness, has been provided in the first chapter. It gives an initial intellectual framework for understanding the *Dharma* that we can start working with. This will be the provisional framework we will initially use to interpret the knowledge and insights gained from our developing practice. We also further build on it as we refine our understanding of the *Dharma*.

We would have constructed our intellectual understanding of the *Dharma* by using concepts from our still deluded mind. It will therefore surely be tainted by the muddled views from our egocentric and discriminating mind. However clearly presented the teachings may be, we would have inadvertently screened them, picked and chose, and additionally attached our biases to the emerging intellectual structure. If we had incorporated any wrong or delusionary views into this framework, and further bound it up by trying to interpret and to cast our experiences into this faulty structure, we will be introducing more faults. If we start with a wrong basis, we will then be only piling up even more hindrances to our development.

The *Dharma* which we know about, is therefore intrinsically flawed because it would be our version of it.

We have interpreted it our way, using our discriminating mind. This flawed *Dharma,* which we recognise as provisional, is to be left behind — when we have outgrown our conditioned and discriminating mind.

Let us, for a moment, step back, and consider all this from a different viewpoint. Let us imagine Mr. Dharma exiting the glass panelled office block, and stepping out on to the street. He waves to the florist at the stall just outside and she waves back. She may likely see him as the customer who is warm and generous, from the many times he had ordered flowers for his family celebratory occasions. "Nice gentleman and what a smart dresser," she may be thinking to herself. The shoe shine boy sees Mr. Dharma from a distance, and notices his well-polished shoes. "Guy in a hurry, no business for me," he thinks to himself, and does not even venture a second look. Mr. Dharma quickens his steps as he nears his car parked by the road. An old man with a walking stick steps on to the pavement, from the road in front of the car. He catches sight of Mr. Dharma, but is miles away, carrying a picture of Ginger, his pet cat, in his mind. He is thinking of getting a tin of cat food as a treat for Ginger, and smiles to himself. A young executive type brushes past, and cannot help noticing the elegant briefcase that Mr. Dharma is carrying. He thinks to himself, "Rich fella, nice burgundy leather finish, just the type I am looking for," as he raises his hand to hail a cab.

In all these situations, Mr. Dharma was a different personality to each of the persons perceiving him. The different perceivers come from different backgrounds, and have different priorities, tastes and biases. Similarly, the *Dharma* will be shorn of its true beauty and profundity, and will be shrouded in a mist, when perceived by our mundane mind, which is intensely caught up with mundane issues.

Knowledge about Mr. Dharma's dressing, his briefcase, or how he parts his hair, is only superficial knowledge. If we further spend more time to study his daily schedule, his credit card bills and his eating habits, we can know a great deal more about Mr. Dharma. We may impress others in a conversation about Mr. Dharma when we roll off the names of the restaurants which Mr. Dharma frequents. We may even be able to name his favourite pub brew. However, do we really know Mr. Dharma? We may have perhaps gathered some detailed knowledge about much of the superficial things about him, but what we know, is of no help to us. Mr. Dharma is still far removed from us; we have not yet connected with him.

To really know Mr. Dharma, we need to start by perhaps inviting him over to our home for a meal. We can then establish a good relationship with him and open up to him. Mr. Dharma may then tell us about his growing up years, or share with us his hard earned experience in fruit tree grafting and planting crab apples. We may come to feel the loss he felt, when he lost both his parents in a recent car accident. Similarly, it is through deep study and practice that we will grow to understand the heart of the *Dharma*. Attaching to its forms and outward expressions may be a pleasant distraction, which may equip us with much quotable details about the *Dharma*, but this is of limited use for our development. In fact, it can easily be a hindrance.

By now, we will have an intellectual grasp of dependent-origination as the unceasing process of conditioned arising and coming-to-be, non-arising and not coming-to-be. The word "grasp" used here is quite appropriate. When a concept is made known to us, we form ideas about it. When we have a mental picture of it and think we understand this concept, we say we have "grasped it". We keep on doing so, creating more intellectual constructions to "grasp" and bind more ideas. We now have a provisional framework of ideas we can throw about; we can verbalize it; we can bounce it off another person and invite his impression of it. However, this concept of dependent-origination still remains external to us. It is still something we bounce about.

We can further illustrate the limits to intellectual understanding, with the analogy of learning to drive a car. We can read up about how the man-machine interactions; such as releasing the handbrake, engaging the clutch, or using the accelerator pedal, work. However, no matter how much book learning we may have about driving a car, all that will be empty words if we do not have the true experience of actually driving it. We have to get behind the wheel, and practise on the road. We will then appreciate the difficulties with driving in heavy rain, snow, or ice. After driving becomes second nature to us, we can discard the operating manual. But before we know how to drive, we have to diligently study the operating manual and use it to guide our training. So it is with our practice of the *Dharma*. We have to go through the stages of study and practice, before there is realization. It is by doing so that we gain entry into the realm of true knowing.

Through deep insightful experiences arising from our practice of the Noble Eightfold Path, we break down the rigid conceptual structures. The deeper the transformational insights, the deeper will be the level of our assimilation of the *Dharma*. It then becomes a part of everything we do. When we speak, we will have it speaking, when we act, we will have it acting. At that stage, we will be able to use the *Dharma* freely and creatively, and not be bound by what were originally just rigid concepts.

The *Dharma* is taught by the Buddha as a means to impart to us the profound truths which he had realised. We do not want to mistake these teachings for the true realised wisdom that flowers from practice. We do not want to grasp on to the intellectual presentations of the *Dharma*, and to mistake the finger that points to the moon, for the moon.

The Buddha forewarns us, with the simile of the raft:

"When you know the Dhamma to be similar to a raft, you should abandon even the teachings, how much more so things contrary to the teachings."[(27)]

The Buddha likened his teachings to a raft, which will have to be left by the river bank after one crosses the river. In the same way, we have to continually be discarding anything else we outgrow. The raft of the teachings may have served us well when we were crossing the river. If we are to carry it with us after the crossing, and bring it with us when we start traversing the forest, we will be bringing along an encumbrance. It will make our work much more difficult. When we next start to climb the mountain, it becomes practically impossible to make progress if we have to be hauling the raft along. So when we start to delve deep into our practice of the *Dharma*, we begin to go beyond our initial conceptual constructs. Ultimately, we will have to go beyond any concepts; beyond even the so-called Buddhist concepts.

This is very beautifully expounded in the *Heart Sutra* (which is further introduced in Chapter 9):

"The Bodhisattva of Compassion (i.e. the Bodhisattva Avalokitesvara)

When deeply coursing in the Prajnaparamita,

Sees the five skandhas are of the emptiness

That liberates from all suffering." [(28)]

From the viewpoint of *anitya*, *duhkha* and *anatman*, the five aggregates (*skandhas*) are empty of any inherent selfhood and are impermanent. They are therefore unreal and empty. When we see into the emptiness of the five aggregates, we should simultaneously also see *anitya*, *duhkha* and *anatman*. The outcome of this realisation is that we will be awakened to the freedom from suffering, fear and delusion.

It does not stop there, and the *Bodhisattva* Avalokitesvara further expounds:

"...

So therefore in emptiness,

No form, no feeling, thought, choice or consciousness

No eye, ear, nose, tongue, body, mind

No sight, sound, smell, taste, touch or objects of mind

No realm of sensory cognition and

No realm of mind consciousness.

No ignorance or end of ignorance and till

No aging and no death,

Nor end of aging or death.

Neither is there suffering nor origination of suffering

No cessation of suffering or path to end suffering,

(i.e. the Noble Eightfold Path is negated)

There is no wisdom and no attainment." [28]

So we finally also leave behind the Noble Eightfold Path, and even the attainment of wisdom. Actually, the so-called "Buddhist" concepts are merely conceptualizations of the *Dharma* which we have developed, at the time when we were trying to interpret those teachings. They will be marred by our own lack of understanding. We had originally built them up as paradigms which are only provisionally correct, so therefore only of limited use. We had built them all up from a mind of limited understanding. As we gain deeper insights from our practice, we will have to continually discard our provisional understanding of the *Dharma*. Ultimately we have to let go of our conceptual knowledge of Theravada, Mahayana, Vajrayana or Ch'an (Jpn: Zen).

The stone tablet on which the teachings were engraved has to be finally smashed. However, we would do well to clearly bear in mind that this is not something we do upfront — while we are still in dire need of the teachings as a raft to convey us across the treacherous river of phenomenal existence. We still need, for now, to reverently follow these teachings, which protect and guide us. At the same time, as the *Heart Sutra* teaches, we should be prepared to relinquish them. We do not want to bind ourselves to an understanding of the *Dharma* because any such understanding will change as we continually grow in the direct experiencing of the *Dharma*. We should not constrain our growth.

The path of spiritual development in Buddhism pertains to our developing the means to see deeply into the nature of things; into the processes occurring in natural phenomena (including our own selves), and then to break out from our conditioned existence. The only question is whether we have the capability to do so, and whether there is a clear and precisely defined way to go about it. The Buddha had demonstrated that we have this capability, and he had also mapped out the path of training. In the time that has passed since he taught, his teachings have seen further tremendous developments and reformulations, to meet the needs and capabilities of the aspirants from the different cultures and countries, which his *Dharma* has been brought to.

We may have asked, what it is that makes life meaningful. To some, the answer may be the fulfilment of a dream, achievement of recognition, pursuing a passion, or nurturing a child to grow up to be successful. Another may find meaning in having beliefs which give what he or she considers to be a sensible interpretation of the phenomenal world, and his or her place in it. Yet another may find comfort in the belief of divine intervention into her personal affairs, or the promise of everlasting life in a heavenly realm.

Having something to live for, or having a goal in life, may give us direction and some respite from the vexations of life. However, if this is based on us having to make an acquisition, then by the nature of it being acquirable, it will not be lasting or permanent. It can be lost or changed and cannot give us full satisfaction, or be relied on always. It may also turn out to be different from our expectations, as the outcome is not within our control.

If we derive comfort from our beliefs, we will want to be certain that we have the correct beliefs. If we have made a clear assessment and have found that the beliefs are indeed reliable: that they will lead to our well-being and the well-being of others; that they do not subject us to illogical fear or bind us unquestioningly to them, then we may at least have some basis to take them on. Even so, we may ask why we need to subscribe to any beliefs at all. In any case, we should not need to compromise our ethical sense, or our freethinking and questioning mind.

The Buddha was well aware of these approaches to exploring the meaning of life. He delved very deeply into them and discovered the complete freedom from the unsatisfactoriness of life, right here and now. That the Buddha's teachings have lasted more than two and a half millennia, is testimony to its relevance to the human condition. It teaches the method of training for release from the bonds that bind us to the unsatisfactoriness of our existential experience. In his wisdom, the Buddha did not cast the practice of the *Dharma* into any absolute dogma which does not allow for personal investigation and assessment, or critique.

Direct Engagement and True Detachment

Words such as "dispassionate", "detached" or "non-attachment" are often used to describe the Buddhist practice. In conventional usage, these words may be taken to imply non-involvement, abrogation of responsibility, lack of sympathy, or having a cold, unfeeling attitude. This misinterpretaion has brought about some damaging misconceptions and wrong ideas about the Buddha's *Dharma,* and what living a Buddhist lifestyle is about.

When we understand the context in which they are used in explaining the *Dharma,* we will in fact see that Buddhism deals with the full engagement and direct understanding of what living life is about. The Buddhist approach is to develop mindfulness, which we can describe as a direct experiential awareness of the happennings within the field of our perceiving and experiencing, in the here and now of the present moment. This mindfulness is the key to awakening from our deluded and aimless mode of experiencing ourselves, and the world around us. It is very much the opposite of being indifferent or unresponsive.

The Buddhist approach is not to be "detached" in the sense of being cut off from feeling and interacting with the world. Instead, the practitioner learns to be fully cognizant of his person, and the environment around him. He directly apprehends his wants and needs, and understands his emotions and mental states which arise in his interactions with the environment. He is clearly involved with trying to understand himself; to have a true engagement with himself. This is where we start; by working on ourselves.

It is only when we really know ourselves that we can know the world. We interpret our surroundings and thoughts through our senses and our mind. Our impressions of the world are blended into our own sense of ourselves. If we are immersed in a murky pool of water, then whatever we will come to know of the world will be but a murky view of it.

With this understanding, we can start to appreciate all that is around us. We learn to "see things as they really are". We begin to see worldly phenomena, including our psycho-physical makeup, in terms of the three marks of being: impermanence (*anitya),* unsatisfactoriness (*duhkha*) and no-self (*anatman).* It is in this context of full acceptance and understanding; when selfless compassion and wisdom is active, that one can be truly "detached" or "dispassionate". The state of being "detached" or "dispassionate" referred to here, is therefore not the mundane indifference or aloofness we sometimes feel. The "detached" and "dispassionate" used here, describes the mind of one who is well on the way to awakening. It refers to the serene, tranquil, and non-discriminating mind; the mind which has relinquished aversion and clinging.

In the transcendent dependent-arising as taught by the Buddha in the *Upanisa Sutta* [29], "disenchantment" develops after insight is sufficiently established in the disciple and can support the abandoning of sensual clinging. This disenchantment with the phenomenal world further conditions the arising of "dispassion". So the "detachment" and "dispassion" referred to, in the *Dharma*, are lofty states in one who has already seen into reality. It is when one can dwell in the wisdom of emptiness, i.e. when one has overcome his impediments, and can be "detached" from the habitual self-referencing mind, that compassion can fully manifest.

We therefore have to be careful; not to try to be "detached" or "dispassionate" in this sense, if we have not yet seen into no-self, or have yet to develop the non-discriminating compassion. We cannot try to act in a "detached" way before we have developed true understanding and compassion, simply because we will not know what the "detached" way really means. Practice comes before realization.

A Buddhist is very much engaged with the well-being of himself, his family, community, environment, and of the world at large. As he develops and penetrates deep into the understanding of the nature of things, he moves away from operating in harmful ways. He will naturally lose interest in pursuing things which are harmful to the development of calm and insight. In other words, his priorities in life change. He will no longer want to be involved in searching for distractions, or be enticed into wasteful or harmful activities. He will also feel the wish for others to realise this.

"My heart does weep
With the sweat of the bricklayer
In the hot noon sun,
With the intent eye of the
Roadside shoe mender keen on his work.

When man strives in honest work
For a meagre living wage,
My heart does pray

Don't let it be after vain strivings
Or things wearisome
That your labour's pledged" [(30)]

As he develops and enjoys the resulting happy and peaceful states of mind, he feels compassion for all beings. He understands pain and fear, and does not wish them on anyone. He acts to support the well-being of others. He makes his living by ethical, harmless means. He practices generosity, sows harmony, and maintains caring and healthy relationships. He will no longer want to imbibe intoxicants to the extent that he loses clarity of mind, for he does not want to let a confused mind give rise to actions which may affect the well-being of himself and others. He restrains himself from speaking hurtful words. He cultivates his understanding of the *Dharma* through mindfulness and meditation, and gains the transformative insights which further refine his development.

When we discover that we have been holding on to a way of life or to habits which have caused much pain and suffering, what should we do? We do not just intellectually "detach" from them. When we discover we have been holding a piece of burning hot coal, what do we do? There is no need for further deliberation. We just let it go. We drop it.

Why We Need to Do Good

What do we understand by "doing good"? Doing good involves the two components of "doing" and "good". "Doing" is willed action. For us to do something, we would have wanted to do it. We would have had a wish for it to be done. We next would have given it some thought, and then made a decision to go ahead with acting on it; actually doing it. When an act is said to be "good", it is generally taken to mean that it is wonderful, morally right, has integrity, and is of benefit. "Doing good" then implies the willed activity of carrying out a virtuous and beneficial action (i.e. beneficial to others and ourselves). It will require a willingness and the generosity to consider the welfare of another or the general wellbeing of others (also including ourselves) when we give. This "doing good" as a "giving of goodness", is therefore a cultivation of generosity and loving.

Why, we may ask, should we be doing good at all? How does it benefit us to care for our fellow man? Coming from our self-centred mind, this would seem to be a valid question.

We do receive a number of benefits from doing good. We do know that if we willingly lend a helping hand to others, we will feel better by doing so. We feel a sense of achievement. It feeds us positivity and energises us.

We detest folks who are self-centred; who have little regard for others. We will rather be with people who are helpful and kind to us, than with those who do not care for us, or who may even harm us in any manner of ways. If we cultivate virtue and are helpful, we will in turn be appreciated. We will have supportive friends and a wider circle of influence.

We sow the seeds of goodness in ourselves when we help others. A mind dwelling in a state of consideration and sympathy for others, is a mind dwelling at ease; it forgives trespasses easily. It is not wearied by having to carry the burdens of suspicion, nor is it poisoned into suffering the fever of mental and emotional agitation brought on by ill will. It is not caught up with having petty thoughts of being wronged, nor does it continually weigh tit-for-tat revenge. It will instead be relaxed, lively, joyful and be thinking and comprehending clearly. It will be effortlessly in tune with the natural harmony of the cosmos, and not just be preoccupied with a tiny corner of a separate existence. It will then also be very receptive to the *Dharma* of unbounded compassion and wisdom.

This attitude of helpfulness and consideration for others is a gem. It is a joy to behold, when we see it manifested in the way children treat their parents with love, or in the way strangers treat one another with consideration and respect. When we put ourselves in the shoes of others, and respond skilfully to their needs as we would to ours, then we are cultivating loving-kindness, compassion, and emptiness. By so doing, we reinforce the positive emotions of love, joy, and contentment within us. As we develop the positive emotions and clear out the negative ones, we will naturally be happier.

If a person is vindictive and hateful, he will be dwelling with the mind of enmity and vengefulness. Hate and bitterness will easily sprout in his mind, and he will be habitually gripped by vengeful emotions. This is not a good state to be in. The feelings of hatefulness insulate him from clarity of mind, strangle his joyful happy thoughts, and stifle his feelings of calm and peacefulness. Similarly, if a person is inconsiderate or conceited, he will be dwelling with the mind of "me and mine only". This is the mind which is closed in on itself, deadened to the life and goodness in others. This is also not a happy mind. The Buddha taught his disciples to develop forgiveness, compassion and loving-kindness as antidotes to these negative energy-sapping mental states, which hinder our access to joy and happiness; the nutriments for our spiritual growth.

The attitudes of helpfulness, caring, and kindness, which we develop towards others, will also be the attitudes we will use on ourselves. We will be kinder to ourselves and will treat ourselves better, if we treat others better. We will forgive ourselves easier and love ourselves more, if we easily forgive and care for others. This is the natural way.

On the other hand, we do not only aim to be a do-gooder. We do good with a measure of wisdom and discernment, as to the appropriateness and timeliness of acting out our good intentions. We do not do good only to be nice, as that will be pandering to our self-importance and the self-view of our niceness. This means we do good with a clearly discerning mind, fully aware of what it is we are doing. We do good to benefit both the person on the receiving end of our actions and us.

We may be taking on some risk when we invite another person into our living space, when trying to help them. Our doing good has to be done judiciously, with knowing the situation at hand. I recall once when a friend from a foreign country received news of her father's passing away. Her fiancé who was a fighter plane pilot, was also recently killed in a war. She was in a very difficult period of her life. My wife and I offered her to stay with us for a while, so my wife could watch over her as she grieved. She stayed with us for two weeks, and we were glad she recovered from that difficult period. However, this may not have been the skilful thing to do if my wife was not with me at that time.

As we grow out of being driven about by destructive tendencies, we cultivate virtue. We will have a clear conscience when we do good, as opposed to be doing harmful deeds. We certainly should not cause harm or suffering intentionally, or be indifferent and rest in indolence. The clear conscience sustains our happy states of mind. Good deeds will bring good results. We can see the immediacy of this in the positive mental states which arise when we do virtuous acts. There are also the longer term good karmic results which will come to fruition at an opportune time. Even if under some circumstances, we do not feel up to doing good, then at least we do not cause harm, or inflict suffering on ourselves or others.

Karma is willed action. It is the consciousness of intent and the resulting actions that plant the karmic seeds, which may bear immediate or future fruit. Seeds of goodness will bring about conditions for happiness and growth. Seeds of self-serving actions will further condition the habitual mind to greed, hate and delusion, which result in pain and sorrow.

There cannot be spiritual growth without the cultivation of virtue. It is one of the three pillars of virtue, concentration and wisdom, which support our spiritual endeavour. By the practice of cultivating virtue and doing good, we develop a lifestyle of consideration and compassion for others. However, if we only do good without concurrently developing an understanding of the *Dharma*, it is an incomplete effort and may not ensure progress. Compassion has to be guided by wisdom, the same as wisdom has to be tempered with compassion.

With regard to the cultivation of goodness, we need to bear in mind the words from the *Diamond Sutra* [31]; that from the viewpoint of *Prajnaparamita* (the Perfection of Wisdom), when there is really no one doing the cultivation of virtue, when there is no virtue that is cultivated, only then is there true cultivation of virtue. This is a profound teaching on emptiness, which is applicable to our way of doing good (i.e. cultivating virtue).

The challenge for one on the path of spiritual growth is to continually maintain a heartfelt sincerity in the assessment of where one is — both in terms of the state of one's level of practice and of one's shortcomings, every step of the way.

The Path of Transcendent Dependent-Arising

It is by disengaging from the endless cycle of ignorance and distress, which has been described earlier in the dependent-origination, that we can be liberated. It is in the moment-to-moment process of the arising and disbanding of the "I" ego in the cycle of dependent-origination, that we can make the leap out to a new mode of being. The chains which have held us in servitude and bound us to the endless rounds of conditioned existence can be cut.

In the exposition of what is called the transcendent dependent-arising, the Buddha teaches that the disciple can take leave of the cycle of dependent-origination by developing "faith" as an offshoot from the link of "suffering" — instead of being caught again in the next link of "ignorance" and making another turn in the endless cycle of (the mundane) dependent-origination.

The disciple sees the wholesome results arising from his practice of the Noble Eightfold Path and with insight into *duhkha* (unsatisfactoriness or suffering), he is convinced of the efficacy of the *Dharma*. He is then armed with the "faith" that enables him to venture out from the wheel of becoming (the dependent-origination which characterises the flow and the web of causal conditioning rooted in ignorance). This blossoming of "faith" out from the mundane cycle of dependent-origination is followed on by other links, which signify growth on the spiritual path, which leads from the mundane to the transcendent; to liberation.

In the *Upanisa Sutta*,[32] the Buddha gives the analogy of how the droplets of rain falling on a mountain top will become rivulets flowing down the mountain to fill gullies and creeks. Their rising waters then overflow to further fill up pools, then lakes, which then brim over to fill up the streams and rivers, which finally flow to reach the wide ocean. The progress on the spiritual path is similar in many ways to this.

The dependent arising of the transcendent path starts with the arising of faith from the suffering of *duhkha* as its conditioning cause. Faith is, in turn, the conditioning cause for the next link of gladness. The transcendent path then follows on with ever higher states of being. The path of the transcendent dependent-arising is the conditioned arising of: faith → gladness → rapture (as conditioned by gladness) → tranquillity → happiness → concentration → knowledge of things as they really are → disenchantment → dispassion → liberation, and finally → (the last link of) the knowledge of destruction of the corruptions [33].

Herein is the supramundane path to the inconceivable liberation. From our direct experience of the unsatisfactoriness of being bound in the endless rounds of ignorance, unease and suffering, and also seeing the suffering and distress of others, we seek a better alternative for ourselves. We look for a way out and start on the path of practice. On realising the benefits of our practice, finding that it results in wholesomeness, happiness and wellbeing for ourselves and others, we start to develop faith in the Buddha, his *Dharma* and our boundless capacity for positive transformation.

As we explore and have further insights into the *Dharma*, we feel even more inspired, and grateful. We realize that we are indeed fortunate to have the *Dharma* made known to us, given to us as a refuge, and to have a common bond with the *Sangha* — those awakened or are also on the path to awakening. Our faith grows as our practice deepens.

The disciple's spiritual growth can now really start to take off; his practice starts maturing and uplifts him to heightened meditative states. He experiences rapture, tranquillity and happiness in his practice of meditation and is able to dwell in deep concentration. He can now sustain ever illuminating insights and even more clearly see "things as they really are". Compassion for all beings arises as he begins to understand the nature of suffering and derive much benefit and joy from his practice. He is even more inspired to further grow and develop on the path to emancipation. The various workings of phenomena can no longer hold him in enchantment.

This disenchantment is a turning away from the earlier fascination with conditioned phenomena. By now, with dispassion, the disciple experiences deep penetrating insight into emptiness. Dispassion here refers to the pure activity of wisdom and compassion, which manifests in the *Bodhisattva* when reactivity and the discriminating mind are cleared away.

The dispassion and disenchantment on the spiritual path indicate the mind which has, to a large extent, relinquished the passions and enchantment arising from self-conceit, greed and enmity. It is no longer enchanted or passionate about itself. No more is it seeking indulgences, placated by shallow superstitious beliefs, or languishing in a false sense of security. If we do not attach overtones of conceited selfhood to the "disenchantment" and "dispassion", we will not feel negative about this.

This "detachment" conditions the breakthrough into the enlightened mind from the mundane mind. The phenomenal world no longer can entice. The *Bodhisattva* breaks out into the supramundane and enters the stream of the *Dharma*. His treading of the path has reached the stage of non-regression, and nothing can stop the gathering momentum as he tears ahead with vigour, to where full emancipation awaits.

We may now understand why the spiritual path is often described in the negative — as in the emphasis on suffering, getting rid of this or that, not to hold on to this or that. This is because the spiritual path is primarily the path of getting rid of accretions of entrenched conditioning, and wrong views. A major clean-up of our whole being is required to clear away the contaminating dross — so we end up with a mind without any fault lines; a tough, but pliable mind. This mind has to withstand the heavy blows of the forge hammer of emptiness, which pulverises any remnants of the attachments to the unreal self.

The transcendent dependent-arising teaches that we can cultivate the good in this process of conditioned change. We can direct this process of *anitya* (impermanence). We will be changed, but then, through our understanding of *anitya*, we should also realise, when we enter the realm of *anatman* or no-self, there is really no substantive "we". Therefore from that perspective, there is really no change. In fact, with understanding *anatman (no-self)*, we may say that ultimately, there is really nothing to change. There is only the continual flowering of the heart-mind, the blooming of the thousand petalled lotus.

The Individual Choice of Practice

It is misleading to say that Buddhism demands one to forsake the love of family, or feelings for one another. The practitioner actually forsakes the destructive energies of greed, hate and delusory thinking, which then allows for the development of love, compassion and the true understanding of the nature of reality. The Buddha encourages his householder disciples to cultivate friendliness and virtue, and to be responsible members of the family and the community. He goes into some detail on how to actually go about doing this (refer to Chapters 3 and 7).

Every individual will have come from a different background, inherited different responsibilities, and will therefore be in a different situation. Each person will have different priorities and for perhaps very different reasons, will decide on how he or she will pursue the very personal path to awakening.

A mountaineer, an Olympian athlete or a trekker, may subject himself (or herself) to intense training away from home, for long periods in a training camp. In the pursuit of his dream of conquering an unscaled mountain face, winning an Olympic gold medal or completing an arduous journey through barren lands in extreme weather, he may abstain from stimulants and be on a regulated diet, in order to achieve the physical fitness and dexterity that he needs to achieve his aim.

So too, there may be those who seek deeper immersion into the practice of the *Dharma*. They may have the option to subject themselves to the rigours of spiritual practice in the supportive environment of a spiritual community. They may take it upon themselves to subscribe to a discipline which facilitates their practice. The compass of the *Dharma* guides them as they traverse the unchartered and ever-changing landscape of their mind, where the thickets of false views have to be cleared, to gain the transformative insights in their quest for awakening.

It is a matter of personal choice of how each person treads his path of development. There is no right or wrong way. We simply need to step forward naturally from where we are at.

Chapter 3: Engaged Joyful Living

Happily Being in the Present

Beyond Suffering to Joy

Enjoy More with What We Already Have

Engaging Joy

Enjoy the Simpler Life

Life is full of choices. We make choices every moment. Do we turn right or left? Shall we smile or frown? Shall we speak up or not? Shall we walk away or lend a hand? Shall we give or take? However, usually before we make any choices, we will have drawn upon our whole personal sense of what feels right or wrong, and whether we will be comfortable with the likely outcome. Any willed action of ours, will have been filtered through layers of habitual thinking and past conditioning, which has become part of our "self". We continually consult this "self" for all our conscious responses as we go about our daily living.

The Buddhist path of awakening helps us to penetrate through these thick sediments and layer upon layer of conditioning, and the notions we have of ourselves. We progressively clear away the clinging dirt, which insulates us from the luminosity of our true nature. The unruly habitual discriminating mind, which continually serves up restless thoughts and feelings of conceit, envy, regret, or greed, begins to be tamed as our practice deepens.

We can then begin to enjoy the pristine beauty all around us. We start to reach out to feel tenderness and love. With this sensitivity, we also come to delight in the *Dharma* which keeps our experiences whole, and which engenders the development of further good and happiness within us.

Happily Being in the Present

When we mindfully stay engaged in the present moment, we will always have a fresh appreciative mind; neither encumbered by our past, nor caught in speculations about the future. We will be experiencing life in its fullness, relishing the present, and embracing life as it continuously presents itself to us; in the present.

However, we are too often caught up in the past or the future. We are attached to our past experiences, our strong beliefs, our misdeeds, disillusionments and conflicts. Similarly, we may be caught in grandiose dreams; arising from infatuation with our overblown self-esteem. We may also be lost in the future if we attach to our imagined incapacities or weaknesses, which may have arisen from a lack of confidence or all sorts of worries. If we hold on to the past and future in this way, we will have kept the joyful experiencing of life at the door, and insulated ourselves from fully living life.

Let us work instead on inviting in the true appreciation of life. To do this fully, we will need to give up our habit of inculcating self-referencing into our experiencing of life. We need to be continually relinquishing ourselves every moment. This requires that we understand *anitya* and *anatman* (impermanence and no-self) in cultivating the mind of emptiness. It requires that we develop a free mind, which will allow this freedom of action, and accept positive change.

We need to learn to live mindfully in the present, deeply experiencing ourselves, without being distracted by our habitual discriminating mind which churns up thoughts and worries from the past, or of the future. This is the way to usher in happiness and well-being. We cultivate being ever mindful, which means being fully aware of the present moment, in the present moment. When we are fully in the present, we will perceive the past and future to be thoughts which arise and cease. Let us drop our attachment to these thoughts, stop pursuing them, and with an uncluttered and undistracted mind, live in the wonder of the present moment. We will then be opening ourselves up to directly experiencing life. No imagined preferences or comparisons will come to contaminate our direct experience, when we live in the present moment.

When we smile, let us smile from the heart-mind of the present moment. Let it be a smile unencumbered by undue reservations from the past or about the future. When we love, let us love with our being in the present moment, not with an imagined "self" from the past or future. When we rest, let us be resting in the peace of the present moment, leaving behind all thoughts of the past or future. Let us be happily and fully resting, in the ever present moment.

Let us do a little exercise on being mindful in the present moment. Make yourself a nice fresh cup of tea (or coffee), and settle yourself in a comfortable place. As you read this, loosen the tension in your shoulders, relax your body and let your arms hang loose. Relax the facial muscles of your forehead and cheeks. Relax the muscles around your eyes and close them lightly. Manage the slight hint of a smile.

Take a deep breath, let it out slowly and feel the relaxed tone of the muscles in your body. Be fully present and relaxed, breathing normally. Feel the calmness in the ever present now. Then for about five minutes, stay loose and relaxed, enjoying the peaceful present moment. If you hear any sounds, just listen quietly; letting any sounds that you hear come and go as they please. Hear them, but do not run after them with interest. If any distracting thoughts arise, let them be. Just stay with the peaceful and relaxed mind of the present moment.

Now lightly open your eyes, and you are ready to enjoy your cup of tea in the present moment. No other thoughts need to be there to distract you from the full enjoyment of your cup of tea. Slowly and mindfully, reach out for your cup. Hold the cup lightly in both hands, and feel the warmth from the cup on your palms. Be with the cup and be with the tea. Slowly and mindfully, raise the cup to your mouth. Be aware of the fragrance from the tea. As you put it to your lips and take a sip, be aware of the sweetness in the tea. Fully enjoy the drinking of tea.

Remind yourself, as you take a sip of the tea:

"There is cup,
There is tea
There is fragrance
There is sweetness
That is all!" [34]

Then continue taking small sips, staying mindfully aware of your movements, the fragrance and flavour of the tea, as you drink.

We thereby experience the emptiness of drinking tea. We can apply this mindfulness of drinking tea to all our daily activities, savouring each moment mindfully, without allowing commentarial thoughts to distract us from what we are actively involved in, in the moment of the activity happening right there and then. This is a good stress-busting practice. In the midst of the daily hustle and bustle of going about your work, take a ten minute break, and enjoy the restfulness of mindfully drinking tea. Enjoy the emptiness of mindfully drinking tea.

When we begin to experience the joy and ease with dwelling in emptiness, we are also developing a mind to relinquishment. It is when we have relinquished the past and future, that we can stay mindful in the present. Relinquishment can be pleasant and joyful. It can give us a whole new way of experiencing life in fullness. We infuse this sense of well-being and joyfulness with being in the present moment, into our everyday living. That is how we can be fully enjoying tea, and how we can be fully enjoying life.

Beyond Suffering to Joy

There may be occasions when we may be stricken with disease, or be suffering from a disability. When we are sick and in pain, we can acutely feel *duhkha*. We directly know the pain of emotional and physical suffering. We may even already feel we are living this suffering.

However, we also know we are not unique in this respect. All beings along with us, are subject to suffering. We sometimes forget about it when we are having a great time, or are distracted by the many myriad forms, thoughts, pleasant sense impressions, enjoyable experiences and the activities of getting on with living. It is during times when we are acutely feeling the discomfort of duhkha that we will have a keen sensitivity to the teaching of *anitya* (impermanence). If we allow ourselves to further contemplate *anatman* (no-self), we will see a new perspective on suffering. We will understand that there is the feeling of pain and discomfort in suffering. There is, however, only the feeling of pain and discomfort, with no need for any other entity to be in that experience of pain or discomfort. Though we say we are suffering, there is no substantial entity in the "we" which is suffering. We learned this from the teaching on the emptiness of the five *skandhas* (the five aggregates of form, feeling, perception, volitional activity and consciousness) which the *Bodhisattva* Avalokitesvara expounded in the *Heart Sutra*. If we see our pain and discomfort this way, we will not claim that the pain and suffering belong to us. It may still feel to be painful, as that is the nature of a painful feeling. We acknowledge it, but need not be drawn further into it.

The Buddha taught that we need to fully understand the cause of unease and suffering; the compounded things (i.e. the five aggregates) which decay and change, are inherently unsatisfactory. They are not to be clung or attached to. When we realise we have been unendingly caught in the cycle of the dependent-origination (which describes the mundane conditioned arising and ceasing of material and mental states of being), we will then begin to understand that we have brought much suffering upon ourselves.

The way out of suffering, is by relinquishing the clinging to our experience of the phenomenal world. It is our mind which develops the attachments to the objects of sensory experience. The fault does not lie with the physical or mental objects which we come into contact with, or which we experience. There is nothing wrong with the world or with the processes of impermanence, decay and death of mundane existence. Similarly, there is nothing good or bad about our feelings, or experiences which can be pleasant or unpleasant. All of these are the sensory and cognitive processes, which the natural environment has evolved and brought into being. However, our self-created idea of an enduring and separate "self", and our blighted vision which sees the world around us as lasting entities with their own separate innate existences, give rise to the discriminating mind with likes and dislikes. The discriminating mind then conditions the arising of clinging. It is with gaining the insight into this that we begin to awaken.

The Noble Eightfold Path is the method of practice for doing so. It can guide us into spiritual growth, along the course of the transcendent dependent-arising. It is then that we directly resolve the issue of unease and suffering. We have recourse to this tested path, to transcend suffering and enter into the realm of true ease and comfort, for the benefit of all beings.

Enjoy More with What We Already Have

It is pretty obvious we will suffer, if we are attached to the material things in life. The material things do not last and we have to worry about their safekeeping. Besides the money we would have spent to purchase a beautiful piece of sculpture or a painting, which we may have bought on a passing fancy, we worry whether they will keep well. We worry when families with unruly kids drop by for a visit. If we have spent a princely sum on a new high performance car, we will have to take extra care when going over potholes on the roads. A scratch on the paintwork or a dent may likely drive us to delirium.

There is also the effort we would have expended to accumulate the money for these acquisitions, the time we would have spent in making our selection, getting all the associated accessories, on top of having to later take good care of them. If we can well afford to do this, and doing this on the whole does give us satisfaction and well-being, then the trade-offs seemingly may be worthwhile. If doing this only gives us more problems, or a short-lived satisfaction, or if it chews up too much of our time, which may be better used elsewhere, we may then want to reconsider. When our tastes change, we find that the things we used to like have become not so alluring anymore.

In our practice of the *Dharma*, we learn how pleasure or enjoyment is related to relinquishment and attachment. In relinquishment, we are not really giving anything up because there was never anything that is ours. Still, we can relinquish only to the extent that we see emptiness; the emptiness of the physical or mental object to be relinquished, the emptiness of ourselves as the person who is relinquishing the object, and the emptiness in the act of relinquishment itself.

It is not a trade-off; as in relinquishment versus enjoyment. It does not mean that the more we relinquish, the less we can enjoy. Rather, what we are doing, is to relinquish our clinging to enjoyment and not necessarily the enjoyment itself. We relinquish the attachments which we have developed in the first place. We are relinquishing that which we have brought into being. If we relinquish these bonds of our clinging, we will be free from the vexations that arise from the attachment. We are thereby relinquishing a worrisome burden we ourselves have taken on. Would that not be a cause for rejoicing?

Enjoyment or pleasure, is a feeling that is part of our experiencing the phenomenal world. It exists, the same as our senses exist. We have pleasurable feelings, the same as we have painful feelings. If we arc told to relinquish any attachment to painful feelings, then that appears to be not a problem at all. This is because painful feelings are not pleasant. We are happy to part ways with them. The case is seemingly different with pleasurable feelings, towards which we easily develop attachments.

The relinquishment of the craving and clinging to enjoyment does not equate to the relinquishment of enjoyment. We can be fully inspired by the wonderful scenery before us, and when we leave the scene, we need not hanker after it. We can enjoy our possessions without endlessly craving to acquire more of them. We may be enjoying every tasty morsel of the main course of a dinner, and when we have finished eating, we can fully move on to have dessert and enjoy that too. We can derive inspiration from the sights, sounds and smells around us and enjoy the beauty of nature, where each stone is nestled in its happy place. We can enjoy the beauty of a deep relationship where we experience giving and sharing. We can marvel at the beauty of human endeavour expressed in art, architecture, literature, music or poetry.

"Feel the sap that flows
through asphalt roads,
swims with the fishes along
river beds,
rising with concrete towers
along the wrinkles of the old man's face,
shaped into a claypot that
melts in a peal of laughter,
and sweat,
and light around, above,
feel its twists and turns,
laughing as it dances on..." [35]

When we are in such a pleasant state of consciousness, we are immersed in the object of our experience, which may be a harmonious musical piece, tasty food, or visually beautiful artwork. We are experiencing them deeply and there is nothing wrong with fully enjoying them. It is, however, often not easy to draw the fine line between feeling and craving; the next link on from feeling, in the cycle of dependent-origination. The problem arises when we so often continue on from the experiencing (feeling) to developing attachment (craving), and then clinging indulgently to the enjoyable experience. We should not delude ourselves that we will not have any attachments, when we go beyond just pure enjoyment, to further indulge ourselves. It takes some degree of insight and mindfulness, to be able to simply enjoy our sensory experiences, without further grasping and clinging on to them. However, this is what we have to learn to be proficient at doing.

We can enjoy, but we stay mindful not to cling on to the enjoyment or the objects of enjoyment. If we can do so, we will then truly enjoy without the taint of clinging (which will have arisen from ignorance). Otherwise, we will be again and again caught in the cycle of samsaric existence and suffer for it. The extent to which we understand the Four Noble Truths and develop ourselves on the Noble Eightfold Path, will reflect the extent of our freedom from having to suffer the effects of clinging to that which can never satisfy.

It is when relinquishment and clinging are all left behind, that one can fully experience without attachment. There is then only the pure enjoyment in the realm of emptiness.

Engaging Joy

We can engage ourselves deeply, creatively and with clarity when we are not intoxicated. Intoxication is a state of being stupefied, drunk, or exhilarated to a condition of diminished mental or physical control. We can be intoxicated by drugs, drink, or by our senses. It may be tempting to seek intoxication as a way to lose ourselves, in the midst of our dissatisfaction or boredom.

We may feel that we lose our unhappiness and suffering when we are in the exhilaration of intoxication, but they are actually only out of our sight for a while. They are just around the corner. When we sober up, or when the effects of intoxication wear out, they reappear to vex us. The so-called "happiness" we get when we are intoxicated, or on a "high", is but a "happiness" in delusion. It does not last. So being intoxicated is not a real escape from our troubles or pain. It cannot be an escape because we get caught back again and again. As it goes on this way, we may be sucked into even deeper dependency. This is not to say we cannot sometimes enjoy a glass of good wine or a nicely chilled can of beer. We enjoy it in moderation, and ensure we do not take on so much that we become diminished in mental or physical capacity. If we cannot do so, then we will want to stay clear of it.

Our vexations are not objects "out there". They arise and cease in our mind. They arise because we wrongly understand, and wrongly perceive ourselves and the world around us. This may appear oversimplified, as the issues we have to deal with often appear much more complicated. However, it is this fundamental ignorance that is the cause of our suffering.

Let us look at an example when someone falls into debt even though he has a decent income. It may be obvious to a friend of his that the problem is due to him living beyond his means. This person, however, turns a blind eye to his own shortcomings and is more concerned with finding ways to spread out his credit card debts. He may, when things get really bad, even resort to fraud or theft to maintain his spendthrift ways. The problem may lie with his indulgence and craving for the "finer things in life". More often than not, it may also be due to his craving for status and recognition: to be regarded as someone who has "arrived", who has to display the trappings of wealth, and to be extravagant in the company of affluent friends.

In the above example, we see the person is craving for feelings of sensual enjoyment and suffers from conceited pride. He is destroying himself (and the welfare of his family or close ones) because of his excessive craving for the enjoyment of things which cannot truly satisfy. He actually does not need to frequently splurge on expensive restaurant food and drink to eat healthily, nor does he need to spend beyond his means to be well regarded by others. All this stems from a wrong view of himself and not understanding the Second Noble Truth (which states that suffering arises from craving). The person who does not have the means to live the high life would do well to disengage from his circle of affluent friends, and live within his means. If he works on his self-cultivation, he will begin to engage the joy of not having to rely on things which cannot satisfy, and develop a steady and happy mind unaffected by praise or blame.

With this understanding, let us next look at how we can engage joyfulness and be free from our vexations. We can start with making a firm resolve to aspire to clarity of mind and living mindfully. We then develop the mindfulness to truly know ourselves better, to understand our mind and the nature of our thoughts and feelings. From having changed the way we conduct ourselves, we already will begin to feel happy with knowing ourselves better and seeing the improvements in our behaviour and relationships with others. We support our deepening understanding with virtuous conduct and develop emotional positivity, calm and discernment. We gain the insights which will further consolidate our development, and establish ourselves in gladness and peacefulness. This is the innate potential within every one of us. We will find that we can handle the issues of life with confidence and clarity, as we develop our practice. Our troubles will then not look to be unsurmountable anymore. This is one way we ought to love ourselves.

Just as we may be intoxicated by our so-called attainments, we may also be intoxicated by our virtues and be blind to our faults. Honesty with ourselves is therefore most important as we grow in our practice. It helps to anchor us in the here and now, in the reality of our present condition, so that we do not get muddle headed and all puffed up.

Enjoy the Simpler Life

We can help lessen our burdens if we make our lives simpler and therefore easier to manage. We will want to loosen our attachments; to cut down on and have less of the unnecessary that weigh us down. We then seek more of that which will inspire us, which can help us cultivate a clear and positive mind.

We look to simplify our relationships, our lifestyle and our needs:

- *It is not necessary to satiate our senses, when we can mindfully derive full enjoyment from the simple pleasures.*

- *It is not necessary to fill our minds to no end with gossip or irrelevant facts, when we can develop clarity of mind and know ourselves directly and deeply.*

- *It is not necessary to be well connected or to crave recognition, when we can develop and appreciate our own worthiness.*

- *It is not necessary to rush and run, when we can take the time to explore and enjoy our connectedness to nature, our community, and our environment.*

- *It is not necessary to be worn out from having to maintain many acquaintances and be involved in many celebrations, gatherings and dinners, when a smaller circle of understanding friends that are appreciative and supportive will suffice.*

- *It is not necessary to pursue too many interests, when we only feel truly passionate for a few.*

- *It is not necessary to go to great lengths to impress, to look wealthy or imposing, when we can be happy with being ourselves.*

If we cultivate the strength of character, which derives from understanding the *Dharma* of non-attachment, we will be emotionally strong, have an overflowing positivity, and be able to go about living our daily lives with an unassuming quiet joy and a song in our hearts. When we have developed the steady strength, clarity of vision and joyfulness in our practice of the *Dharma*, we can then be a support for others who are caught up or lost in the vicissitudes of life. We can be a true friend, to be able to point them to, and help them along the way to true contentment and happiness.

Chapter 4: The Freedom that Comes from Relinquishment

If we have a potted plant indoors, we may worry about it not having enough water. This worry can be easily settled. We make a commitment to water it on alternate days and with that commitment to responsible action, we no longer need to worry about our potted plant drying out. Let us say the plant flowers. The purplish pink flowers are such a delightful sight before we leave the house for work in the mornings. All too soon, the flowers wilt and fall. We feel a loss, but we get over it rather quickly, because we know it is not any fault of ours, nor that of the plant. It is simply nature taking its course.

When we understand the true nature of things, we do not suffer, because we will have the wisdom to accept reality. It is in the nature of a flower to wilt away. That is the process of *anitya* (impermanence) at work. That is just how it is. However, it seems rather difficult to extend this acceptance to the other things we hold dear. Why is this so? Why do we bring so much distress to ourselves by trying to cling on to that which is bound to wilt away?

There is much suffering that we can learn to let go of. The delusive attachments which bring on suffering or hinder our development should be dumped. Being detached is not enough. Note here, we are using the word "detached" in the conventional sense. True "detachment" on the Buddhist path, as we have seen earlier, is a highly developed state based on having acquired deep understanding into seeing "things as they really are". It arises from deep insight which has kindled the spirit of relinquishment and renunciation in the disciple. When used in the conventional sense, the word "detached" does not bring out the positive aspects of this process of actively and knowingly letting go.

This is sometimes where misunderstandings can arise. There are some who wrongly criticize the Buddha's teachings by saying, "Buddhism teaches detachment from worldly affairs. It teaches not taking responsibility. Buddhism teaches dispassion, which is uncaring. I love and care for my family and friends. I don't ever want to lose them. So how can I even consider being a Buddhist?"

The Buddha taught the *Dharma* which caters to all. He teaches the householder to have care and respect for elders, love for the family and friends, responsible commitment to a wholesome lifestyle, and to live joyfully in developing virtue, concentration and mindful wisdom. An individual may further make the choice to relinquish the householder life and immerse himself in the practice of the *Dharma* with the community of monks. However, not everyone who aspires to this can actually do so in practice. It is not a choice we can live out, if we are not ready for it. True relinquishment cannot be willed into being. This is not something we can wish upon ourselves or others. It can only happen to the extent that the insightful wisdom which sees into emptiness is developed, and when the heart-mind of the disciple is attuned to accepting it. When this happens, the generosity of giving and compassionate love can be fully manifested and the person lives to benefit all beings.

For those who are fully committed to the pursuit of awakening and are ready, the Buddha teaches the practice of total relinquishment. In this total relinquishment, the supramundane detachment and dispassion manifests. It is only then that true detachment and dispassion are possible. They are not the mundane "detachment" and "dispassion" which are associated with alienation, arrogance and repressed urges. Unless we are ready from having practiced deeply, we will not be able to have the true "detachment" or "dispassion", even if we wanted to.

We allow ourselves to relinquish, or to let go, when there is a realignment of priorities. This will happen as we develop insight into the true nature of things. As a mundane example, when we want to lose weight, we may let go of wanting an extra scoop of ice-cream. We willingly do so, and may even also give up our usual tea time snacks. The letting go is made easier when there is understanding to support it, when we realise as in this case, that the letting go will benefit us and help us in our efforts to lose weight.

We let go with knowing the nature of what it is that we are letting go of. True letting go is not a pushing away, not a suppression, not a disdainful blocking out, and definitely not annihilation. The letting go is in the gesture of an opening of our fist and letting what it is that we have been tightly clenching on to, to be wafted away from our open hand. We have mindfully severed our bonds of attachment to it, knowing well that our clinging is a source of distress, and so we allow it to freely go.

When we let go in this way, we are not losing anything. We instead gain the freedom from the bondage of our clinging and attachment. Let us look at what we can let go of, and how doing so will directly help us.

Letting Go of Self and Other's Views

It does help, if we are to loosen our hold on views we hold of ourselves. We do not have to hold on to views that we are of a particular behaviour only because it has been a habit with us to be acting in such a way. Of course we firstly should be aware of what our shortcomings are. We need not hold on to thoughts of ourselves as being quick to anger, unfriendly, unhelpful, lazy, fearful, and stingy, or all the other types of poor behaviour. We have to recognize we are capable of change.

The *Dharma* is all about a major transformation of ourselves. With practice of the *Dharma*, we will definitely change for the better. So we do ourselves a great disservice and are putting obstacles in our way, if we think negatively about ourselves. We can only start from where we are at. When we recognize our weaknesses, we will know what we may especially need to work on, and we release it from our grip. We let it go, as we set out on the path of transformation of the Noble Eightfold Path which covers change in all aspects of our being.

When we tread the Noble Eightfold Path, this change for the better will occur subtly and continually. In letting go of our own self-views, we also would want to let go of holding on to views others have of us, or views which conventional society imposes on us. When we know we are doing right, and are happy with ourselves and the way we conduct ourselves in accord with the *Dharma*, there is no need to seek approval elsewhere.

If we are advanced in years, we have to let go of giving ourselves excuses for not looking beyond our habitual selves just because we are older. We may have to be slower or less physically active. However, we need not stop from being positive, having a bright and agile mind, or further developing happiness and contentment.

We need not pigeonhole ourselves by adopting what we think the behaviourial norms for the young or old should be. We need not impose rigid views on what the words "old" or "young" should mean. The "old" folks can always be "young" and fresh if they let themselves be so, and they should allow themselves to be so. Physical aging is natural, and we want to accept it as it comes; for we start to age from when we were born, moment by moment. Least of all, it should not stop us from pursuing the development of peaceful calm and insight.

When we are older, we have more of the experiences that life will have thrown at us. We will have had more exposure to capricious human nature, and will have experienced more of delight, disappointment, anguish, love and hate. We will have an abundance of examples we can draw on, to support our cultivation of insight into the nature of mind, and to realise the calm and wisdom, which leads to the happiness of release from distress.

Letting Go of Indulgence

Enjoyment need not be by way of indulging in our senses to the extent that it becomes a constant craving for more. It is better to have enjoyment in having the time to pursue our creative activities, be truly experiencing ourselves, and to be free from having to pander unceasingly to the needs and wants from every quarter.

We need not always be on the lookout for playthings or distractions. There is no need to be continually storing up experiences; to end up with large collections of photographs, or repertoires of travel anecdotes. If we burden ourselves with too much memorabilia, we will tend to trap ourselves in the past. We certainly can have fun, enjoyment, and derive inspiration from travel. However, if we are merely craving for and collecting experiences, we will never be satisfied.

When we let go of indulgence, we will be rid of a large portion of our distractions and will begin to be in touch with ourselves deeply. We will be happy with what we are enjoying, in the moment of the enjoyment. Having the time to slowly savour a strawberry tart, or mindfully sip one's favourite jasmine tea, can give us much pleasure and satisfaction. Going on a leisurely stroll when it is calm and cool, or just meeting up with friends to enjoy each other's company can be very meaningful. In fact, simply sitting mindfully, dwelling in the present, perhaps feeling the coolness of the light evening breeze and hearing at times the ringing of the wind chimes, can be really delightful.

When our mind begins to tire of the simple things, we grow restless, and give in to craving for new experiences. If we develop mindfulness in our activities, and relinquish the mind that wants to seek unnecessary distractions, we will begin to develop contentment. We can then enjoy the simple things much more and give ourselves more joy. We will be happy with deriving a deeper appreciation from the simple things we already have. If we develop a clear and sensitive mind, nature in the environment around us will reveal its awesome beauty to inspire us. Perhaps we may say that nature reveals our innate beauty to us.

Ryokan (良寛, CE 1758-1831), the well-known Japanese poet-Buddhist monk writes:

"*The willows are in full bloom!*
I want to pile up the blossoms
Like mountain snow." [36]

Wouldn't you like to join Ryokan in piling up the blossoms?

Letting Go of Painful Experiences

If we have suffered a painful experience, for example cruel physical or emotional treatment, the experience may have been traumatic enough to have left strong unresolved emotions in us. We may be similarly affected if we see our loved ones subjected to such treatment. Whenever the painful experience is brought to mind, thoughts of resentment and hatred may arise. There may also be further complicating emotions of fear or self-doubt, linked to the painful experience, which are affecting us as well. We may then harbour thoughts of revenge or ill intentions.

The actual pain or distress experienced at the time of the actual experience has passed into the past. The pain we are experiencing still, is the pain brought on by a recollection of that past experience. We are suffering from clinging to a recreation of the experience from within our mind. It is now a self-created image and not the real thing. If we can understand that it is our attachment (to that past experience) which is causing us pain, it will be easier for us not to be drawn into it. We can instead, begin to let it go. However, doing so may not be easy, even though we already may be convinced that it is the right thing to do.

We can start with letting go of the fear, self-doubt, and resentment within us. These feelings do harm us, and further strengthen the attachments to our painful past. We have already suffered enough of the pain dealt out to us, from being subjected to that painful experience. There is good reason not to take on more suffering from dwelling in the fear, or from having vengeful thoughts, which further stoke the emotions of self-doubt or hatred within us.

We can move towards being free from the suffering of the painful emotions which are conjured up by our reliving that painful memory. We need to let the past go. We have to disengage from those attachments, to forgive and move on. Our understanding of the *Dharma* tells us that the five aggregates are impermanent, and have no selfhood. They are empty, so we can outgrow our "old" selves. We can let go of the mind which is deluded, fearful and vengeful.

If we want to move on from that painful past experience, the practice of the *Dharma* will allow us to develop the positivity which can sustain our healing. Especially with the practice of mindfulness and meditation, we lay the positive ground from where we look into our thoughts and feelings. The *Dharma* empowers us to change this habitual mind which is the source of the pain. We embark on the practice which can lead us out of this predicament. We start with treading the Noble Eightfold Path of transformation into wellness and restfulness.

On closer examination, when we see into the nature of our feelings and emotions of fear, self-doubt or hatefulness, we will find that they are empty. There are but conditioned states of mind which arise to further stir up empty feelings. In our ignorant state, we are the ones giving direction to the harmful feelings we have allowed to be brought into being. We have to learn to relinquish our hold on to these negative emotions.

If feelings of hatred or ill will, however justifiable we think they may be, are causing us pain, we will be better off to be rid of them. It is better to be happy without being vulnerable to chronic and painful emotional tangles that hatred will return us to. We can do this with anchoring ourselves in a love for ourselves, and then melting away the emotional barriers for us to extend the friendliness to others and even to our "enemies". This practice of loving-kindness (refer to Appendix I) is the antidote for our feelings of hate or ill will. It is when we have let go of ill will that we will be free from having to endure the pain from the emotions which hatred or ill will stirs up in us.

We want to bear in mind the words of the Buddha from the Dhammapada:

"Hatred is never appeased by hatred

Only by love is hatred appeased

This is the timeless truth."

Letting Go of Guilt and Remorse

The Buddhist path of self-development does not seek to condemn someone who had carried out a harmful act, to eternal damnation or suffering. It in fact provides the means to lift the person out from his guilt-ridden mind, and to help him overcome his tendency to be bogged down in remorse. There is the potential for release from suffering in all of us. In other words, we may say that there is the nature of the Buddha in every one of us.

Let us begin with the story of Ahimsaka [37] (the Harmless One) who was from a privileged family in the time of the Buddha. Ahimsaka turned to become a merciless bandit and violent murderer who wore the fingers of those he killed in a garland and thereby came to be called Angulimala (the Finger Garland). One day, the Buddha, after his morning alms round and meal, set out alone along the road leading to the forest where Angulimala was known to be. The other travellers and village folk who he met along the way tried to dissuade him from making his way there. They told him even large groups of travellers have been set on and killed by Angulimala, but the Buddha went on in silence.

When Angulimala saw the Buddha alone in the distance, he thought he will have an easy prey to kill. He girded himself with his weapons, and with a drawn sword in hand, approached the Buddha from behind. Strangely though, no matter how hard he tried, he could not catch up with the

Buddha, who appeared to be unhurried and walking normally. Sensing that something was amiss and as he collapsed to the ground from exhaustion, he shouted out to the Buddha to stop.

We can picture the completely exhausted and humbled Angulimala on his knees, leaning on his sword. The Buddha turned to address Angulimala, "I had stopped. Angulimala, you stop too." Angulimala asked the Buddha for the meaning of why he spoke thus. The Buddha compassionately told him he had stopped forever from violence and the "self" in him had stopped coming to be. At that moment, Angulimala underwent a turning about, deep in his consciousness. Despite all the evil deeds he had done, the seed of goodness in him sprouted and brought forth new shoots.

Angulimala renounced evil, and asked for the going forth at the Buddha's feet. The Buddha addressed him with the words, "Come monk." That was how Angulimala came to be a disciple of the Buddha. We are told that with ardent and diligent practice, Angulimala later attained to *Arhat*-ship. Angulimala, however, occasionally had to endure physical pain and injury from violence done to him by those seeking revenge for his past misdeeds.

Once, when Angulimala the monk was on his alms round, he saw a woman in the difficult and painful labour of childbirth. He mentioned what he had seen to the Buddha. The Buddha told Angulimala that since he was born, he had not killed any being, and by this truth, he should give his blessings to the mother in labour. Angulimala was surprised by the Buddha saying so, for he had taken many lives. The Buddha told Angulimala it is indeed true; he (Anguimala) had not taken life from when he had his noble birth, from when he became a disciple of the Buddha. Angulimala did as the Buddha instructed and the delivery of the baby went well. To this day, in the Theravada tradition, the *Angulimala Paritta* (protective chant of Angulimala) is recited to give blessings to expectant mothers for easy childbirth.

The above *sutta* tells us that the seed of goodness and greatness is in every one of us. We only need, as the Buddha puts it, to "Stop!" We are to stop inflicting pain and suffering on ourselves and others, cultivate virtue, and to do so with knowledge of the *Dharma*. Angulimala would of course have felt great remorse for the suffering he had inflicted on his victims. It would have required from him much diligent effort to overcome the karmic hindrances (the negative imprints conditioning his consciousness) and leave all that behind him, to be "born again" into following the *Dharma*. Though we would not have subjected ourselves to the same predicament Angulimala was in, we need to do the same, to leave whatever misdeeds we have done behind us and move on ahead into the peaceful joy of the *Dharma*.

The concept of "sin" as a violation of the will of an absolute divine power, or a curse which condemns one to unavoidable suffering, is foreign to the *Dharma*. As we do not cater to the dictates from any higher power by way of blind submission to "divine" authority, the concept of committing "sin" from the transgressions of those dictates, have no meaning. We know from the Buddha's teachings that the process of growth and transformation can be guided by ourselves and led by ourselves. This can happen because there is no permanent unchanging "self"; everything is subject to continual change in moments. We acknowledge our mistakes, and feel remorse for the harm we had caused. We come clean as it were, and then we drop it all behind us. We will have to bear the consequences of our wrongdoing, but we do not need to be further bogged down by feelings of guilt which hinder our development. Guilt does not belong to us. We can let go of it.

Though we understand that we should let go of our guilt arising from past wrongdoings and start anew right this moment, our habitual clinging mind will resist this. This is because we still cling to past experiences; even to negative views of ourselves. We cling to the false security of keeping a past outdated "self", even though it hurts us. With an understanding of dependent-origination, we know from the above example that it is the clinging (to an outdated "self"), as conditioned by craving (for affirmation of existence), which is hindering the relinquishment of our burden of guilt. As we practice the *Dharma*, these feelings of guilt and remorse will diminish and then vanish, as we purify our heart-mind in our practice of the Noble Eightfold Path.

To establish ourselves in the letting go of guilt and remorse, we can allow the inspiration and support from the Buddhas and the *Bodhisattvas* into our healing process. One effective method is to do the prostration practice as described in the chapter on "Reverencing the Three Treasures". The prostration practice is especially effective because it involves both body and mind. The physical act of prostration loosens us physically and also helps to relax our mind. When we can do it smoothly, both body and mind are unified in the flowing movements of prostrating.

We do the prostrations with a mindful acceptance that we have in the past done harmful or regrettable deeds. We lay down all of our negativity towards ourselves. We relinquish the past which is already gone, to move on ahead with our practice of cultivating virtue on the Noble Eightfold Path. We open ourselves to inspiration from the Buddhas and *Bodhisattvas*, and invite the joy of going for protection and refuge in the Three Treasures. We end with wishing all those who feel remorse to be quickly relinquishing their burden and to be joyful and happy.

Letting Go of the Past, Present and Future

Wouldn't it be wonderful if we can be fully free from being hounded by past regrets, worrying about the future, and from being unsure or listless in the present? We can begin to enjoy this freedom as we learn to let go of the past and future, and work on our self-cultivation in the present.

We are usually laden with much unneeded baggage from the past. We then take on even more as we journey through life. There are many unhappy thoughts, feelings of insecurity, fear and emotional pain, which we can dump. They are the spoil sports that venture out from the recesses of our mind when baited by the seeds of delusory thinking, hate, envy, or greed, to hijack our calm and happy states of mind. We are especially vulnerable to be suffering from this when we let our guard down and sink into negativity.

We can clear away those unhappy thoughts. Those thoughts are not ours to begin with. As we develop our understanding of the *Dharma*, we will begin to realise that our thoughts have no self-nature (i.e. no inherent selfhood). If we let them be, they will just fizzle away. With mindfulness, we learn to let go of these thoughts, and not bind them to ourselves. We do not hang on to them. Neither do we need to rein them in with chains. We develop a mind in emptiness and those chains of attachment will naturally fall away.

Let us not hold on to what is not ours, or bind unhappiness to ourselves. Those thoughts are but our own imaginings, so let them be, drop them, move on into the light of mindfulness and they will vanish by themselves.

The Buddha has this to say:

"Let not a person revive the past
Or on the future build his hopes;
For the past has been left behind
And the future has not been reached.
Instead with insight let him see
Each presently arisen state;
Let him know that and be sure of it,
Invincibly, unshakeably.
Today the effort must be made..." [38]

Here, the Buddha speaks about the futility of dwelling in the past or the future. We are to cultivate mindful awareness of the present moment, be mindful of "each presently arisen state", and not be bound up with the craving and attachment to that which is presently arising. There is only one place from which to start, and that is from the present moment.

Everything is open to us to act on, in this very instant. This moment is open for us to create a new beginning. Not a new beginning in contrast to an older beginning. Just another step forward, and we decide where we want to be heading. This is always available to us every moment. So why should we not be happy to have such opportunities arising endlessly, moment by moment? If we cultivate an open mind, a free mind, a receiving and giving mind, this becomes an opportunity for growth in our well-being, every moment. It gives us such immeasurable opportunities and freedom.

We will be presented with ever new possibilities for growth if we are to relinquish the past and future, and be mindfully

115

aware of the present without grasping at and clinging to the experiences that life continually presents to us. In that way, we also let go of the present.

"This felt bond of being
Fusion of flowing calm
Silence echo eternal strains
Vanishes in consuming void" [(39)]

Always Letting Go

We want to continually be "letting go" every moment. We want to let go of the habitual discriminating mind, which takes the view of "self and other" whenever it arises. This habitual discriminating mind also gives running commentaries on our initial impressions which arise out of our contact with phenomena. It creates preferences, which give rise to footholds for clinging and attachment.

When we have a view of "self and other", it means we have a view of an inherent tangible self which can be differentiated from the external world. We know from the Buddha's teachings on the Four Noble Truths, on *anitya, duhkha* and *anatman* (impermanence, unsatisfactoriness and no-self), and from the teaching of dependent-origination, that this is not a true view of things. There is no permanent or inherently existing selfhood in all things; not to speak of "ourselves". All things are empty, being subject to ceaseless conditioned change and becoming. That is how it is. The Buddha also pointed out that in this same process of conditioned change, we can also be open to growth and transformative change, and thereby have access to emancipation, release and enlightenment.

In the *Mahasatipatthana Sutta* of the *Digha Nikaya*, the Buddha taught that the complete fading away and relinquishment of craving is the cessation of suffering. [40] The Buddha goes on to state that the Noble Eightfold Path is the way of practice that leads to the cessation of suffering. When we let go of the discriminating mind, we take leave of the cycle of dependent-origination. We break out of it at the transition between the link of "feeling" and "craving", or even in the earlier link, between "contact" and "feeling".

This stepping out from the conditioned dependent-origination occurs where there is the sense perception, i.e. there is experiencing and feeling, but we disengage before the discriminating mind attaches to having likes and dislikes in the immediacy of that "feeling". If we allow the following links of "craving" and "clinging" to arise, we will likely be too late, and will again be ensnared in the cycle of creating the unsatisfactoriness of *duhkha*. As the dependent-origination is a process which applies to every moment of our being, we have to cultivate the mind of always letting go. We have to always be mindful and be aware with discernment, not to be creating bondage.

In the *Malunkyaputta Sutta,* the Venerable Malunkyaputta who was well advanced in age, asked the Buddha for a brief teaching he can work on resolutely. The Buddha taught him:

"...When, Malunkyaputta, regarding things seen, heard, sensed, and cognized by you, in the seen there will be merely the seen, in the heard there will be merely the heard, in the sensed there will be merely the sensed, in the cognized there will be merely the cognized .. This itself is the end of suffering..."[41]

The Buddha teaches us to be mindful when we experience sense impressions. We need not let our experiencing of the object be carried into craving and grasping.

In the same spirit, in Ch'an Buddhism, a direct experiential knowing which is "not relying on words or letters", is emphasised. Many of the teachings in Ch'an Buddhism address the way we conduct our daily activities, and are conveyed in a manner which strikes us directly.

Ch'an Master Yunmen (雲門, approx. 864-949 CE) of the Tang dynasty era, was asked to indicate how a practitioner can gain an entry into the path, i.e. he was asked to give a teaching that indicates the way to awakening.

The Master said,

"Eating gruel, eating rice." [42]

When we are fully aware of whatever it is we are doing, and stay fully in the experiencing at the moment of the experiencing, we are then fully practising in that very moment. Eat gruel and only eating gruel, eat rice and only eating rice. There is no further need for there to be anyone eating gruel or rice either. No need for anyone to be represented in the experience of eating. There is just this eating gruel, just the eating rice.

It is insight, at the level of "dispassion" in the transcendent dependent-arising, which can support this kind of letting go or relinquishment. Even after this stage of letting go, there is further work to be done, to finally uproot ignorance, and to fully uncouple the rounds of the cycle of dependent-origination.

Letting Go of the Discriminating Mind

The discriminating mind is the mind which holds on to differences and preferences. It is the mind which discriminates between self and other, this and that. When we catch sight of a beautiful flower by the roadside, before we can fully feel the fresh beauty of the flower, the discriminating mind will step in to comment that it is just a weed. When we see a celebrity holding on to a clutch purse, the discriminating mind steps in to let us know it will impress our friends if we get one too. When we tuck into a bowl of noodles, the discriminating mind tells us the more expensive offering from another vendor should taste better. These taglines: "just a weed", "celebrity status will impress", or "more expensive is better", are the labels the discriminating mind sticks on to the objects of our senses, and we unwittingly fall prey into harbouring these biased views. We are thereby immediately robbed of the experiencing of beauty, of having an objective assessment of quality and value, or of being able to fully enjoy (e.g. the bowl of noodles). We need to let go of the discriminating mind to have the unencumbered existential experience of phenomena and see into the true nature of things.

There are many levels of this letting go of the discriminating mind, just as there are many levels of insight. We may say that the more we truly understand, the more we will be able to let go. By letting go of the discriminating mind, we are letting go of everything. When we let go of the discrimination of self and other, we let go of the unreal "I" ego, and cultivate the mind of emptiness. Though easily said, this development requires our perseverance, vigorous effort and continual watchfulness.

Letting go of the discriminating mind also means we let go of our pet ideas and beliefs. We let go of "Buddhism" or the idea that we are "Buddhists". Being a "Buddhist" is a conventional definition which has no real meaning from the viewpoint of no-self (*anatman*) and impermanence (*anitya*), or emptiness. However, though we do not need to hold to this view, we still need to use this conventional definition of "Buddhist" in our communications with others. We actually need not "be" anything in particular.

Ultimately, we let go until there is nothing more to let go of. The Ch'an (Jpn: Zen) tradition is rich with anecdotes dealing with this letting go of the discriminating mind. Herein we can see how the *Dharma* has been assimilated into Ch'an Buddhism. We can see that the core teachings of the earlier schools of Buddhism are carried through into the later Mahayana schools. Though with a cursory view they may look so different in their outward forms, we begin to realise that they are very much of the same spirit.

The "Inscriptions for Faith in Mind" (信心铭), is a composition of verses which is much revered by the Ch'an Buddhist School. It is attributed to the Third Ch'an Patriarch Sengcan (三祖僧粲, CE?-606), who lived during the brief Sui dynasty. A patriarch (ancestral master) in Ch'an Buddhism, is the holder of the lineage of *Dharma* transmission of the teaching. Bodhidharma is recognised as the first Ch'an patriarch in China, and is deemed to be the twenty eighth patriarch in the line of transmission from the Buddha.

The first few lines of the "Inscriptions for Faith in Mind" are:

"The Great Way is not difficult,

     just do not pick and choose.

Only with no aversion or attachment,

     will there be correct thorough understanding.

The least bit of difference,

     sets heaven and earth apart.

To have it manifest,

harbour not for or against.

The vying of like and dislike,

is a disease of the mind. " *(43)*

Patriarch Sengcan exhorts us to break out from our habitual discriminating mind which is caught in love and hate; the mind which always has preferences and wanting this and that. It is a profound teaching on the relinquishing of views. We have picked and chosen our views on everything we have come to be associated with. We have views and preferences on who is right or wrong, environmental issues, political leanings, on whether meditation should be with eyes open or closed, and so on. It is when we are prepared to give up our views that there can be fruitful discussion and learning.

Everyone is entitled to his or her views. Finally, however, we will have to relinquish all clinging to views, whatever they are. This does not mean we have the ability to do this now, or that this is the right thing to do now, for every one of us. We do not, in any case, disregard all conventions. We need to have regard for purposeful conventions. They have evolved over time to uphold the social structures which we now have in place and help to establish acceptable behavioural norms.

In the *Dhatuvibhanga Sutta*, (44) the Buddha gave a profound teaching on this "letting go of the discriminating mind" to the monk Pukusati when both of them happened to be spending a night in a potter's workshop. It appears that Pukusati, though he had gone forth as a disciple of the Buddha, had not met the Buddha in person before.

In this extract from the *sutta*, the Buddha taught Pukusati about the discriminating mind which gives rise to all sorts of mental constructions. The Buddha said,

" *'I am' is a conceiving ; 'I am this' is a conceiving; 'I shall be' is a conceiving ; 'I shall not be' is a conceiving; 'I shall be possessed of form' is a conceiving; I shall be percipient' is a conceiving; 'I shall be non-percipient' is a conceiving; I shall be neither percipient nor non percipient' is a conceiving. Conceiving is a disease, conceiving is a tumour, conceiving is a dart. By overcoming all conceivings, one is called a sage at peace.*"

At the end of the Buddha's profound discourse, Pukusati realised that the person giving him the teaching must be the Buddha, and asked for his forgiveness in having just called him "friend", and not given him the respect due to his teacher, and an enlightened one.

When Ch'an Master Yunmen (雲門) was instructing the assembly of monks, he quoted the lines from the *Heart Sutra*:

"There is no eye, ear, nose, tongue, body nor mind."

The Master Yunmen then said,

"Because you have eyes that see, you cannot say that there is no eye. And since you are now seeing, you cannot say there is no seeing.

Even though it is like this, you see everything with your eyes and there is nothing wrong with that. Do not grasp at anything. What is it then about the objects of sound, smell, taste and touch?"[45]

This is in a monastery setting, and Ch'an Master Yunmen is in a dialogue with monks steeped in the practice. The Master is teaching the monks that one does not alienate oneself from what one senses; one is fully aware of the experience of sensing an object. However, one does not need to take it any further. One knows the sense consciousness is apprehending (i.e. the object is sensed) but one does not need to go on to grasp at the sensing. There is then no problem at all with our senses, the act of sensing, or the object. This is a teaching on relinquishment, and the application of the Four Noble Truths to *Dharma* practice.

If we are told that all our beliefs are merely unreal conceptualizations, and that in actual fact we are not to think there is even a thing because there is "not a thing" to begin with, can we then let go of our earlier understanding? Can we let go of our provisional intellectual conceptualizations? Can we demolish our strongly held beliefs with which we had conducted our lives — upon which we had relied to understand ourselves and the world around us, and which have lasted us thus far?

The practice of discerning mindfulness gives us the awareness of the arising mental states. We learn to discern and disengage from indulgence and the excesses we have discussed in the earlier chapters. We work on developing virtue, concentration and wisdom on the Noble Eightfold Path. In the cultivation of skilful mental states and the development of insight, we are aided by the Buddha's teachings on the Four Noble Truths, *anitya, duhkha, anatman* (impermanence, unsatisfactoriness, no-self), emptiness and the dependent-origination (pratitya-samutpada). As we relinquish the false notions of the permanent and inherent existence of our being, we begin to let go of the belief in an enduring separate self. Compassion and wisdom can thereby be firmly established.

The unlimited potential for development which we all have, becomes evident only if we can let go of our attachment to the false "self". This is not a nihilistic view, as the "self" is not real in the first place. Do we then end up with nothingness? Not so, because these false notions of the enduring and separate "self" we will be rid of, are the hindrances to our awakening to our "true nature", for want of a better word. They are the edifices which we, in our ignorance, have constructed out of emptiness and we suffer the pain for doing so. When we forsake the false "self", the light of reality shines unencumbered and a new mode of being in pristine wisdom and compassion manifests.

Let us close this chapter with a profound Chan dialogue. An eminent Ch'an master from the Tang dynasty, Zhaozhou Congshen (趙州從諗, CE 778-897), was asked by his disciple:

"What is it like when nothing appears?"

Master Zhaozhou answered, "Put it down."

His disciple then asked, "But when nothing appears, what is there to put down?"

Master Zhaozhou said, "If you can't put it down, take it out of here." [46]

It is when everything is let go of; when even the idea of having to let go of, or not having to let go of, is dropped and transcended, that one awakens to enlightenment. All that can be relinquished is then relinquished. There is just this.

Chapter 5: Bringing Clarity into Loving and Giving

The Buddha's teachings on compassion, love and forgiveness, are central themes shared by the major religions of the world. These are the virtues shared among all who profess that the well-being of their fellow humankind (or in the case of Buddhism, of all beings), is at the core of their religious practices. This concern for all, needs to be inculcated into the way we humans conduct ourselves; be it in the immediacy of our homes, our larger community, in the way we work with our natural environment, or in the arena of political engagement between nations.

It is the belief in a differentiated separateness that stirs up feelings of resentment and hatred, which then result in us harming and persecuting others. When there is persecution and vile deeds, hatred is also present. None can claim he is on the path that teaches love for his fellow beings, if there is unbridled anger in his heart. None can claim that he is cultivating goodness, if he does not seek to rid himself of ill will and hatred.

A teaching or a way of life, which espouses universal love and compassion, has to be thoroughly inclusive. It has to encompass all life. Only then is it complete and true to itself. So the Buddhist, in having experienced pain himself, is taught to have regard for the suffering of all beings. He will not want to subject any being to further pain, fear or dread. How well he can accomplish this, will depend on how deeply he comprehends suffering (the First Noble Truth), to what extent he can relinquish his self-interest and how well he understands the consequences of his actions in the conditioned causality of dependent-origination.

Mindfulness in Loving Relationships

Forgiveness is an expression of selfless love. There has to be love as support, as a precondition, before forgiveness can happen. We can only forgive to the extent that we love. What we are saying when we forgive is, "You have hurt me, but I bear no grudge." In forgiveness, there is forgetfulness. We leave the misdemeanour behind us and are no longer burdened by it. We can also take it one step further and open our arms to embrace the person we have forgiven, with warm friendship and love.

Forgiveness is not something which can be kept in reserve, to be doled out when someone has hurt us. Rather, we cultivate an always forgiving mind. Forgiveness then becomes a protective coat around us, keeping us free from the agitation of vengeful resentment.

In the family context, parents tend to forgive their children their trespasses easily. When the children are sometimes insensitive, this brings pain to their parents. However, their parents will easily forgive them the pain they have caused. This is because the parents have unconditional love for their children.

If it has been a bad day at work, when the parent is tired and had a bad experience that day, then he or she may be snappy; past infringements are brought to mind and an argument ensues. The parent at that time is led by the "tired" mind, the "bad experience today" mind and not by the "unconditional loving" mind. This is where intervention with mindfulness can change the course of the unfolding events, for the better.

If we are mindful, we, the parent or the children, will have an awareness of anger arising in our mind. We can then rest in the moment, to create a calm space for the arising reactive emotions to come into the light of awareness. When we mindfully do so with positivity, our breathing is calmed; the tension in our body and in the air dissipates. We mindfully relax and everything is brought back into the context of love, sharing and forgiveness. It usually takes only one party to initiate this shift and the situation resolves back to the love and caring mode.

The practice of mindfulness can therefore help us maintain the loving relationships we enjoy; by ensuring that the emerging thoughts of antagonism or ill feelings are recognised before they can precipitate into unkind speech, or harmful action. When we couple mindfulness with the practice of loving-kindness, we will have created an oasis of serene love and friendliness to which we may also invite others to rest in. In the cooling waters of this oasis, any smouldering fires of ill will and anger will be quenched. We recognise these negative thoughts are surfacing and allow the reactive negative emotions, which can further provide them nutriment, to be dissipated in the light of calm and loving mindfulness.

Friendliness and Kindness

Friendliness, is the conduct worthy of someone who one knows, trusts, and is warmly disposed to. Friendliness as loving-kindness, is an equitable translation of the Sanskrit word *"maitri"*, or the Pali *"metta"*. This friendliness of *"maitri"*, is commonly viewed as a selfless and inclusive fraternal love. When one has the friendliness of "maitri", one extends loving-kindness and goodwill to all beings. In the practice of the meditation on loving-kindness, it is consciously cultivated as an antidote to enmity, resentment or hatred.

We would know, from our own experience, that anger and resentment are destructive. They can destroy the relationships we hold dear, and wreck our positive mental states. When we hold anger or resentment in our minds, it is akin to spreading poison on to the seeds of goodness and well-being, which we have planted in our hearts. Anger very often leads to harsh words and thoughtless actions we later regret. If we are easily angered, we need to break out of the cycle of being overcome by anger and then acting impulsively on the anger. The resulting harsh words or hurtful deeds cause harm to another. Once said or done, they cannot be retracted. After the destructive outburst, we suffer the remorse and retribution for what we had blurted out, or thoughtlessly done.

When we submit to anger, we are firstly hurting ourselves even before we hurt the object of our directed anger. We take the first drink of the poison of anger. In that fit of anger, we further punish ourselves by destroying the relationships we dearly cherish, and then have to bear the consequences of our damaging actions.

The practice of the *Dharma* will purge anger and ill will from our mind. The cause for the arising of these negative emotions is ultimately our clinging to the belief in a separate, inherently existing self. The Buddha specifically taught the development of loving-kindness, to rid us of anger, and to stop us from harming ourselves and others. The reader can further refer to the meditation practice on loving-kindness (given in Appendix I), to have a feel for the friendliness of *maitri* which we would want to cultivate. We start with developing loving-kindness to ourselves, and end the meditation practice with radiating it to all beings throughout the infinity of space.

In the adaptation of the *Metta Sutta* given below, we can have an appreciation for how the mind of one who is contemplating loving kindness, would abide. The Buddha teaches us to develop loving-kindness with keeping these thoughts in our mind:

"May all creatures be safe, with peace and joy in heart,

Let none bring another's downfall or slight and cause him hurt,

Let none wish another harm, through provocation or hate.

Just as a mother loves her only child,

So with an unbounded mind,

An all-embracing love, for all the universe,

Untroubled and without enmity,

Let him dwell mindful and unceasing on this,

This is the state divine." [47]

Early in my own practice, when I was a university student, I practiced the meditation on loving-kindness and the recitation of the *Metta Sutta* as given above. This was particularly useful on one occasion when I was on a solitary hitchhiking trip. I was not getting good rides that day and was dropped off a long way from my destination, late in the evening, on a road with farmhouses set far back from the road. It became pleasantly cool as it grew dark, and I walked on with the moon lighting up the road, whenever it was free from the clouds.

Suddenly, I could hear the barking of a pack of dogs in the distance and could hear them making their way towards me. I knew I could not outrun them and had nothing that I could use to ward them off. I could only call on the practice of loving-kindness. I stood still and focused on suffusing thoughts of loving-kindness in all directions, as in the meditation practice. I was then calm and unafraid. The pack of five or six dogs stopped barking when they got to me. After sniffing at my legs, they made their way off elsewhere. This was one of a number of occasions when the practice of loving-kindness was directly useful. On this occasion, it helped to relieve me of my fear. Perhaps the dogs also sensed that I was not fearful and had no ill-intent, and so left me alone.

The *Metta Sutta* can be recited silently, especially when we are relaxed and are in a positive mood. When we bring the *Metta Sutta* to mind and recite it with an open heart-mind, we embrace the unbounded cosmos and bathe it with loving-kindness.

We should feel free to frequently express the friendliness we feel within us, with a smile. Through practicing loving-kindness, our heart-mind grows pliable and warm enough to melt away the icicles of the negative emotions of conceit, enmity and jealousy, which had lain embedded for so long within us. As they melt away, our positive emotions begin to flow unhindered, free to find expression in loving thoughts, deed and speech. We drop the burden of having to put up barriers around our own little "selves". We will feel free to be honest with ourselves: to be like little children again, to smile, to cry, and to be joyful.

Opening Up to Compassionate Loving

As we realise the benefits from our practice and see into the profundity of the *Dharma*, we will also have developed a heart that is thankful. We feel gratitude for the opportunity to have heard the Buddha's teachings and to see how the Three Treasures (the Buddha, the *Dharma* and the *Sangha*) are our true refuge. We begin to understand there is much unnecessary suffering in the world around us. It is with some measure of loving-kindness and a growing certainty of our faith in the *Dharma,* that compassion arises and starts stirring within us. With the ripening of understanding and insight, we begin to open outwards, to share the bountiful treasures that the *Dharma* had brought to us.

Compassion is a deep-seated aspiration to soothe away the suffering of others, to free them from their bondage of attachment, craving and the discriminating mind, which are the root causes of unease, distress and suffering. Compassion laments the wretched state they have gotten into, and welcomes into its arms both the wicked and the good, with the same demeanour. Compassion envelops all sentient existence in its warm love. No one is excluded. Compassion is never at a loss; for though touched by suffering, it is not tainted by it. It will have the wisdom that sees into emptiness, beyond pain and suffering — to be a support for the suffering, the dejected, and the confused.

In the *Bodhisattva*, compassion becomes the reason for his exertions, and gives him the inspired vigour to go about his development to full enlightenment.

"Compassion feels the earnest desire to wipe away the pain and suffering of all beings; to wipe away the tears of sorrow, relieve the tiredness and aimlessness of beings bound to meaningless existence. It at once also feels their sense of being lost with no true refuge.

Compassion wants them to be guided into the light of true knowledge, into the purposeful quest for growth and unto liberation. Compassion wants to hold their hands, carry them in its bosom.

Compassion wants to see the smile and purpose on their faces, the joy and calm in their being. It weeps for their pain.

With tears of compassion, a kinship is felt with the Transcendent Bodhisattvas. One has a glimpse into and touches the heart ground of Maha Bodhisattva Avalokitesvara.

The heart of boundless love and care, the heart of the true Dharma, worthy of the Buddha's smile." [48]

The enlightened state is often portrayed as the state of perfected compassion and wisdom. It takes the loving heart of compassion to wield the sword of transcendent wisdom, which cleaves apart mundane phenomena to reveal its true nature. There must be a caring smile of great compassion together with the glare of blazing insight. Only great compassion can withstand the searing heat from the sword of *prajna,* to actualize the transformative energies of deep insight.

Loving-kindness and compassion are two of the four "divine abidings" of loving-kindness, compassion, sympathetic joy or gladness, and equanimity. The mind absorbed in these four "divine abidings" is said to be on par with being in the realm of the gods. In more common parlance, those who dwell in loving-kindness, compassion, sympathetic joy or gladness, and equanimity, experience a heightened consciousness that is "out of this world".

When we allow compassion and loving-kindness to work in us and so conduct our relationships, we will be at peace. We will know that whatever we do, will be the considered and the right thing to do. Compassion and loving-kindness will have softened our hard shell of the false "I" ego, and will have given us the courage to explore the viewpoints of others. It will allow us to accept that doing right may mean we do not get what we want, but that whatever is done with compassion and loving-kindness will bring happiness and be setting the course for positive development. Relationships are to be cultivated and nurtured, and the nutriment for any positive relationship is compassion and loving-kindness.

In our daily living, there will be many occasions when we have to resolve differences. In a typical scenario, one party may be adamant in wanting to have something done in a particular way which we may find difficult to accept. This may be because it is very much contrary to the approach we are used to. This is especially evident when decisions are to be made for important occasions; for example, how a vacation is to be organized, how a new washing machine cum dryer is to be chosen, how a wedding or funeral is to be conducted, etc. Sometimes, the right thing to do may be to go with the demands of the other party, even if it appears not to be the best approach, rather than to press on with our own preferences. It will help if we can try to understand why the other party feels so strongly about wanting it done their way. This may need some skilfully directed communication to elicit their unspoken purpose or biases. If we can communicate with a heart of compassion and loving-kindness; with the consideration for the welfare of others uppermost in our mind, we will not come across as being unreasonable, or unyielding, in their eyes. We gain their trust, and give them the opportunity to be more considerate in future.

Our development in loving-kindness and compassion are good yardsticks of the progress in our overall practice. If we are just as easily irritated by minor lapses, are easily angered and have little care for the welfare of others, then however much we think we have come to understand the *Dharma*, our understanding is still deficient or lop-sided. We need to have loving-kindness and compassion, along with wisdom, for a balanced development.

In those moments when you are touched by compassion, you may be overwhelmed by the sorrow of the needless suffering you see around you. It may feel to be unbearable, and you may be weeping lightly. However, you will also feel an inner gladness of being nourished by the *Dharma,* and the certainty of your own practice. It is normal that we may sometimes feel sadness when we are touched by compassion. When it feels as such, we know we will need to pair it with developing the wisdom of seeing into emptiness. We will then be led into equanimity.

Acting on the Thought to Give and Share

Giving to others can take the form of giving what we have acquired, what we have in our possession or what we can control. It may involve giving understanding, sympathy, time, energy, emotional support, or material things. When we give, we interact with the recipient and therefore at the same time, also receive. We receive the responses which are conditioned by, and which arise from, our act of giving.

When we give thought to others, we are giving consideration to their welfare and well being. We can further follow on from those thoughts with action. For example, if we know of someone who has fallen sick, we can give our time and effort to bring him to a doctor. We can wait for him, and then send him home. We can check he takes his medicine and is comfortable. We can perhaps further ensure he has food readily available. We can help stock up his refrigerator with some basic groceries to last the few days he may find difficulty in going out to shop. In times of need, especially in times of sickness, caring help goes a long way to relieve pain and discomfort in the sick person.

Oftentimes, we would have just settled on to a comfortable seat and are caught up with an interesting article in a magazine. We are relaxed and are in a pleasant state of mind. If at that moment, we become aware of a situation where someone needs help, we can be easily "detached" from it. Our flatmate may have just come in with heavy groceries and may be having some difficulty with locking the door, but we can be easily "detached" from the thought of wanting to help. We may mutter some words like "Do you need help?", but we stay put in our comfortable chair. This is the "detachment" of absolving ourselves from the actual acting out of a virtuous thought; when the discriminating mind hijacks the cycle of virtuous action.

We should instead, be free to act on that which will benefit another. We want instead, to be detached from self-interest and the craving to be in a state of comfort. The Buddha teaches this kind of loving detachment. With loving-kindness, we naturally rise up to offer help.

However, we also have to be skilful in how our help is offered. There may sometimes be other overriding considerations, so that being helpful may mean not directly or immediately offering help. Sometimes, the recipient may not be forthcoming with appreciation for the help received, but that need not matter to us. What we did was done with consideration for the well being of another; it was the right thing to do, and we are happy to be in a position to do it. We leave it at that. A compassionate or considerate action may be for the benefit of others, but it also creates a positive frame of mind in the doer and contributes to his feeling of worthiness.

It is always a good practice to give presents. These need not be expensive, but should be a gift which will delight and bring joy to the recipient. This communicates that we have caring thoughts and concern for him or her. For example, if we happen to see some freshly baked tarts in the window of our favourite bakery, and we remember a friend of ours needs some cheering up, then buying a few tarts for her will make a good present. There may not even need to be any reason; there was just an opportunity to share scrumptious freshly baked tarts.

The small little things, which we do to help another, may go a long way towards giving them comfort and joy. We should not underestimate the power of giving presents to the little ones as well. I recall with much fondness the wooden toys my grandpa made for me. He made small cars of wood, with coins for the wheels. He painted them a silvery grey, with what appears to be leftover paint used for the roof of our house. The car windscreens, windows and doors were lined out in red markings. That memory has become an inspiration for me to draw on. It was indeed a wonderful present.

One of my fondest memories from a two-year work assignment in the United States was at my farewell get-together, prior to the luncheon. My manager brought in two large apple pies as a surprise for the farewell gathering and we had a good laugh. He knew I was fond of apple pies. I would very often have a slice of the delicious apple pie when having lunch at the staff cafeteria. He was giving me the present of a delectable lunch dessert and a pleasant finale to the many memorable lunches at the staff cafeteria. This kind of thoughtful consideration shown in the workplace helps foster thoughtfulness for others and contributes to a pleasant work environment.

We certainly will derive much satisfaction from giving the little things which may come to mean a lot to both ourselves and the person receiving it.

Giving Respect and Care

The giving of respect to those worthy of our respect is an energising practice. This is when we acknowledge there are qualities we deem are worthy, in the person to whom we are giving respect. This is an especially important practice with regard to our conduct in a family setting. We naturally give respect to the eldest in the family. This is respect for them having discharged their duties as a grandparent, parent or elder, which has brought about harmony and stability, in the establishment of the family household.

If the elder has shortcomings which weigh heavily on us, we can still give respect, by way of the position that she (or he) holds in the family. Of course if she had acted responsibly and had discharged her duties as a family elder well, it would have made it easier for us to be more forthcoming in showing respect to her. If we reflect on the pain our parents would have endured and the sacrifices they have made; to feed, clothe and bring us up in the world, we will feel a deep sense of gratitude. In any case, we always maintain the decorum of being respectful. In doing so, we maintain the closeness in the family relationship.

After his attainment of Buddhahood, the Buddha returned to his former home with the gift of awakening to *Arhat*-ship for his father, wife and son (the Buddha's mother had passed away seven days after his birth). The Buddha teaches us to respect our parents and honour them;

"Mother and father are helpful to their children: they raise them, nurture them and show them the world... They are worthy of gifts from their children, for they have compassion for their offspring. Therefore a wise person should revere them and show them due honour, serve them with food and drink, with clothes and bedding, by massaging and bathing them, and by washing their feet ..."
(49)

Such reverence for one's parents may seem out of date, as most elders nowadays may desire to be independent and may not want to rely on help from their children. This may partly be due to the ease with which we nowadays can get access to clean water, food and medicine. Also, in the olden days, water for bathing would have to be drawn from a well. Food did not keep well, and had to be freshly cooked. We can show care and respect to our elders in many ways. I recall that as a child, I would bring my dad his house slippers and helped him with taking off his socks, when he got home after making his frequent trips to a nearby town on business. I would also bring him a cup of water to quench his thirst. Being a father myself now, I know my dad must have been pleased he was appreciated and respected.

We can never repay the debt we owe our parents who brought us into the world, cared for and fed us. We also can never repay the debt we owe all beings who have played a part in our growth and development. We can never repay nature: the source of all sustenance and nutriment which has nurtured all of humanity and upon which all beings have relied on. We can, however, help to ensure that this sustenance continues to be available to all. We can use the

138

natural resources available to us without waste, and responsibly maintain the environment which is entrusted to us.

As for our parents, we can always give them time, for example, by patiently listening to what they have to say and keeping company with them. We would also want to give them easy access to the refreshing natural environment around them and those close to them. Even if they may perhaps be too feeble to actively interact with those around them, they will surely enjoy being around their loved ones.

We can give a smile to the elders, inquire after their health, or give a pleasant greeting when we meet them. When we do so, we are also giving the elders an opportunity to respond and communicate in a positive way. We can similarly wish a family member a "Good morning", when we first see them in the morning. By doing so, we kick-start the process of communicating respectfully and this helps to set the tone for the rest of the day. There will then be less of a chance for harsh speech to arise and there is the acknowledgment that everyone has a place in the family. A good practice prior to eating at mealtimes, is to respectfully invite everyone seated at the dining table to partake of the food, with the eldest being invited first; as the French would say, "Bon appetit (enjoy your meal)." Again, this helps to reinforce the tone of respect and appreciation of the elders, which will undoubtedly spill over into a healthy appreciation of everyone in the family.

If we get undeserved condescension or indifference when we give respect to someone, then we need to skilfully reconsider our future interactions with that person. We will have to discern whether we are actually helping the person or us by doing so. We may want to maintain an evident self-respect and not aggravate an unhealthy relationship.

However, we sometimes may not have much of a choice and will have to put up with poor behaviour; especially if that is the tolerated norm, in some of the social circles we have to operate in. In any case, we ground ourselves in our practice of compassion and loving-kindness, when we find ourselves in these situations. We need not become part of the unruly crowd.

We would want to also show respect to those younger than us; also to the little children. They are at a sensitive age. The words we use and the way we treat them, can leave deep impressions. If they see us conducting ourselves with generosity and consideration for others, they would more likely learn to cultivate these behaviours. We would want to teach them to differentiate intentions and actions that are beneficial, from those that are harmful. We should encourage them to think independently and handle issues confidently, with consideration for others.

There is a general emphasis nowadays, for children and young adults to be encouraged to be assertive and confident. Some are, however, taught to cater to their self-interests first, and are further encouraged to be aggressive. Aggressiveness should not be confused with assertiveness. Snatching another's toy, or shoving another away to be first in the queue, is not being assertive. Speaking loudly out of turn and being self-centred or disrespectful, is definitely not self-confidence. If we do encourage the growth of these poor traits of character in children, we are giving them empty shells, which can be easily shattered. This is not the type of character trait which we will want to inculcate in them. It is only showmanship, and lack of consideration for others, which is rather superficial and will be a burden to them later. When they later need to confront deeper issues in life, they will tend to jump, shout and lash out, rather than calmly and sensitively weigh the matter and communicate. They may later also find difficulty in developing long lasting positive relationships, and may spread much unhappiness, if self-centredness is at the core of their actions.

We instead should teach our children the confidence that comes with knowing themselves deeply and knowing what they are capable of. We will want to teach them to discern the true from the false, to have appreciation and consideration for others, to be helpful and to understand that generosity in helping others is a privilege.

Mutual Understanding in a Marriage Relationship

The Buddha taught mutual respect between husband and wife:

"... Both husband and wife are endowed with faith, charitable and self-controlled, living their lives righteously, addressing each other with pleasant words. Then many benefits accrue to them and they dwell at ease." (50)

The committed relationship between husband and wife, or partner, is a rather complex one. The parties in the relationship will have many differences arising out of past upbringing, pet peeves, individual pursuits, the different work related issues, and having different opinions on family financing, relationship with the in-laws, bringing up children, etc. It is therefore of fundamental importance that the sharing of love and trust between husband and wife or partner, be robust enough to allow the relationship to weather any contentious issue which may arise. Committed effort and self-sacrifice is required to keep the relationship loving and harmonious.

Each couple will have together made many sacrifices for each other to be living together, raising a family and sharing all the hardships and the good times that they have already been through together. These bonds of a shared commitment may have been forged over a long period of time. Both partners have had to provide generous attention, love and care for each other and to be sensible about and be sensitive to the needs of each other. At the same time, there has to be understanding and forgiving of each other's shortcomings.

Many couples do have arguments now and then. There has to be recourse to a method which will help manage these arguments; to keep the relationship harmonious and loving. Mutual respect, love and commitment, should be allowed to come to the fore when the anger that fuels an argument arises. We can enlist the support of our practice of mindfulness to help us out in this regard.

With mindfulness, we step on the brakes and let the argument cool down. We hold back from spouting words which may arouse further discord and reactivate our caring and understanding mind. After an argument, be the one to first say "sorry", or to reach out to hold the hand of your partner. This shifts the focus back to the relationship, rather than the argument. Contentious issues can be worked on later in a rational manner, after both sides have reconciled. We let the focus be on love and understanding in the relationship, and not on the issues that may need to be discussed in a calm manner; facilitated by mindfulness and giving. It should not be the contentious issues which get the upper hand in a committed loving relationship.

The relationship between husband and wife has to rise above the usually petty squabbles and issues. We may be somewhat more task oriented at work, but at home, there has to be special emphasis on the relationship. From that primary orientation and commitment to mutual respect and love in a marriage, we work on the other secondary issues.

It is helpful to share the expression of love and concern in acts that show our sincere appreciation and caring for each other. Saying, "Darling, I love you," as a frequent restatement of our commitment, helps us keep this in mind.

Our spouse and family members are, in most cases, the ones who are most dear to us. We may find fulfilment and happiness in being there to share our life with them and to always be there for them. From the preceding segments, we have seen that the Buddha teaches us to have gratitude and reverence towards our elders, and to cultivate love and care for our family.

Giving Praise and Comfort

We are cultivating generosity when we give encouragement or praise. When we see that something is done well, we will want to give acknowledgement. The doer will derive some enjoyment and fulfilment from a compliment, and is thereby encouraged.

If we deliberately do not give any good words or acknowledgement, even when the thought of giving a compliment comes to mind, we will effectively be cultivating an ungenerous attitude. We have allowed our petty jealous mind to stop us from being generous and true to our positive feelings of appreciation. By doing so, we will set up barriers to our development. We had the opportunity to develop generosity and warm-heartedness with well-wishing, but instead chose to ingrain in ourselves more coldness. This will certainly not help our friendships or ourselves. Our blocked emotions, which are left to fester, will then need to be resolved in future.

We have to be mindful not to let our thoughts and feelings of jealousy overwhelm the sparks of generosity and warm heartedness coming forth from our mind. If we are mindful, when such negative thoughts arise, we know of their arising and we let them be. We instead focus on giving expression to our generous thought of wanting to give a compliment, and let that carry through into actually verbalising it. We will then witness the joy which springs up in our friends when we give our sincere compliments. When we further share in that positive experience with equal joy, we will be also developing sympathetic joy (*mudita*).

Giving Space to Grow

In the course of our practice, we may sometimes feel critical of the behaviour of others. As we develop mindfulness, more of the workings of the relationships we are in, and the state of mind of others who we interact with, will become clearer to us. We may become more acutely aware when there is insincerity or lack of consideration. When we start to feel this way, it shows that our development of loving-kindness and compassion have not caught up with our quality of mindful discernment. Our observations and awareness have become sharper, but our supporting positivity is lagging and has not allowed us to overcome our discriminating and judging mind. We have begun to attach to differences and comparisons.

We will then need to remind ourselves that this is the discriminating mind at work. We have to move away from creating a separation based on critically judging the behaviour of others. We learn to accept that just like us, every person has his or her own shortcomings and preferences. By doing so, we cultivate an accepting and forgiving mind. We will then be not affected by their unseemly behaviour which may otherwise disturb us now and then. We will be in a better position to support them because we will be open and receptive to their needs. An analogy we can use here is that we allow the horses of the mind of others, with their different dispositions, to run freely and not be constrained in a corral built up by our discriminating mind. We give them the space to roam freely — to fully be themselves. We learn to accept them as they are.

We may know of long standing relationships which were disrupted because one party took offense to something that was said. The offending words may, however, have been just an unthoughtful remark. If that person had been given more space, it would have been easier for the offended party to accept that though what was spoken may have been hurtful, it was just part of the sometimes belligerent nature of that person who needed some space for expression. If we understand this, there will be unspoken forgiveness for the hurt; we will not react negatively and will avoid harming the relationship. We just drop the issue, make nothing out of it, or laughingly brush it off. The person then knows there was no offence taken, and it becomes a small matter. If we can further sense that the person is receptive, we may want to point out in a skilful way, that what was said was not appropriate. This helps the person to grow and derive benefit from that experience. The relationship is kept whole and both parties will appreciate each other better.

Giving Fearlessness

We can give fearlessness to one who has a mind filled with fear: be it the fear of death, his own helplessness in a particular situation, or fear of loss. It sometimes may not take much to comfort our fellow beings in their time of need, but it may be crucial they receive support at that time.

As supportive parents, we can let our growing children know we will be there to support them — regardless of what they do or what they had done, we will always be there for them. This gives them additional confidence to face the troubling times they may have, through their growing up years.

Giving fearlessness can also mean giving acceptance. If we see another holding back with some trepidation about a task he (or she) has to complete; not having the confidence that he can perform it well, we may be able to first give him acceptance, and inspire confidence in him. We let him know we accept him for who he is, and that he need not fear failure if he does his best.

Sometimes, giving fearlessness can take the form of giving calm. If we see someone hurt or disoriented, we can, before help arrives and if appropriate, hold her hand until she feels comfortable enough to get back on her feet again, or until help arrives. We remain calm and just stay there with comforting her, to help her feel at ease.

It is when we have attained to true fearlessness that we can give to others the fearlessness which comes from truly knowing the *Dharma*. This fearlessness is based on the insight which comes from seeing emptiness and knowing reality. Even as we learn to be fearless by practising the *Dharma*, we will be able to soothe the pain of those who are fearful, by showing them to that tested path to fearlessness.

Heartfelt Giving and Receiving

When we give, and if it is appropriate, we should look the person we are giving to in the eyes and hand over the gift with both hands. This signifies an open, sincere giving. We smile as we hand over the gift, saying with our eyes, "Enjoy this gift, may it benefit you." When we receive a gift, we do the same; we receive with both hands, look the giver in the eyes, and say with our eyes, "I appreciate your thought, I appreciate your gift, and I receive it with thanks and much gratitude."

By doing so, we allow the giver to be able to fully experience the act of giving. We mindfully stay in the positivity of this communion, not allowing other negative thoughts or emotions to dampen this sharing of giving and receiving. Both the giver and receiver can then participate fully; the giver gives with a full heart and the receiver accepts with a full heart. Both are practising generosity and giving, at the same time. Both are experiencing the emptiness of a selfless exchange.

We should be happy that we have the opportunity to be giving. Perhaps we feel we have been blessed by an abundance of what it is we are giving. So when we give, we should also feel gratitude because we have abundance to give. We cultivate the mind of great abundance when we give. It is because we have an abundance of love that we give of our time, caring, energy and material possessions.

If we are mindfully aware when we give, we will learn a lot about ourselves. We may often see the assertion of the unreal "I" ego making its appearances throughout the process of giving. This is the discriminating mind which compares and judges critically from a self-centric perspective. We do not need this intrusion which interferes with our expression of generosity. When we give sincerely with a full heart, we experience the carefree joy of the emptiness of just giving. We then feel truly enriched and gladdened.

The Generosity of Not Giving

We can sometimes be giving or generous when we actually do not give away something we have, or something coming into our possession. For example, when we feel anger arising in us, we will not want to give vent to the anger and pass it on; to induce the state of anger in the mind of another. We instead employ mindfulness to dissipate the arising anger and flush it away with loving-kindness.

We are also giving when we do not pass to others the worries we have. We learn to work on these by seeing into their causes, and work on transforming ourselves. We transform the worrying state of mind which comes from having strayed into the past, being bogged down by past regrets and failures, or from having thoughts about future insecurity and uncertainty. We instead, learn to be fully in the present and to be calmly addressing issues. We have dealt with this approach in the "Letting go of past, present and future" section, in Chapter 4 of this book.

We therefore are giving when we do not pass our burdens and troubles on to others. This means we take responsibility for our actions. We will want to uphold the principles which will help us lead a lifestyle which does not give rise to such problems in the first place. This is the harmless way of going about living. It is harmless in the sense that we do not carry out unskilful actions which we know will bring unbeneficial or harmful results. The resulting problems bring harm to those who are in our circle of friends and our family or community. In that way, for example, by committing to a marriage relationship and not indulging in sexual misconduct, one will not cause problems which would be saddled on everyone in the family. One is therefore being generous and giving when one acts responsibly.

The Generosity of Taking

Sometimes we actually are giving when we take from others. When we take on the burdens of others, we are being generous by giving our time and resources to help. It may be in simple everyday activities, as for example, when we lend a hand to help out another. We take on a heavier load and carry the heavier burden. If there is a plate of not so palatable food to be eaten, we will be giving if we try to finish what is on our plate. If we are offered pastries by a friend who is keen on learning to bake, we may want to take more on our plate, to give that friend encouragement to do better.

It is in the spirit of the *Bodhisattva* that we take on the suffering of others. If we see someone in pain, we can wish we take away and bear their pain, and we wish them freedom from pain. We generate the thought, "Let me bear your pain. May you be happy and be free from pain." If we see someone confused, we can wish we take away their confusion and give them clarity of mind. We generate the thought, "May you have clarity of mind. May you be mindful." We do so with developing the mind to compassion and find the skilful means to help others, to free them from suffering. If we hear voices being raised in a harsh exchange of words some distance away, we can generate the thought, "May there be calmness, may there be understanding and friendliness." and forward it to where we hear the commotion. We may not be physically present where it is occurring, but we can help with our thoughts.

The Highest Gift

When we give someone a teaching by pointing out how something can be done better, we are giving that person an opportunity for growth. We can also give a teaching on the *Dharma*. This, in the Buddhist tradition, is the highest of all gifts, because it represents a giving of the means to the attainment of great ease and freedom. To give a teaching well also involves being skilful about the right way to present the teaching; at the right time and in the right setting. We will have to understand the disposition of the person, and may have to guide him (or her) to be in a receptive state of mind. We will have to present the *Dharma* in a manner which will let him understand its usefulness and profundity.

The *Dharma* can only be shared with someone who is receptive. Sharing is both giving and receiving. So, for true sharing, there has to be someone truly giving and someone truly receiving. It belittles the Buddha's *Dharma,* and we may also be doing harm in planting the seeds of disinclination in the other person, if we overzealously try to force the *Dharma* on someone who is not ready for it, or who does not want to receive it. The Buddha himself did not suffer the insincere and the undeserving.[51] There are sometimes strong karmic influences in the way of someone not being able to accept the *Dharma*. If we are skilful and patient enough though, we may still be able to make the person receptive to living a better lifestyle or cultivating virtue and good roots.

Chapter 6: Restfulness and Effectiveness in the Work Environment

Awareness of Our Physical and Mental Conditions

Knowing Ourselves

Getting Along with Our Peers

Doing It Well – No Need to Rush

Handling Stress at Work

Giving Understanding and Sympathetic Joy

Responding to Aggressive Behaviour and Being Assertive

Cultivating Leadership – A Buddhist Perspective

If we are holding a job, we will likely be spending a large portion of the day in the work environment. We may be in a very competitive work environment, which is highly stressful, with tight schedules and high workload. We may sometimes feel drained at the end of the workday and head for home bringing with us our tired body and weary mind. To better handle the challenging work environment, we can seek guidance from the Buddha's teachings on "Right Mindfulness", "Right Speech", "Right Action" and "Right Livelihood", which are especially associated with the practical and ethical aspects of the Noble Eightfold Path. It may not be directly possible for us to change our work environment, but if we equip ourselves with the right mind-set and is discerning, we will learn to be happy in that environment and perhaps even induce some change to it. We start with physical and mental relaxation, and getting better acquainted with ourselves.

Awareness of Our Physical and Mental Conditions

One useful application of mindfulness practice to the work environment, is in maintaining a relaxed condition of our body and mind. Having a relaxed body helps relax the mind. If you have a desk job and spend much time sitting or working at your computer, you may likely have a pet muscle ache that is related to your working posture. The neck and shoulder muscles are especially prone to this. You will want to ensure the ergonomic setup; the positioning of your body at the workspace, is adequately catered to.

When you walk, try relaxing your shoulders, arms and hands to the tips of your fingers, and allow your arms to swing naturally. You may want to give your fingers a twiddle now and then as you walk, so as to remind yourself to do this. If you are practising the mindfulness of breathing meditation, you can extend your mindfulness practice to your daily activities by keeping a loose awareness on your breath throughout the day. When you do that, it helps keep the mind settled and also gives you a quiet joy as you go about your work.

Being mindful in our daily activities is a key *Dharma* practice. When we are mindfully aware, we know the condition of our mind and mental states. We will be aware of the reactive thoughts which surface in our mind when we are presented with a new situation. We can then exercise self-restraint, or be creative and respond in a way which will help the situation at hand.

When we are caught up in traffic while driving to work, the practice of mindfulness lets us know when anger arises. Before we are about to again launch into a tirade against an errant driver, mindfulness gives us the opportunity to choose not to respond in that way, and we instead, "keep our cool".

We maintain mindful awareness on our feelings and our thoughts, and we can just watch them arise and disappear. We reserve comment, just mindfully watch with discernment, and we can see the emptiness that is *anitya*, *duhkha* and *anatman*, in our daily activities. This gives us the clarity of mind, which will allow us to be objective and able to pursue the beneficial course of action. We thereby are empowered to develop the Right Action of the Noble Eightfold Path.

Knowing Ourselves

It is through knowing ourselves deeply that we can confidently move forward in our self-cultivation. Knowing oneself is well recognised as a prerequisite when preparing for competitive pursuits: be it in adversarial combat, in competitive sports, in boardroom politics or at work. When we understand our strengths and shortcomings, we can seek ways to address them, to plug the gaps where our shortcomings may be and to work on improving ourselves.

In the work of antiquity: *Art of War* (孫子兵法) by Sunzi (孙子), which was probably written about two thousand three hundred years ago (about 400 BCE), he writes:

"For he who knows the enemy and knows himself,

Victory is ensured in all battles.

For he who knows himself but not the enemy,

Victory and defeat are an even outcome.

For he who knows not himself,

Every battle will be perilous." [52]

The Art of War is highly regarded as a military classic. It has been influential in the thinking of many military strategists and is nowadays also applied by sports and business management team coaches. Sunzi utilized all means including diplomacy, tactical deployment, intelligence gathering, deception and surprises, as part of his stratagem for winning battles. We do not ever advocate war and we would not want to use tactics which are ultimately damaging or destructive. However, we would agree with Sunzi's emphasis on the need for knowledge of self and the enemy for the warring factions.

In our practice of the *Dharma*, the battle on our path to awakening is not with another, but with our own selves, fought in the battleground of our mind. We train in the *Dharma* and deploy mindfulness and discernment to be rid of our attachments, greed, hate and delusion. We win our battles by developing the insight to cut through our attachments, and to sap the energy from our enemy of deluded thoughts and negative emotions, which arise from our discriminating mind. As we keep up our practice of cultivating ethical behaviour, mindfulness and sincerity, we may even come to recognize our "enemy" as a friend who gives us the opportunity to practise. The more we practise, the deeper we will know ourselves and victory is thereby assured in all our battles.

Getting Along with Our Peers

Earlier in my own practice and career, I had a difficult relationship with a particular co-worker from a different department. I needed his consent to allow his subordinates to support some work I was doing. As I did not expect he would change his ways, I had to start working on myself. We cannot expect others to change their behaviour to accommodate us, but we can always change ourselves or change our outlook. I used the meditation on loving-kindness (refer to Appendix I) as the method to effect the change. He was my "enemy" in the practice. It took some practising before I could change my own perception of the situation and was able to accept him as he is. When that happened, he could no longer sense any enmity from me. My body language or the tone of my speech did not show the negative responses he expected to elicit from me anymore. In the end, he stopped trying to instigate the anger or frustration in me. Maybe he found that working positively with me gave him more satisfaction. Whatever it was, I had to change myself to elicit the better behaviour from him. Change has to come from, and starts with our own selves; we have to take the lead. The outcome is worth it; it is good for all.

The practice of friendliness or loving-kindness will help us to empathise with our colleagues and understand their concerns. We can then approach the issues we are working on together with them in a positive manner. In a team comprising of members from different organizations and with different agendas, the various self-interests have to be meshed together to achieve the aims of the endeavour that the team is working on. The practice of loving-kindness helps us stay above any pettiness, differences in opinion, disruptive behaviours, cultural differences or irksome personality traits. We can then devote our full attention to focus on the job at hand.

This does not mean we cannot be firm. We can be firm but considerate, and can get on with doing things with gentleness at the same time. If we do this consistently, we will be recognised at the workplace as a fair and considerate player.

We should practise generosity and seek to share knowledge, as this will contribute considerably to the development of positive relationships with our colleagues. We can press our views and argue vigorously for what we feel is the best way to handle a work related issue. We should not withhold information, or indulge in activities which are hurtful to others, just for personal gain. We always stay mindful of our fundamental practice of giving, friendliness and compassion.

We know how nice it is to be greeted with a smile and to be in a friendly, peaceful environment that induces restfulness. We would have felt the stifling and lethargic mind when we have to endure an unfriendly and highly strung work environment brought on by unfeeling and inconsiderate colleagues or bosses. If an organisation is to have friendliness as a workplace culture, there will certainly be benefits from increased productivity arising from better workplace relationships, more sharing of ideas, lessened agitation and more restful minds which will think clearly. We can contribute to this end by being friendly. At least this will affect the tone of friendliness in the circle of our immediate co-workers and perhaps through them, this circle of friendliness will widen. The effects of a friendly and restful workplace will be far reaching, even with helping to improve the home environment. If we can end every workday with a happy and relaxed mind, we will be bringing those conditions back home with us to our families.

Doing It Well – No Need to Rush

If our working environment requires intense focus on the work at hand, and we are likely to be continually addressing issues with having to meet tight schedules, it will be easy for us to develop a "tensed-and-hurried" mentality. This is the mind working in overdrive mode. This is when everything needs to be done as soon as possible, and we feel we do not have time for much else other than getting the work done soonest. We feel rushed when everything on our work list is "high priority". We feel we have to "multitask"; be attending to everything simultaneously, and working on them in high gear. When that happens, we need to step back and create mental space for ourselves.

Getting the job done does not equate to rushing about restlessly. In fact, if we want to do a good job, we will want our mind to be thinking clearly, addressing the issues calmly and thoroughly; knowing where to draw the line between what needs more work, and what will suffice. This is where being mindful helps.

In this particular application of mindfulness, we are mindfully aware when the mental state of wanting to hurry arises. This tensed-and-hurried mentality is our habitual mind worrying too much about the outcome of the work we are doing or should be doing. We are then concerned about a future outcome, while actually working in the present. When we become aware of this, we can mindfully disengage from being drawn further into this mentality. We drop our attachment to that mental state and let it pass, without acting on it.

So we note, "Ah! It is the tensed-and-hurried mind!", when it comes into our mindful awareness. We then withdraw our attention from the tensed-and-hurried mentality, and go about working things out calmly, and complete our work in a relaxed manner. We let the hurried mind go; let it be gone without pushing it away. With practice, we will no longer need to cater to this tensed-and-hurried mind. We can work fast when haste is called for, but we need not be tensed-and-hurried when doing our work.

The tensed-and-hurried mind may also make an appearance when we have to be on time for an appointment. If we have to drive to an appointment and have to be there by a certain time, we will tend to rush to get there if we are running late. We may then tend to drive fast and overtake with less care than we normally do. Our tensed-and-hurried mind has taken over the steering wheel. When we drive, "Safety First" should always be uppermost in our mind. We should not allow this priority to be usurped by the tensed-and-hurried mind. It would be much better to leave for our destination a few minutes earlier, to avert having to rush and be unsafe on the roads.

Handling Stress at Work

There is typically always some level of stress in our lives. In normal circumstances, the stress that comes from a change in the environment, new demands on our work or a change from our normal routine activities is manageable, and may even precipitate a change for the better in us. The stress and upset which we experience when exposed to the unsatisfactoriness of *duhkha*, may cause us to reflect on, or to re-evaluate, our way of living.

We may encounter excessive stress at work if we feel we are not coping well with what we are tasked to do, could not fulfil the requirements of the job, or meet our own expectations of the quality of our performance. Sometimes, it may happen that the work demands which come with a new posting are not matched to our abilities. We may also feel stressed if we do not share in the goals which have been set for us, lose our enthusiasm and begin to lose interest in our work.

We respond physically to stress, and if we are exposed to persistent stress, we may start to display symptoms such as irritability and anxiety. If the stress is prolonged and intense, we may further feel emotionally and physically fatigued. Stress can be debilitating.

There may be times when several things come together at the same time to burden us and subject us to stress. At an early stage of my work career, I was posted to a new job assignment which required setting the operating targets, monitoring product qualities, and designating the product disposition and dispatching schedules. If there is a hiccup in the production or dispatch, the financial consequence will be high and this weighed heavily on me.

It was also when I took up the new position that my second child was born. I suffered from lack of sleep from being woken up during feeding times for the baby, on top of getting late calls from the processing plant or laboratory whenever there were production or quality issues to be addressed. The work was also new to me and I had to learn on the job.

I used a number of methods to cope with the stressful situation. All these centre on efforts to bring the mind back to the present moment; to be mindful of the activity in the present moment. This being in the present moment lets our mind dwell restfully in the experiencing of whatever it is we are doing in the present moment. I learnt to compartmentalize my time. I would devote a fixed allotment of time even when there was urgent work, to not be disturbed when having periods of restful activity such as having a cup of tea or just quiet moments during the day. By doing so, I gave myself space to fully lay down any thoughts about work, to restfully experience myself being in the present moment and to recharge. I would also try to take my mind off from getting caught in trying to solve the work issues while getting to work. To keep my mind focused and inspired, I would silently recite the Buddhist *sutras* which I have learnt by heart. This helps to close the door of the mind to wandering thoughts or mental agitation. The mind is roped to follow the recitation and not be distracted into thinking about work issues. These issues can always wait for our full attention when we get to the workplace. In the evenings, I would try to fit in the reverencing and meditation practices.

By the end of the first year in that assignment, I was moved to handle another product line which was even more demanding, with higher production rates and limited storage capacity, which meant having to expedite product batching and dispatch. By then, however, I was ready to take on the additional challenges and not have any more issue with stress. It became just a heavier work load at times. The job challenges also turned out to be rather satisfying.

I have found it important that whenever I feel restless or stressed, to take "time-out" to reassess the situation. It is also a good practice to have short segments of time when we do something other than work, such as tidying up our work area, making a trip to the pantry to fetch a cup of tea, having a short sharing session with a co-worker, taking a brief walk out of the office, etc. We can introduce intervals of calm and restfulness throughout the day, to ground ourselves back on to the mindfulness of the present moment. We will then be reinvigorated and rested.

We would also want to be involved in activities that help us de-stress; which open us to higher inspiration, give us peace and calm, and let our hectic and stressed minds have a respite. For that, we may do the chanting and meditation practices. Physical exercises or involvement in activities that require full but relaxed participation and involvement, also help to alleviate stress.

The prostration practice is especially suited for calming us down when we are restless or agitated. The physical nature of doing the prostrations in a focused manner helps vent off some of the mental agitation. When we do the prostrations wholeheartedly, we will be both mentally and physically involved. We also invite the blessings of the Buddha and *Bodhisattvas* into our practice. As we get attuned to the relaxed mind, we can move on to meditate. If we have already developed our meditation practice, even a short period of meditation can put our minds back into restfulness and calm.

The practice of mindfulness helps us to focus on the job at hand, and it can also give us relief from the restlessness and worry that often comes with stress. Whenever we feel overwhelmed with work, we can make a cup of tea (or coffee) and sit by ourselves in a quiet place, to fully be with the cup and tea and slowly savour every sip. We place ourselves at ease and as we sip, we can bring to mind the tea drinking gatha[53]. There is only the tea and the experience of the drinking of tea, and nothing else to complicate the emptiness of drinking tea. In that short break, as we experience the emptiness of drinking tea, we will be reinvigorated.

The above practices may be enough to help us to de-stress. If not, we may need to give further thought to understand the underlying causes of what it is that is actually causing us the stress or distress. The forementioned methods may give us a breather and allow us to soothe away the stress, but the better solution is to lift ourselves out of being under stress altogether. That is, we can aim for a full cure; a fuller and more satisfying resolution of the issues around the stress; not just addressing the symptoms.

If we do not like our work and that is causing us undue stress, we either have to change our mind-set to accept what we have to do, or we look for feasible alternatives. If the stress is due to a working environment which appears to be cold and unfriendly, or overly immersed in office politicking, then mindfulness may help us to be more aware of the personal dynamics at work and help us to better handle the various situations which could initiate stressful responses in ourselves. Under such circumstances, it is often the practice of loving-kindness which will be most effective. It will alleviate the effects these negative influences can have on us.

In the practice of loving-kindness, we effectively shield ourselves from the swirling currents of ill will or unfriendliness, with an outpouring of friendliness. We will not be weighed down by the negative atmosphere, and will in fact be able to help improve the environment we are in. When we are sustained by loving-kindness, we will not be in the grip of negativity and can rid ourselves of that stress. We can then enjoy our work, maintain our zest for life and bring back to our families or our home a hale and happy mind at the end of every work day.

Giving Understanding and Sympathetic Joy

I have worked as the project manager on a number of multimillion dollar petrochemical and refining investment projects. These projects were typically schedule and cost driven and the work required much interaction and interfacing with all the stakeholders. I invariably find that people will treat us the way that we treat them. If we give due respect and understanding to the folks we interact with, it typically comes back to us.

In the workplace, we will likely have met people bent on pursuing their career advancements at the expense of others. Some will be playing at spreading distrust or misconceptions about the capability or behaviour of their "adversaries". We often hear disparaging remarks such as: "Looks like he could not handle what he is doing." passed on someone who we know to be very capable. Some may have taken to be putting others down by passing seemingly innocuous remarks such as, "You don't look so good today," or "You look stressed out today," and the like, in the company of unconcerned colleagues or within earshot of their superiors.

These are not the practices we want to indulge in. When exposed to such situations, we can turn such unskilful activity to benefit our practice. We can use these instances for developing our loving-kindness, or with the application of mindfulness and discernment, look into the characteristics of *anatman*, *duhkha*, *anitya* and emptiness in the process unfolding before us. We mindfully observe what is happening, understand what is happening and with awareness of that, we can address it with clarity and let it go with a smile.

We need not be arrogant or display power to intimidate others. We want to be able to grow in our practice and not have to deal with the negativity, which operating in the manner of an intimidating and arrogant egoist, will deal out to us later. Sometimes, it may be skilful to display firmness with emphasized speech, in full view of the team members. The team members may need to know of our seriousness, when the urgency and importance of an issue requires that we communicate it in such a way. If we handle our work with mindful awareness, we will be able to see through the pretensions at work, both in ourselves and in others clearly and can work to avoid the pitfalls.

In supporting a positive atmosphere in the workplace, there will be many occasions when we can show and develop sympathetic joy (*mudita*). This is the shared joy in the good fortune, success and happiness of others. When we see that someone is happy, we let the sympathetic joy within us flow out to join in celebrating that happiness. When someone is given recognition, we let the sympathetic joy within us join in the happy occasion. Sympathetic joy is one of the four "divine-abidings" of loving-kindness, compassion, sympathetic joy and equanimity. These are the very powerful positive mental states which melt away our negative emotions and remove the hindrances to the flowering of our heart-mind.

When we feel for the happiness of others, we will not be caught up with feelings of jealousy or envy. Instead, we find joy in the well-being of others, so that our joy transcends caring only for ourselves, or feeling only happy for ourselves. The practice of developing sympathetic joy dismantles the barriers which prevent us from being happy with the happiness of another. It frees up another avenue for our happiness to grow. We are then able to let our feelings of happiness flow freely. How wonderful that we will have much more occasions to be joyful and happy, when we additionally further share in the happiness of others!

Responding to Aggressive Behaviour and Being Assertive

Being aggressive is typically defined as being combative, and even hostile. In some organizations, this is apparently an endorsed workplace behaviour, and workers are supposed to be aggressive to land the top job. However, what is this energy that is associated with being aggressive at the workplace? In aggressiveness, the focus is on a self-serving display of combative energy, looking to strike out at the object of the aggression, at taking down whatever it is that appears to be in the way of achieving an end result.

The overtly aggressive person, in applying this aggressiveness to the work environment, will be the person who steamrolls his way, and wades into whatever he is doing with a "My way is the right way," or "Get out of my way," mentality. There may perhaps be some short term benefits in getting a job done that way, but it definitely creates more harm than good, and will not be sustainable in the long run. Aggressive behaviour is self-indulgent, and it comes across as an inconsiderate and dismissive attitude. The aggressive behaviour may also be an outlet for pent up feelings of insecurity which take on the guise of a false sense of asserting control and is expressed as aggressiveness. Aggressive behaviour undermines goodwill, caters to self-centric conduct and creates mistrust, all very much anathema to what leadership by example entails. An organization which supports teamwork and consultative leadership will not condone this type of behaviour.

It is better to emphasize assertiveness, rather than a destructive aggressiveness, in the workplace. In being assertive, we express ourselves clearly, and show a consistency of action which may be forceful at the times when that is required. We do so calmly and without hostility. Our focus is on the message and its conveyance in a convincing and if need be, in a bold manner. Sometimes, we may want to let it be known that aggressiveness, which is tantamount to harassment or bullying, is not acceptable.

An example of this was when I was called into a meeting to resolve a pressing issue arising from a facility modification which would have significant cost impact. As I sat down, the contractor manager launched into playing the blame game and tried to put us on the defensive. He ranted on about how we are at fault, without giving any positive suggestions as to how the issue can be addressed. I interrupted his ranting, and directly told him I was there to help with working out the issue, that he was not helping with getting the job done, and that we need to work as a team. As he appeared unready for further constructive discussion, I suggested we reconvene when there is clarity on what is on the table for discussion, ended the meeting and left the room. We may sometimes need to make a strong point that we do not subscribe to such bullying behaviour.

How else can we deal with an aggressive person at the workplace? It may not be easy if we cannot appropriately raise this issue to our manager, or it could be that it is our manager who is prone to such behaviour. We may feel trapped in our work situation, fearful that we may lose our employment, and at the same time be stressed by having to put up with the aggression. Let us look at the options for handling this predicament.

Firstly, we have to decide we will not respond in a way which will demean our practice; we will maintain our practice of loving-kindness and focus on the work at hand. We do not want to be in a confrontational situation, and instead, will try to work out creative positive responses. If we do not feel up to the challenge, we may consider moving to another position where we do not need to deal with the aggressive person directly. However, if we have no choice but to stay where we are, or if we are willing to take on the challenge, then we will have to deepen our practice of loving-kindness so that we do not bear ill will to the aggressive person. We will then not indirectly harm ourselves with giving rise to feelings of enmity or hatred. With the searing cloud of enmity out of our way, we are no longer held hostage by the reactive emotional responses and can then take the right actions with clarity. We will also be giving the person an opportunity for reform and growth.

If we want to be happy for the long term, responding to aggression with hatefulness is not an option. We need to put on the armour of loving-kindness, to protect ourselves from the negativity of aggression. In doing so, we are also directly laying siege to the ill intentioned mind of the aggressor with loving-kindness. We then look into his motives and actions with calm discernment, and skilfully act to address his sphere of negative influence. In addition to our practice of loving-kindness, it may be that doing nothing more about it is the right answer. It may well be that we need to also address some of our own weaknesses. For example, we may need to change the way we communicate with our superiors. We need to understand ourselves, understand the situation, understand our options, and then work the solution.

Sometimes, we may land with an aggressive person in our team who does not support our work. We may then be concerned that we may be wrongly perceived as not getting the job done well, or that we may be misrepresented. If an area of overlapping roles and responsibilities is part of the issue, we can start with clarifying that. We put in the effort to make sure our workplace superiors know what our job scope and work responsibilities are. This is best documented after discussion and endorsement from them, and communicated to all involved. We can also enlist emotional support from our mentors or those who share our values. They may be outside our work environment, but they can give us support. By doing this, we are being assertive because we are giving expression to our conviction that good begets good, that care and concern is the nature of our practice, and we are doing it in a skilful, consistent and bold way. We are also being creative in employing resources that are available to us, to help us meet the common objective of getting the job done effectively, in a friendly workplace environment.

A person with aggressive behaviour may resort to underhanded means to work his or her advantage, for example, by belittling our efforts, and undermining our position. This would be a manipulative, covert aggression, which may involve back stabbing, late submission of supporting reports that hinder our work progress, misplaced blame, or inaction and so on.

To address these, we have to positively enhance our work contributions in a way which is apparent to all. We inject clarity into our role and participation in the workings of the organization. We let the stakeholders in the endeavour know the different areas of work we are handling, the good contributions we have made in those areas, and how we have resolved the many challenges and taken responsibility for their outcomes. We clearly document our good efforts, identify issues which need further evaluation or follow-up and define where the resources will be coming from. We widen our circle of communication and raise our profile, so that our area of responsibility or stewardship is known to all involved.

Having deadlines for closure of any outstanding issues, and identifying the persons responsible, is key to getting a job done well and on time. There will then be no uncertainty in everyone's mind as to their own areas of responsibility. It will also be obvious who is responsible for work yet to be completed. By doing this, we lift a load off our minds, as it will then be apparent to all when we have completed our job responsibilities, or how well the work we are handling is progressing.

We have to be happy with the contributions we make, and publicise it to those who may derive meaning and benefit from it. We can let this issue of handling the aggression be an opportunity, which we take on consciously, to spur us on to develop our career. This may require additional effort on our part to clarify our responsibilities and to ensure our work progress is effectively communicated, but it will be well worth it. If we do this in a consistent manner, we will make it clear we are focused on getting the job done well and will be recognized for being able to rise above the rancour of petty office politics. We can skilfully use this approach to drive, on the one hand, improvements in our performance and capabilities, our communication and interpersonal skills, and on the other hand, our practice of loving-kindness and generosity. In other words, we develop assertiveness by our way of mindful awareness, firmly and skilfully addressing issues which arise at the workplace, in the spirit of graciousness and friendliness.

If, however, after having tried the abovementioned approaches, we still find that the situation is too taxing on our mental and emotional well-being, it may then be time to make a move out of the organization we are working in. An organization which supports the kind of aggression being dealt out to us may be having a systemic inadequacy, or a wrong company culture which may be too much to be handled by us alone. As with any change, there will be risks with finding new employment elsewhere, but our well-being is also paramount. We should not languish in a working environment which does not support our development. We should not subject ourselves to deadening and energy sapping negativity at the workplace if we can help it. Ideally, we would try to find employment in a Right Livelihood environment. Having a Right Livelihood as part of the Noble Eightfold Path taught by the Buddha, is a key factor in our development. If we have the right opportunities, we may ourselves be in a position to start a Right Livelihood business which gives employment to others, in an environment which enhances everyone's well-being and growth.

Cultivating Leadership - A Buddhist Perspective

Let us explore how we can carry out the duties of leadership and cultivate leadership in a manner which supports our practice of the *Dharma*. Leadership is commonly referred to as being in charge or being in command, being in the principal position and having the power to institute the position of being in command.

From the Buddhist perspective, one does not aspire to leadership as an end in itself, nor does one aim to cling on to power and influence. Rather, we aspire to provide for the well-being and welfare of others. In the workplace, we can contribute towards making the work environment a positive, energizing and friendly place, where the supporting conditions for Right Livelihood can be met. We do not need to be a designated leader to contribute. We can do our part in every little way by using any opportunity available to us. The leader, especially if he is in a senior management position in an organization, has a key role to play; in giving support to his workers through the day, and taking steps to ensure they leave the workplace safe and on a positive note at the end of every workday.

The person in a leadership role has to bear in mind that there will likely be many heated arguments as to which of the alternative options for solving a problem is the best one to pursue. A final consensus on the way forward has to be found so that the next stage of implementation will be a fully endorsed commitment by all stakeholders. In this process of guiding the discussion to consolidate the many divergent views to achieve a clear objective, the quality of loving-kindness is particularly relevant. The practice of loving-kindness in such situations helps tremendously towards having healthy discussions, and will make it apparent that there is no ill will or resentment in the discussions; that one is not out to take advantage of, or to shame anyone else. Everyone can then feel the warm invitation to freely contribute, in an atmosphere which sustains spirited but friendly discussion.

The leadership role may sometimes be a brief one, as for example, when we may be called to lead a study group, a review committee, or a profit enhancement exercise. In any case, the principles of leadership still apply with regards to the conduct of a leader and the typical issues he may be exposed to.

In most organizations, there will likely be broad guidelines which help to establish the way it goes about doing its business effectively. A system of management which establishes the controls and work processes for the conduct of business would typically already be in place. The check and balances, and oversight of work practices would have been implemented to sustain operational excellence, together with adequate governance. The challenges of taking on a leadership role in such an environment can be made easier if one understands the many different demands on someone in a leadership position. Below are some of the approaches I have found useful for working effectively in a leadership role.

Know the team members and support them

The leader has to know her (or his) team. She has to understand the cultural sensitivities, strengths and weaknesses of her troops. She has to know what their core capabilities are and the resources they may have at their disposal. She has to know what help she will need outside of her arena of direct influence, and the internal and external interfaces she has to deal with. The leader can be a good support for her troops only if she knows them and the situation well enough, to be able to assess what support they might need as the work develops.

She has to know the resources which have been designated for her use, usually as specified in the organisational structure. She will also want to know the answers to these questions: What are their levels of competency in their area of expertise? When will they be available for deployment? Will they be available on a part time or full time basis? Do they work well in a team, or are they individualists? Do they take on responsibility or do they tend to shy from work? Do they take the initiative or do they have to be directed? Do they know how to manage upwards and downwards, or do they need to have an eye kept on them always? Are they sensitized to the cultural differences of the people they are going to be working with? What further training do they need? How about the availability of specialized (e.g. process, equipment, technical, safety, environmental, permitting, cost control, etc.) resources? How are these to be shared or managed?

When the leader knows her troops and the resources available to her, she can then prioritize what else she may need, or how she can fill the gaps. She will have a better idea of whether she will be able to meet the milestone timelines and cost schedules with what she has, or whether she will need manning up, or to ask for more funding. By doing so, she can address any shortcomings early, and those supporting her will not be later overstretched or be subjected to unnecessary work pressures. If she is leading a team of office personnel, the considerations are similar in making the assessments on whether she can take on more work or meet tight schedules, handle training requirements, or assess what risk exposure she may have in terms of resource capability and availability.

The practices of mindfulness, letting go, compassion and loving-kindness all have key roles in our leadership activities. With these practices, we can develop a clear sensitivity to the different needs of the different people we are dealing with. We can support them better if we understand them well. We can back them up by giving them adequate resources to do their work better, and nudge them gently to corrective actions when it becomes apparent such direction is needed.

We set the tone of friendliness and fairness in building and sustaining our team by cultivating loving-kindness and being ourselves mindful of the interactions around us. When we apply our practice of letting go, we will not be judgemental and will not be bogged down by emotional reactivity or prejudice. We will, with calmness and clarity, be able to rise above the many trivial misunderstandings, to influence the team positively, and align it to clear objectives.

Listen mindfully

In the various discussions we will have in the conduct of our business, we will want to listen mindfully. We can then better distinguish the real from what is made-up, or the protective mechanisms thrown up by parties playing on the defensive. If we are listening mindfully, we will be able to discern the group dynamics at work, and we can then fruitfully steer the team to positive and forward looking strategies. We cut through the inconsequential, and address the real issues affecting the work at hand.

When we cultivate discernment and detachment, problematic issues will be clearer against the backdrop of *anitya* and *anatman*, and the path forward will be viewed with clarity. Self-interest or the fixation on prior assessments or prior actions, which have resulted in either good or bad outcomes, are seen in their proper contexts. We do not let them mislead our judgement or unnecessarily complicate matters in going forward.

Be Aware of Cross-Cultural Differences

Cultural sensitivity is a very important aspect of communication. The leader has to be aware of, and be sensitive to, the cultural background of his audience in his communications with them. An overly brash manner does not work well with folks used to measured and milder behaviour. I have been in meetings where arguments can be vigorous, but where the discussions remain respectful. I have also been in meetings where a manager conducts himself in a culturally insensitive and disparaging manner. The discussion then quietens down as the sharing of views and ideas comes to a halt. It is not conducive to having fruitful discussions when another party feels that he has "lost face" and was belittled, or has been subjected to condescending or demeaning behaviour.

When we need to work with other cultures, which do not have a good command of the English language, we do have to be extra patient. We need to ensure we have understood correctly and we are not misunderstood. Though the production rate for your plant may have been "ramped up", you may however be told instead, that production has been "screwed up"!

Sometimes in a different cultural setting, the major decisions are not made by group consensus during meetings. Meetings may be deemed useful only for gathering information and sounding out sensitivities. We may have to lower our expectations when going into these meetings.

The telling of jokes that play on cultural differences in a cynical or demeaning way has no place in the work environment nor anywhere else. Humour of this sort is insensitive and prone to be misinterpreted. It is likely to further have an exaggerated impact on someone from a different culture.

Stay humble and accept criticism

Leadership is not about crushing will, nor bending and shaping members of the team to meet the job requirements. It is rather about evaluating what needs to be done and how best to go about it with the available resources in hand. The leader guides his team in the execution of the work plan with a willingness to help, in the spirit of mutual support and mutual respect.

The leader therefore has to be continually in touch with the folks on the ground. He has to "walk the talk". He has to be humble enough to accept criticism, to be honest in his dealings, and to be respectful of those around him. In the same manner, he should give honest criticism when that is needed.

Lead with clear direction

The leader has to set the direction for the team and make sure his priorities, key areas of focus and milestones, are well thought through, and then clearly communicated. He keeps in mind Right Speech, and communicates civilly and with sensitivity, with focus on the issues being worked. He does not let communication be hijacked by egotistical self-interest.

He does the legwork to ensure there is "buy-in" to significant changes in the implementation plan; to get early endorsement for the changes he is trying to implement. Obtaining "buy-in" from all stakeholders in the endeavour is critical. The "buy-in" has to be inclusive, and should be done early at key stages in the development of the work. Sometimes, after considerable progress has been made, the odd comment from someone who was inadvertently left out of the discussions can cast the proverbial spanner (e.g. with questions as to the viability or correctness of some key assumptions, or whether enough consideration was given to some past difficulties experienced in a similar situation, etc.) into the smooth implementation of the project.

When work is in progress, the leader ensures it is progressing safely as planned; with the correct order of priorities, and meeting work scope specifications, quality, cost, and schedule requirements.

Resolving Conflicts

Conflicts may arise from differences in opinions, or may be due to differing requirements for conformance to procedural practices or differing assessments of the situation at hand.

An example of a conflict situation I was involved with was when the contractor specialists (located overseas) were at odds with our own in-house specialists with regards to the design of a major piece of plant equipment. As I followed the technical discussions in the thread of emails between the two parties, I could see their positions becoming entrenched, until it came to a stalemate. The contractor threatened to withdraw his guarantee of operational and safety compliance for that piece of equipment if we did not accede to having his requirements incorporated into the equipment design.

As the project manager, I had to resolve this conflict before it led to a delay in the equipment construction. I arranged for the contractor specialists to fly in, and closeted them with our in-house specialists in a face-to-face meeting. It was a vigorous and argumentative meeting. However, it helped sort out the common ground. In such a meeting, the leader has to be present, to guide the group back to the project priorities, whenever it tries to veer into indulging in personal preferences. Even though there was no full agreement at the end of that meeting, a path forward was agreed upon. The whole issue was then resolved in a fortnight. It is with experiences like this one, that I have come to believe in the efficacy of having face-to-face meetings instead of communicating via e-mails, or having teleconferences, when complicated issues have to be addressed head on and be promptly resolved.

Be fair and honest

As leaders, we will have to make sure that those committed to working for us are fairly treated, and get something out of working with us. At least, it should be a pleasant experience which gives both parties some degree of satisfaction. We want those who have supported us to feel they have been appreciated, that they have developed on the job and that it has been worth their while in having spent their time with us. This may require some upfront planning to let them have opportunities for exposure to new learnings. Again, this is done with consideration for their welfare.

As a leader, part of our responsibility is to provide feedback to those who are working for us, as to the quality of their work or the manner in which they are handling it; be it good or lacking, so they can improve. It is also our duty to sell them, to promote their good achievements or attitudes, so they will be recognised outside of the team.

Stay infectiously happy

If we are happy and therefore have an easy smile, we will be contributing towards developing a positive and pleasing environment to work in. This can have a far reaching effect on everyone around us. It induces peacefulness and calm; which are sorely needed with all the fast moving activities happening around us.

It helps that we do not get too emotionally caught up with work issues, and to instead develop a clear and positively energised mind so we can think straight. The outflow of positivity comes from a peacefully settled mind which is at ease with itself. To be established in this state, we firstly have to be happy with ourselves, and to then share this friendliness of loving-kindness (*maitri*) and the sympathetic joy (*mudita*) with those around us.

Improve leadership skills

We can always do better as a leader. There is always room for improvement, and we should take the initiative to change for the better. We should be humble and accept responsibility for whatever happens on our watch. We learn from any mistakes, oversights, or missed opportunities.

Taking on a leadership role typically means taking on additional responsibility. There may be occasions when a job clearly needs to be done, but there are no takers. This is an opportunity for demonstrating leadership, if one knows that one has the capability to handle the job. It may require additional work on our part, but if successfully concluded, the effort will certainly be appreciated.

As practising Buddhists, we should be keenly aware that what we do will affect those around us and we will want to affect them in a positive way. Our leadership style should attest to that attitude. We should demonstrate consideration and care for others in the team while being firm in action, and having clarity while in the midst of meticulous and quick execution. We should be effectively mentoring the less experienced, and those willing to learn. Above all, we conduct our activities in a spirit of friendliness, with calmness, clarity, and focused determination.

Leadership in a crisis

It is in times of crisis when leadership is needed and tested. In times of crisis, the leader has to transcend his normally defined role, and take up the challenge. He has to call up his commitment, his resolve and the creative energies within him, to steer rapidly unfolding events to a satisfactory resolution. A good example of this, was the leadership demonstrated by the third Secretary General of the United Nations, U Thant, during the Cuban Missile Crisis. This was in October, 1962 when the USSR and the US almost came to a naval clash, and was at the brink of nuclear war.

The US learnt about nuclear ballistic missile launching sites being constructed in Cuba, and imposed a "naval quarantine"; short of a "naval blockade" which would have been a declaration of war. The "hawks" in the US presidential team of advisors advocated destroying the missile site with air strikes and an invasion of Cuba. As the standoff between the two superpowers worsened, the US military alert for the Strategic Air Command (SAC) was upgraded to Defense Readiness Condition level 2 (DEFCON-2). This is one level below the DEFCON-1 for imminent nuclear war. DEFCON-2 was the highest DEFCON level that the US military was subjected to in US history. In the midst of all the tension, a US U-2 spy plane was downed in Cuba, killing the pilot.

Secretary General U Thant decisively approached President Kennedy of the US, and Premier Kruschev of the USSR, with a direct urgent appeal for a moratorium. He also urged President Castro of Cuba to suspend work on the missile facilities, and offered his services to help resolve the impasse. He then took on the role of mediator, and gained the trust of both superpowers with his fair-minded, calm and sensitive handling of the issues as they developed. He urged restraint, sought assurances, and gave hope to both parties that there will be a way out of the quagmire if there is giving and taking.

U Thant's role was recognized by both the US and the USSR after the crisis was defused. President Kennedy praised U Thant's efforts in helping to resolve the crisis and said that U Thant has put the world deeply in his debt. U Thant was reappointed UN Secretary General [54] by unanimous vote of the UN Security Council in 1966. He refused a third term as Secretary General and resigned in 1971. U Thant passed away in 1974 at the age of sixty-five.

U Thant had said that his upbringing as a Buddhist taught him to be tolerant, and to especially cherish modesty, humility, compassion and equanimity. It was when he was rushed to the UN in the early hours when the Six Day War (1967 Arab-Israeli War) erupted, that he mentioned he had, for the first time in his memory, left home without doing his morning meditation[55]. U Thant practised the meditation on loving-kindness in his daily practice of extending goodwill towards all beings.

When exercising leadership, we should take up the mind of a *Bodhisattva*, cultivating a field of rich harvest with everyone sharing in the work, and employing skilful means to bring joy and restfulness into the realm of work.

Chapter 7: Enriching Positive Relationships

Growing Relationships

Knowing Where We Stand

Sincere Communication

The *Mangala Sutta*

Whether we like it or not, we are immersed in relationships. We are involved in relationships with family, friends, neighbours, the lady at the convenience store check-out counter, and the person at the other end of our phone line when we call in for an order of takeaway pizzas. There are also relationships we have with our pets, our love-hate relationship with the pantry drawer that slides out grudgingly, and so on. Life is a series of ongoing relationships. We tend to think the basic "problem" with relationships is that they involve another party besides us. We tend to always think the problem is with someone else and not with us. We are nearly always wrong, for it takes two hands to clap.

How we go about relating to one another will affect us considerably. Every one of our relationships will be special and different. Good relationships enhance the positivity of the social environment we move in. They support the growth and development of the partnering individuals in that environment. Relationships need routine maintenance, the occasional patching up, and at times extra careful handling. We also cannot rely on the other person in the relationship to be the one making the effort to change for us. The responsibility finally lies with us.

When we have developed an understanding of the teaching of no-self (*anatman*), we can begin to let go of our hold on to the erroneous view of an unchanging self. As we apply the *anatman* teaching to the way we relate to ourselves and others, we gradually become more amenable to be accepting of positive change in ourselves. We will be able to empty out the hardness in us; becoming soft and pliable enough to round out the sharp edges. We then begin to loosen up and enjoy being at ease with our joyful selves.

Growing Relationships

We may not always want to respond immediately to help another person out, so as not to overdo the nurturing part of the relationship. For example, we may not want to right away pick up a child who has fallen down. We check if he is hurt. If he does not need immediate help, we may want to let him be, for a short while. We let him learn to pick himself up. By doing so, the child will learn to help himself to grow in confidence, and not to wail and cry in anticipation of an extended hand every time he falls down. So when we then reach to pick him up, it is an affirmation of care and love. Some will need this approach more than others; to be weaned out of their overly dependent nature.

Parents with growing teenagers may not find it easy to adjust to the changing phases of their emotional growth. We have to be aware whether we are handling their issues from our own self-affirming approach, which limits their experiencing themselves, or with consideration for their emotional development. Being mindful is the key to doing what is beneficial. It may be tempting to be constantly watching out for them, but that may not always be the right thing to do. Dashing to the kitchen to get them their bowl of cereal and milk when it looks like they may be late leaving for classes, may not help with their cultivating the responsibility to be punctual. Missing the occasional breakfast will not be detrimental to their physical growth. Hunger from a missed breakfast, or scolding from a teacher for being late for class, may be a good lesson for them.

We have to make an assessment of what is helpful for the occasion. As with any relationship, we will also be learning and growing together. We have to take care not to come across as being too prescriptive when we share our ideas and opinions. We also have to be mindful we do not cling on to the "I know what is best for you", or the "I know better" mentality. In any case, we will want to let them know we care for them, and that we will always be there to support them in any way we can.

When there is a change in our lifestyle, there will be adjustments to be made. When a person gets married and enters into a new phase of being husband or wife, there is tremendous change; especially if both partners have not lived together before the marriage. Marriage is a deep commitment which calls for much give and take. There is the attending to each other's well-being, sharing of the responsibilities of running a household, bringing up children and resolving issues together. This calls for much understanding, loving and forgiving. We will likely find that we cannot easily change the longstanding, ingrained traits in our partner. We should also not go about trying to change the person directly. Being married means we have accepted each other as we are, warts and all, in a committed relationship.

We can instead, work on ourselves, such that we indirectly influence the outcome of any misunderstandings. If our partner is prone to anger, and on occasions when we feel it rising, we need to stay even calmer. We stay mindful not to bring up the reactive mind which is very quick with raking up past misdeeds and not to further add fuel to fire. We work on guiding the tone of the communication and lead it back to calmness. When we do this, we are making it clear that we will put effort into developing a loving relationship which is anchored in giving and caring.

The practice of mindfulness can be very helpful in giving us an awareness of the situation at hand, and an awareness of our mental state in that situation. With mindfulness, we can then act clearly to achieve a happy outcome. This is not being cold or calculating. To be cold and calculating means acting to gain an advantage and alienating our partner. This is not the case here. What we are mindfully doing, is to bring the other person softly into our arms and embracing him or her with tender care. With mindfulness, we will always be prepared to respond with warmth and understanding. For two persons to have support and love for each other, to care for each other throughout life and further be the support of other members of the family, is a wonderful undertaking.

A good relationship will be fertile ground for the growth of the individuals in that relationship. We would hope everyone grows with involvement in the relationship. The relationship should not be binding us in an exclusive dependence which is restrictive and stifling. Instead, it should allow us to communicate deeply and honestly; bringing trust and understanding into the relationship. We would wish the other person will grow in freedom, self-reliance, and develop good attributes in a relationship which is based on mutual understanding, love and respect for each other. It starts with us understanding that the relationship can be changed for the better and then making that change happen by working on ourselves. This is employing the Right Understanding and Right Aspiration (Right Resolve) of the Noble Eightfold Path.

In relationships which are centred on growth and self-cultivation on the Noble Eightfold Path, and are in accord with the *Dharma*, the participants will be part of a loosely knit community of the *Sangha*. Members of this spiritual community will enjoy the kinship of interaction with fellow pilgrims on the path to awakening, sharing the positive environment of friendliness, sincere communication and the joyful certainty on the path. This will be a very supportive environment for growth and development.

Knowing Where We Stand

It is important that we truly understand the nature of the relationships we are in. We may be painting a rosy or a dark picture of a relationship, depending on our views and biases. We carry that picture with us and it affects the clarity of our interactions with the other party. If we are biased, we will then be actually working against ourselves, by having created these false views.

We will want to ask: Is the relationship a healthy companionship? Is there a sharing of individual interests, hopes and understanding? Is there insecurity or emotional dependence in the relationship? Do we try to make the other person in the relationship truly happy? Do we feel we are being exploited? Do we feel appreciated? Have we done enough to be supportive? When we discern our role in the relationship, see how it is affecting us and how we are affecting others, we will understand it much better. The practice of loving-kindness (*maitri*) and the discerning mindfulness will be indispensable to help us move on with the relationship. However, in some cases, we may even want to dissociate ourselves from that circle of influence if it is overly affecting us negatively.

Relationships will definitely change. They may someday come to suffer the strain of accessibility and physical remoteness if there is a physical relocation. There may also be changing commitments as we go through the different phases in life. We have to give the changing relationship sufficient leeway. We should not be dismayed when we think we have been let down by a relationship which has cooled. If we have done what we can to help remedy the situation, then perhaps its time is up. If that is the case, we will want to let it de-energize naturally. We may have lost the closeness we once felt, but we can rejoice that our paths have crossed and we had shared in the joy of friendship. We allow loving-kindness, compassion and the discerning mindfulness to guide the way we conduct our relationships.

Forgiveness is the glue that keeps relationships whole. Forgiveness is perhaps the greater love. It sustains the joy of being in a relationship. If we have caused hurt to another, we ask for forgiveness, learn from our mistakes and move on from there. We would also want to forgive ourselves our inconsiderate actions and stupidity. It is never too late to rebuild a relationship which has gone unattended, or perhaps even turned sour. We first need to forgive the past. The starting ground for the required repair work is always in the present and it starts with us forgiving the past. Do not underestimate the power of forgiveness and loving-kindness. Forgiveness lets us leave the past behind and gives us the fresh start. Loving-kindness empowers us to create the new beginning and nurtures it.

Relationships within the family will be affected when there are lifestyle changes, as for example, when we make the change from a regulated work life in an office to a home environment due to taking up the duties of a homemaker, or when we leave the working life, or retire. If we are then spending more time at home with other members of the family, there will be more interactions we will need to adjust to. Any adjustment will be made easier if it firstly comes from us. We have to be open to be doing things differently. What may seem to be little things to us may matter a lot to others. For example, the kitchen may have earlier been completely run by our spouse. When we spend more time in the kitchen, we have to be mindful of her needs and her way of doing things. We give ourselves time to adjust and ask for forgiveness if we are not helping out well enough. With mindfulness as our guide, we should adjust well to our new roles.

Sincere Communication

Sincerity is an oft used word. It is usually described as not feigned, honest and even pure. So being sincere is being truthful and being honest. However, there will not be sincere communication if we are not, in the first place, truthful and honest with ourselves. This means knowing and accepting our strengths, weaknesses and shortcomings.

Communication is a two way process. The key to a good relationship is good communication. However, our communication with others, because of our faulty self-view, will be distorted. It will be tainted by the selective masking, or be enhanced and augmented by our self-view modifications, in the process of being conveyed to others. We may not be as kind a person as we would like to think we are. There may be parts of ourselves we do not consciously want to accept or acknowledge. Under these circumstances, our communication and interaction with others will be inherently flawed.

If our mind is grounded in sincerity and honesty, our communication with others will then be meaningful and sincere. The starting point on the way to sincere and honest communication is therefore with ourselves. We have to get in touch with ourselves and know who we really are. We will also want to anticipate how the other party we are interacting with, will take what we are trying to communicate. They will have their own biases and self-views. They may not be ready to share and communicate at the intensity or in the manner we would wish for.

We may be hurt by insensitive words spoken to us, especially when they are from those whom we hold in high regard. We may have similarly hurt another. What was said can never be retracted, but we can move forward with forgiving or asking for forgiveness. This should be done as soon as we realise the foolishness of our actions, to re-establish the relationship back on a positive footing.

If we speak false words, we are punishing ourselves with having to live that falsehood. We will burden ourselves with having to carry it with us; mentally referring to it before we speak and perhaps feed it more lies. If we do this often, it makes it easier for us to utter the next lie, until lying becomes second nature to us. We will then often succumb to be telling lies to escape from being inconvenienced, to hide our blemishes, to slander another person, or for personal gain. The chances of being caught telling a lie increases as more lies are told. Lies are remembered, and time will improve the chances for the truth to surface.

When a person is branded a liar, any communication from him (or her) will be questioned. There will be devastating effects on his career development, his relationships and his standing in the community. False communication easily destroys relationships.

What form does sincere communication take? It will be communication which engenders friendliness, conveys support and understanding, is clear and truthful, builds trust and is for the betterment of all.

We therefore do not want to waste time and effort to indulge in gossip. Useless gossip can turn out to be a detrimental practice in rehashing cruel remarks, reliving unhelpful experiences, making slanderous accusations and inciting hatred or distrust. One comes out of an interaction of this sort feeling negative and emotionally drained. It is better to part company with those who incessantly incite mistrust and slander others. Sincere communication, as in the sharing of life experiences, or even just lending a sympathetic ear, enriches and is helpful. It deepens trust and bonding.

Our communication should be with the intent of bringing concordance, spreading goodwill and understanding. If there is opportunity, we will want to share the *Dharma*, for the communicating and sharing of the *Dharma* brings countless benefits to all. We innately will subtly impress on others the beauty of the *Dharma* if we participate with sincere and honest communication. This is the "Right Speech" of the Noble Eightfold Path.

The Mangala Sutta

In the beautiful *Mangala Sutta* [(56)], the Buddha gave a discourse on those practices which are particularly relevant to the householder; which lead to lasting happiness. *Mangala* means "a blessing" or "an auspicious sign" in both Pali and Sanskrit. *Sutta* is the Pali word for the Sanskrit *sutra* which means a thread of discourse or a teaching given by the Buddha.

External signs are believed by some, to portend good or bad tidings, for example, the belief that bad luck will befall one who crosses path with a black cat. In the *Mangala Sutta*, the Buddha taught that one need not be affected by the seemingly inauspicious, and does not need to depend on external signs of auspiciousness to derive good outcomes. The cultivation of virtuous conduct and understanding of the *Dharma* are the truly auspicious signs that usher in good tidings. The quotes below are adapted from the *Mangala Sutta*, and they deal with relationships between the householder, his family and the community in a practical way.

1) *"Not keeping company with the foolish, but associating with the wise, honouring those worthy of honour - this is the highest blessing."*

The "foolish" are the deluded and those predisposed to selfishness, to harmful speech, to all manner of excessive indulgent behaviour, or those who harbour jealousy and ill intent. If we associate with the foolish, we will be exposed to their foolishness, and thus be unwittingly affected. There is also the danger that not just ourselves, but also those close to us, will be inadvertently drawn into that association and be adversely influenced. The mindful discernment which we cultivate, will give us the clarity to see into their obsessive mind and false pretences.

The foolish who are preoccupied with acquiring fame and wealth, are stingy and have strong self-centred views, will find it difficult to part with any of their possessions. They will tend to gauge their actions, and the extent of any help they proffer to another, in terms of gain or loss. The foolish who are conceited, will not acknowledge our good attributes, especially when in the presence of others. They are therefore unreliable and will not likely be of much help when approached for assistance. The foolish will therefore end up in the company of the foolish. The wise will not seek them out, nor suffer their foolishness.

There may be occasions when we may be able to offer them guidance or clarity. We can encourage them to cultivate sincere giving for the welfare of others. However, when we do so, we have to be mindful and exercise care to not be caught in their world of deluded views and negative tendencies which have arisen from their having very strong attachments.

We seek the company of the wise; those who are clear sighted, virtuous and have deep understanding of the

Dharma. It is a true blessing if there are wise persons to whom we can go to for counsel and guidance; those who can inspire us in our practice.

2)   "To reside in a suitable locality,"

If we reside in a safe and secure environment, we will not need to worry about how we get to work, the need to secure our home or the whereabouts of our loved ones. Ideally, we would want to be in surroundings, which are conducive to our practice, where the social environment emphasises mutual respect and tolerance.

3)   "to perform meritorious acts, "

If we cultivate virtue through meritorious activities, these will bear fruit and positively support our practice. We will have a happy frame of mind from having known that we have done good deeds. Virtue is one of the three pillars (the other two being concentration and wisdom) which support spiritual growth.

4)   "and to set oneself on the right course - this is the highest blessing."

If we have directed our efforts to the cultivation of virtue, concentration and wisdom, then this is certainly a blessing, for it leads to release from pain and suffering. This will be a blessing not just for ourselves, but also for others associated with us, who are open to our learnings. We will be a source of inspiration and a blessing to them as well.

5)   "To have much learning, be skilled in a craft, be well trained in discipline,"

Having a good education or training in a specialised skill helps us have a good livelihood, and a respected place in society. All this will, however, come to naught, if we lack discipline or are not controlled in the way we conduct ourselves.

6) *"and to be of pleasant speech - this is the highest blessing."*

This is equivalent to having a good level of the emotional quotient, and being able to communicate proficiently. Our communication should not be harsh, coercive, or arrogant. It should be pleasant and in a friendly tone, open-hearted and inviting a positive response. The way we communicate will need to be tailored to the audience. If we are in a business discussion, we communicate civilly and pleasantly. We will not want to appear overly friendly; for in that context, it may be taken to mean submission or a lack of confidence.

As always, we need to be sensitive to the different cultural nuances when communicating cross-culturally. The society at large nowadays appears to be somewhat alien to the expression of friendliness from strangers. So we should not be surprised when the reaction our *maitri* (loving-kindness) is sometimes a cold stare.

7) *"To support one's parents, to cherish wife and children,"*

Having carried out our responsibilities to our parents and family, and treating them with respect and concern, ensures that we will have harmonious family ties. We will then have a happy and joyful home environment to go back to at the end of every day. For some, especially the smaller families, it may not be a feasible option to fully take on the burden of caring for the infirm or aged parents. It will be a blessing if we do ensure they are well taken care of by other caregivers. In some cases, our parents may not need our financial support, nor be living with us. We can still provide them emotional support and give them joy with our love and care. We and our children will in turn, be blessed by their wisdom and love.

8)   "and to be engaged in peaceful work - this is the highest blessing."

In having a livelihood aligned with our practice of harmlessness and friendliness, which is free from having to deal with the uncertainties of our safety, income and position, we will have a calm and relaxed atmosphere to work in. It is a blessing if we are in a supportive work environment, and are not subjected to extreme stress, danger, worry, or uncertainty in our daily work.

The Buddha taught that amassing wealth is praiseworthy if it is legitimately acquired and used for meritorious deeds:

"The one enjoying sensual pleasures (i.e. a lay person), who seeks wealth lawfully, without violence, and makes himself happy and pleased, and shares it and does meritorious deeds, and who uses that wealth without being tied to it, uninfatuated with it, not blindly absorbed in it, seeing the danger in it, understanding the escape – he may be praised on four grounds ...'He seeks wealth lawfully without violence...makes himself happy and pleased... shares it and does meritorious deeds ... and uses that wealth without being tied to it...' Thus one enjoying sensual pleasures may be praised on these four grounds." [(57)]

9)   "To be generous, be of upright conduct, render help to relatives, and be blameless in deeds - this is the highest blessing..."

In the *sutta*, the Buddha next goes on to teach the practices of the Noble Eightfold Path.

When we conduct ourselves beyond reproach, and are generous and helpful, we will be easily accepted by the community we live in. Our many friends will give us reliable support and we will be welcomed with friendliness and respect wherever we go.

If we accept that we can change for the better, we will be more receptive to the needs of others, and be responsive to the dynamics of our interactions with others. We will have shifted the normal centre of reference outside of ourselves, and into the relationship. We widen our field of awareness, and act with clarity and consideration. Communication can then be naturally open and flow without hindrance.

For a relationship to deepen, we have to open ourselves up, and invite the other person to also do so. We must also, at the same time, be mindful whether the other person is ready to handle the deeper level of interaction. There are those who may be suspicious and misconstrue our sincere actions. If they are not ready, doing this may result in an awkward response. If so, it will be better to let the relationship mature naturally.

The above considerations also apply to our relationships with our spouse, or other family members and our wider circle of friends and acquaintances. We can always act to the best of our understanding, to help others understand and grow themselves. In the process of doing so, we give expression to our vision and insight, and that is our practice.

Chapter 8: The Practice of Meditation

The most direct practice on the path of self-cultivation is the practice of meditation. When the Buddha was approached by a disciple for instructions, he would teach with some pointed words, or he would give a short discourse. The disciple would then go about his meditation practice ardently, to contemplate what he had been taught. Though we may feel encouraged to meditate and know that meditation pays big dividends, we are to approach the practice of meditation with a mind which is not seeking results. We let our practice naturally unfold from within us; without any prodding, without any aim to be getting anywhere.

The Approach to Self-Cultivation and Meditation

Overall in our practice, we cultivate an open mindful awareness. We cultivate an awareness of our physical condition, awareness of our mental condition, and awareness of our surroundings. With the awareness of our total condition, we will know how the environment around us affects our mental states. We then know when we need to be inspired, and when we need to push ourselves, or rein ourselves in if our practice has become slack. We will also know when we need help to further develop our practice. The practice of mindfulness will be carried into our practice of meditation, and our meditation practice will in turn contribute to our developing mindfulness. We then mesh all this together with our family and work activities, to have a holistic, sustainable and effective practice of the *Dharma*.

Meditation is not about thought control, shutting out thoughts, or trying to have only "good" thoughts. We are not out to control our thoughts by trying to force all thoughts out of our mind, or by trying to force our "bad" thoughts to become "good" thoughts. In fact, we are not too concerned when any "good" or "bad" thoughts show up. The Buddha taught that all "good" or "bad" thoughts are equally no-self, and are empty. In meditation, we need not distinguish between "good" or "bad" thoughts. They all belong to the realm of the five aggregates and are therefore illusory. They only distract us from our meditation practice. So when they show up, we just do not bother about them, and by denying them this nutriment of attention, these distracting thoughts will vanish away.

The meditation practices of the mindfulness of breathing, development of loving-kindness and walking meditation (see Appendix I), are practices which are good for everyone, and are not easily subject to misinterpretation or

196

malpractice. The Buddhist practice of meditation is directed towards developing calm and insight. It is much more than just a feel good practice, though we undeniably will feel good when developing our practice.

A few pointers for the beginner to note — the meditation practices start with us being in touch with ourselves, with our feelings, thoughts, mental states and consciousness in the present moment. There should be no alienation of our meditation experience. This means we are directly experiencing the meditation in the present moment. We are not doing any thinking about meditation, neither dwelling in the past nor in the future. What we are doing is deeply experiencing ourselves in the present.

There are a confusingly large number of different types of meditation practices available in the public domain. It may be enough for one seeking to be relaxed or restful, to continually chant a few syllables and thereby attain to some degree of restfulness or calm. It is, however, another matter altogether if we want to delve deep into the nature of mind, and to awaken to the nature of phenomenal existence. For that, we need a far-reaching method of practice.

In the course of meditation practice, we may have experiences which if incorrectly interpreted, may cause confusion, or which may bind us to deficient concepts or flawed interpretations. These may hinder our longer term development. Here we can rest assured that the Buddhist meditation practices have already been vetted by enlightened practitioners, covering more than a millennia of experience.

I first started learning meditation when I was an undergraduate at university and was practicing the martial arts. The senior instructor taught me to focus my attention on the energy centre below the navel. During one practice session, I lost the sense of my body, and felt an expansion of consciousness outwards beyond the room. I was confused, and when I asked the instructor what that experience meant, he said to just ignore it, and to continue with the practice. It was when I began practicing Buddhist meditation and the *Dharma*, that I came to understand what my experience meant, and how to proceed further with my practice.

When properly developed, the meditation practices will lead to deep calm and insight. As we get deeper into the practice, guidance from an experienced teacher will help to ensure we stay on the straight path, and not deviate into unsuitable practices as a result of our own emotional bias or self-indulgence. In any case, meditation with a group, or with a teacher will give us added morale and support for our practice. We will not then be distracted, especially in the beginning, with niggling doubts that we may not be doing something correctly, for example, even something simple, like not having an upright sitting posture.

The practice of meditation can give us benefits such as better concentration, a more relaxed mind and a happier disposition; which help us handle our daily work and life issues better. During meditation, we relax body and mind. We free the mind from distracting thoughts and allow it to rest in a natural calmness. In that lucid calmness, we directly confront and experience ourselves.

At a later stage, after we have developed sufficient concentration and an understanding of the *Dharma*, we can delve into directly investigating the nature of things. We may look into the nature of the arising and disbanding of our feelings, thoughts, and consciousness. Meditation is the most direct way of self-cultivation. When we develop joyfulness in our meditation practice, we will look forward to our daily practice.

We should be prepared to change and adjust the tone of our practice as we progress. We need to adjust the practice accordingly; not too severe or too taut, and not too loose; to be just comfortable for where we are at. We are going for the long haul, so we need to work with that in mind.

When we initially experience the relaxed and yet pointed state of calm, some of us may feel as if our body is floating or we may lose the feeling of the presence of our body. We may, because of this, feel unnerved. Recognize that these are normal experiences which may arise with the initial experience of the focused state of mind. The bodily senses recede to the background, and the unadapted mind which is new to these experiences may be somewhat disconcerted. We just let it be, and continue with our practice, without giving any importance to these experiences. We certainly do not want to be drawn into any speculation or delude ourselves as to their importance. They are not any attainment; nothing special at all.

As we develop our practice, we may on occasions, experience a release or outburst of internal energy, usually accompanied by feelings of being at ease both physically and mentally. It can especially happen when we are in a state of heightened awareness. We may even feel it building up and coming. If you sense that "something is brewing", do not try to accelerate it. Just let it be, be aware of it, and let it develop at its own pace. You may feel a build-up of an inner stirring, and when the floodwaters breach the dam and burst through in a huge swell, you may then smile, or be letting out a loud laugh, or you may be weeping.

This can be disconcerting to those who happen to be around you; who do not know what is happening. You, however, will clearly know that your mind is lucid. You are deeply experiencing yourself and giving expression to what may feel like a groundswell of inspiration. Perhaps something which has been clogging up your system, or a barrier hampering the free flow of your energies, has been demolished. This may have been brought about by an insightful experience which had shattered a barrier in your mind. In any case, it will feel good. So there is no need to worry; it is a good sign, but do not think that this is some kind of attainment, for this is really far from it. It is nothing special. We just continue with our practice.

Developing Calm and Insight

We may practice developing calm by the mindfulness of breathing practice; by the counting of our breaths (refer to Appendix I).

How, then, do we handle thoughts and mental distractions which arise during meditation? We let them go. We do not "join in the party". Let them go of their own accord. If we do not add fuel, and do not further dwell on them, they will leave. We need to be mindfully aware of them, know them for what they are, and then let go of them. We do not cling to them, try to control them, or follow them.

We develop an empty awareness: an awareness which does not get involved with the object of awareness. There is "just this"; just awareness and knowing; without any further involvement. The mind then will be clear and calm, alert and comfortably at ease.

Ch'an Master Xuyun (虚云老和尚) has this to say about deluded thoughts:

"We are all afraid of deluded thoughts which we find difficult to tame. I tell you folks, be not afraid of deluded thoughts. Do not waste your efforts to subdue it. You only have to be aware of it. Do not cling to, follow it or push it away. Only let it be and not have any dealings with it and it will, by itself depart. As in the saying 'With awareness at the moment of arising of the deluded thought, the deluded thought will be immediately dispelled.' If you can

incorporate deluded thoughts into your practice, watch when it arises, you will come to know that it has no selfhood and it is empty.... " [58]

When we are familiar with the meditative awareness, we can carry that awareness into our daily living, to be aware of our thoughts and the quality of our thoughts, as we interact with our surroundings. We bring in the element of discernment into our mind, and besides seeing the quality of these thoughts, we look into their nature and anything else surfacing in our mind. We thereby extend the practice of mindfulness with the practice of insight, into the way we conduct our daily activities.

In meditation, when the mind is calm, there will be a component of joyfulness in that state of calmness. We welcome the calm joy. There is no need to try to consciously enhance that feeling, or to hold on to it. We just experience this fresh joyfulness. We let our body and mind be invigorated in that serene joy.

You may, when you are in the calm state, look into thoughts that spring up in your mind, without any "investment". See where they arise and look into their emptiness; to know for yourself that they have no inherent self-nature, and are transient and illusory. Penetration into this will give rise to transformative insight. The same can be done for any of the five *skandhas* (form, feelings, thoughts, volitional formations, and consciousness). We see their workings; we see into their nature. The Buddha tells us that our mind consciousness (*vijnana*), as with the rest of the five aggregates, is empty. It is *anitya, duhkha* and *anatman (i.e. impermanent, unsatisfactory and no-self)*. We need to delve deeply within our meditation practice to directly experience this liberating insight for ourselves.

The Blade of Mindful Discernment

In the Mahayana (The Great Vehicle) tradition, the transcendent wisdom (*prajna*) which sees the face of reality, is represented by the adamantine sword of transcendent wisdom. This is the double edged fiery sword wielded by *Bodhisattva* Manjusri, the *Bodhisattva* of Wisdom, and it cuts the bonds of ignorance. This is a beautiful symbolic imagery with *prajna* wisdom likened to a sharp edged sword which can cut any delusion that stands in its way.

Though we may not yet have the sword of transcendent wisdom, we do have the sharp blade of mindful discernment in the *Dharma*. We do not need to slash at the false or wrong thoughts in a violent manner, nor do we need to destroy them. What we want to cut are the bonds with which we have allowed ourselves to be tied to those thoughts. We just let the delusionary or distracting thoughts arise or disappear as they wish. We do not want to control them or do any violence to them. It is with a knowing smile that we let them be gone.

We wield the blade of mindful discernment to sever any attachments to these wayward thoughts like cutting the lines we attach to kites. We do not have a liking or disliking to these "kites". We know they originate from our minds and are illusory. We let these "kites" fly away of their own accord. We detach from them, and we are not to be concerned with where they go, as they vanish away. When we do this we also gain an understanding into the impermanent nature of thoughts; that they do not have any self-nature. They can be here one moment and gone the next. By the associative reflection that our empty thoughts have brought about other thought-conceived ideas of an owned "self" or our own "self", we may perhaps have an understanding into the impermanence, no-selfhood and emptiness of our "self".

We always have the blade in hand; it is always ready for use. We cut off the "kite strings" we attach to the five aggregates and just let them float away naturally. The blade of mindful discernment is a tool, a method which we use, and we do not lay claim or ownership. We do not engrave our initials on it. To brandish the blade of mindful discernment and to wield it with ease, we need to develop a mind which is accepting of its power. We have to be sufficiently grounded in emptiness; in the truths of *anitya*, *duhkha* and *anatman*; so we can accept our true nature, and when we have that, we can start to really let go. We strip off all the labels we have stuck on to all objects of our perception. Whether something is black, white or grey does not trouble us anymore. We let them all be as they are.

Thus:

"The prajna sword is not a sword...

And certainly, it is not your sword

Just as any thoughts are not your thoughts, and are

Not really thoughts.

The same is true for your feelings, mental constructs, and your consciousness.

It is just because the prajna sword is not a sword, and is not your sword,

That it blazes with such radiance and

Works with such majesty and power that

Nothing can resist it or stand in its way." [59]

So now, have you really learnt anything from this book thus far? Depending on who is asking, and who is listening, one may say, "Not a thing! Nothing at all!"

Ch'an Tradition Huatou and Gongan

In the Mahayana Ch'an Buddhist tradition, there are the uniquely Ch'an meditation practices of the gongan (public case, 公案), the huatou (lead or head of word, 话头), and mozhao (silent illumination, 默照) which may suit oneself. In essence, however, these practices are similar in approach and practice, to the other meditation practices used in other Buddhist traditions: for example the Theravada tradition practices of *samatha* and *vipassana* (tranquillity and insight), or the mahamudra (great seal) and dzogchen (great perfection) practices of the Vajrayana. There are the elements of developing concentration, tranquillity, and insight, in all these Buddhist meditation techniques. In the mahamudra practices, for example, the mind is stabilized in tranquillity, and in that state of lucid cognition, the nature of mind is to be directly recognized.

Especially in the Linji school (临济宗, Jpn: Rinzai-shu) of Ch'an Buddhism, there is the practice of using the huatou. It refers to the state before a thought or word is conceptualized. A huatou typically is a phrase or word which has no conventionally definable meaning. It is sometimes derived from an encounter with an enlightened master which is recorded as a gongan; which describes a "public incident". An example is the "Wu" (no, nothing, or there is not, 无) gongan.

A monk asked Zhaozhou (赵州, the revered Ch'an master from the Tang dynasty), *"Does a dog have Buddha nature?"* The master answered, *"Wu,"* which means "no, or there is not". But the monk knows, according to Buddhist teaching, that all beings have Buddha nature. So why does Zhaozhou say "Wu"?

This "Wu" is used as the meditation object in a huatou Ch'an practice. It serves to invoke a fully focused mind bent on seeking for an answer to "Wu". This "Wu" is wielded as a sword, like the flaming sword of *Bodhisattva* Manjusri. However, the allegory does not give the full picture because there is actually no handle to allow the practitioner to grasp on to this "Wu".

The practitioner uses "Wu" to cut through all other thoughts or distractions; anything that stands in the way of his practice of *"What is Wu?"* There is both the practice of tranquillity when his mind is fully absorbed into "Wu" and insight when the mind probes deeply into his consciousness of "Wu."

In Ch'an, there is a saying;

"When you meet the Buddha, chop off the Buddha. When you meet a demon, chop off the demon." [60]

It means one has to let go of everything; one abandons all attachments. Even attachment to holiness and attainment is abandoned; not to speak of abandoning defilements. In this very graphic way, in a very total sense, and in its rather unique way, Ch'an communicates the Buddha's teaching of non-attachment.

This Ch'an presentation of the teaching of non-attachment may not initially strike a deep chord in one who does not have a cultural leaning which is open to working with such conundrums. This approach may not seem to be suitable for someone brought up in the tradition of erudition or where the dialectics of philosophical argument are emphasized. However, on the other hand, with skilful means, the application of this approach in a seemingly contraindicative culture may be where even greater energies for transformation may be tapped into.

The use of such metaphors is not unique to Ch'an Buddhism. The Buddha himself used this approach in the *Kesi Sutta*. [61]

When asked by the Buddha how he disciplines a horse, Kesi the horse trainer answered that he would train a horse either gently, sternly or both kindly and sternly, and kill a horse which would not submit to discipline, so that the guild of his teacher will not be disgraced. Kesi then, in turn, asked the Buddha how he would discipline a person to be tamed. The Buddha answered Kesi in a similar fashion, but with different meanings to his words. He said he would discipline one person gently; dwelling on the development of virtue, or sternly; dwelling on the retributions to misconduct, or gently and sternly; dwelling on both the development of virtue and the retributions from misconduct. Kesi then asked what the Buddha would do if the person would not be disciplined by any of these methods. The Buddha replied, *"Then I will kill him."* This greatly surprised Kesi, who protested that the Buddha is not allowed to destroy life! The Buddha then explains that when he said to *"kill him"*, he meant the person is not to be taught further.

Sincerity in Our Practice

It is the sincerity with which we approach our practice that enriches it, and keeps us from straying into the many distractions and dead ends. We have to watch our practice, and be mindful of how it is developing. It is sincerity together with mindfulness, which gives the clarity we need to guide our practice. Mindfulness gives us the awareness of the quality of our experience, and sincerity gives us the unbiased discernment of that experience. Our meditation experiences and insights have to be subjected to the unwavering light of sincerity and truthfulness. We will then not grasp on to self-serving or self-promoting delusions, nor feel excited over the so-called "attainments". If ever any taint of the "self" is evident in any aspect of our practice, let it be a forewarning, let it be put to the sharp blade of mindful discernment and be released from our grasp. Let this sincerity with ourselves and our own practice be our teacher, ever guiding us along this life affirming path to calm and liberating wisdom.

Some people may not have the background in the *Dharma,* or may initially not have sufficient maturity in their spiritual sensibility, nor have the psychological makeup, which will allow them to fruitfully practice meditation by themselves unsupervised, or without group support. One's faith in the *Dharma* and sincerity need to be rather developed before one can practice by oneself over an extended period. If one is not prepared, there are pitfalls which may slow progress or even mislead one down the wrong path. It is therefore recommended that the beginning meditator starts his practice with a recognised teacher or with a group, in a positive setting; so as not to succumb to any self-serving needs which may turn the practice away from its true purpose. Sometimes, we may not be able to see the implications of carrying on with doing what we do not clearly know. We need to have the humility to forgo conceit, and be receptive to teachings from those more accomplished than ourselves.

If it is not already apparent, let the reader be reminded that progress in meditation also depends on progress in the practice of virtue and the other factors of the Noble Eightfold Path. The Noble Eightfold Path as it were, loops back on itself. As we progress, we progress on all fronts. Our practice of Right View will align with the insights we have gained from our practice. Our Right Aspiration is energized by our progress. Our Right Speech reflects the refinements in understanding we have gained. Our Right Action further affirms our growth and development. Our Right Livelihood sustains our practice in a supportive environment. Our Right Effort sustains the vigour in our practice of the development of virtue, concentration, and wisdom. Our Right Mindfulness increasingly gives clarity on our mental state and actions. Our Right Concentration then further illuminates our understanding, and develops further with the support from all factors of the path.

Practice with Non-Attainment

In our meditation practice, there may be occasions when we may have experiences which seem out of the ordinary. This may involve any of our sense perceptions. A beautiful scene may unfold before us in brilliant colour. We may perceive an object appearing before us in such detail that we can make out the tiniest thread of colour. We may see *Bodhisattva*s reclining and decked out in full splendour. On the other hand, we may see the unsightly and the ugly. In any case, all these are illusions. They are all mind created and are *anitya, duhkha* and *anatman* (impermanent, unsatisfactory and no-self). They reveal to us the innate power of our ordinary mind, which however, is still in the mundane realm of the five aggregates (*skandhas)*.

If we think we thereby have experienced some attainment, then there is the tendency that we will want to try to relive such an experience. If we succumb to this indulgence, we will be constricting our practice, as we will be imposing our delusions into our practice. We are then grasping and clinging to our so-called attainment. This is unhelpful as what we are then doing, is tying down the development of our practice to the confines of the mundane, and holding it back.

If we develop any sense of attainment in our practice, then we are feeding our deluded self-importance and conceit. We should also not boast of what we deem to be attainments. We should not create problems for ourselves; problems we later will need to address or to uproot.

We do not want to attach to these ephemeral experiences, no matter how wonderful or exciting they seem to be. They are not any mark of true attainment, so do not take them to be such. In any case, we need not interfere with their unfolding before us. We do not get involved, and do not try to instigate, or manipulate them. They are nothing special. We let them be, and stay with the calm awareness and clarity of our practice.

There may be instances when we may be struck by some strong insightful experiences. If there is an occurrence of true insight, it will stay with us. We will recognize it as such, if we are sincere in our practice. It will not bring up any feelings of having attained to something special. We will be naturally driven to nurture that insight with further practice, and that is even less a thing to worry about.

The *Heart Sutra* affirms that the *Bodhisattva* dwells in non-attainment. This should be the basis of our meditation practice. We should impose nothing on our practice. We just let it unfold and develop by itself. There should be no sense of gain or wishful craving for attainment or achievement. We instead, dwell on the beauty of just doing the practice and enjoy the positive calm and joyful states without attaching to them. Let the heart-mind lotus of a thousand petals bloom of its natural accord. There is no need to rush things.

Practising with the mind of non-attainment also means practising with the mind of no-purpose, or the objectiveless mind. We may be practising to develop ourselves, perhaps to realise awakening, or if we are inclined to the *Bodhisattva* ideal, we may be practising for the benefit and welfare of all beings. However, in a deeper sense, we should be practising with the mind in emptiness, without any thought of attainment, and also without any purpose. There is just the practice. We just let the profound *Dharma* unfold and manifest in us.

"Who", said the lamp post,
"Who", said the roadway sign,
And bowed. [62]

The Discipline of Practice

We will find that to have tangible results from our meditation practice, we need to practice consistently. It is helpful to set a particular time slot in our daily routine for our practice. It is better in the beginning, especially when we are developing calm, to have undisturbed practice. Fix a schedule which will allow you to be free from having worries about being on time for something else. If you find that you can meditate well during a particular period of the day or night, try to block out a period of time then for your practice. Usually, the best times for meditation practice are in the early morning or in the later part of the evening; that is, before the start of the day's work and after the day's work is done.

The environment for our meditation practice is important. We will want to have a clean and tidy place, which helps to impart a sense of relaxed calm. We may want to have a picture of the Buddha or the *Bodhisattva*s hung or placed in a position that we look up to, when we sit. We can offer flowers or incense as a token of respect and gratitude for the *Dharma* and the practice which we are using to cultivate ourselves.

To help us settle into the meditative state, before we start our meditation, we can bring to mind or recite the verses which help to loosen us from our usual self-centricity and allow us to "let go". We then will not be carrying any baggage with us into our meditation practice, and will be open to spiritual insight.

We can recite the following meditation gatha, with palms joined in reverence:

"I pay homage to the Buddha;

The Fully Enlightened One,

The Serene One, Knower of the Worlds,

Unsurpassed Teacher of Gods and Men.

I pay homage to the Dhamma; the Teaching of the Buddha, the path we tread.

I pay homage to the Sangha; the steadfast, wise and virtuous followers of the Way.

Cultivating the Bodhi mind, I relinquish the past, present and future.

Cultivating the Bodhi mind, I relinquish all hopes and dreams.

Cultivating the Bodhi mind, I relinquish all defilements, hindrances and attachments.

Cultivating the Bodhi mind, I relinquish myself.

For the benefit of all beings,

For the welfare of all beings,

With body speech and mind,

I dedicate myself." (63)

211

Ch'an Master Xuyun (虚云老和尚) has the following to say with regards to the prerequisites for Ch'an (Jpn: Zen) practice:

"Putting down all entanglements, Delusions disappear of themselves.

Discrimination not arising, the mind is distanced from grasping.

Without the arising of even a single thought, self-nature manifests bright and pure.

Thus arriving at the condition for meditation.

Further diligently practice, cultivate and investigate

To realise mind and see into self-nature." [64]

In this teaching, Ch'an Master Xuyun points to the ongoing discipline of practice. It is after the deep calm (from the stilling of all thoughts), and after one has had a direct glimpse into emptiness that true meditation practice begins.

Vimalakirti's Advice

In the *Vimalakirti-nirdesa Sutra*, the *Bodhisattva* Vimalakirti assumes the guise of a not so ordinary layman, and employs "skilful means" to develop living beings. He appears wealthy, but lives a life of purity and mixes freely with all levels of society. This *sutra* is also called "The Inconceivable Liberation". It conveys the deepest teachings of the Buddha couched in magical "out-of-this-world" visionary allegories, and is indeed a very delightful teaching to study.

In the passage below from this *sutra*, Vimalakirti is giving a teaching to the Venerable Saripurta, who is known as the foremost of the wise, among the disciples of the Buddha.

The Venerable Sariputra was in deep meditation at the foot of a tree in the forest when Vimalakirti dropped by and spoke to him.

"Reverend Sariputra, this is not the way to absorb yourself in contemplation. You should absorb yourself in contemplation so that neither body nor mind appear anywhere in the triple world of desire, form and no-form. You should absorb yourself in contemplation in such a way that you can manifest all ordinary behaviour without forsaking the cessation of Nirvana. You should absorb yourself in contemplation in such a way that you can manifest the nature of an ordinary person without abandoning your cultivated spiritual nature. You should absorb yourself in contemplation so that the mind neither settles within nor moves without toward external forms. You should absorb yourself in contemplation in such a way that the thirty-seven aids to enlightenment [65] are manifest without deviation toward any convictions. You should absorb yourself in contemplation in such a way that you are released in liberation without abandoning the passions that are the province of the world..., those who absorb themselves in contemplation, in such a way are declared by the Buddha to be truly absorbed in contemplation." [66]

This teaching of Vimalakirti left the Venerable Sariputra speechless. He did not know how to respond to Vimalakirti and kept silent. In the context of this Mahayana *sutra*, the Venerable Sariputra here represents the *Arhat,* who has to further develop in the final stages of the path of the *Bodhisattva,* to attain the supreme enlightenment of Buddhahood.

In this passage, Vimalakirti points out that the meditative poise, has to be able to transcend itself, to allow full functionality and interaction with the world of phenomena. We should seek to incorporate the meditative poise into our daily living activities. This is something we will always need to be reminded of, and to strive for, in our practice.

Some Guidelines for Meditation Practice

Here are some useful guidelines for the person who wants to dive directly into the practice of Buddhist meditation. One can definitely start with the meditation practices as given in this book. They are: the mindfulness of breathing, the meditation on loving-kindness and walking meditation. Refer to Appendix I for the details on these practices.

For the sitting practices, one can start with either the mindfulness of breathing or the meditation on loving-kindness practices. Both practices can lead the practitioner to the attainment of the meditative absorptions (*dhyana*). These meditative absorptions are of increasingly finer and more subtle states of consciousness. The meditator will experience states of joy and bliss, one pointedness and equanimity, which are "out of this world", in these meditative absorptions. Though these states are unmistakably beyond our normal consciousness, and have been referred to as states of super-consciousness, they are nevertheless still in the realm of conditioned worldly phenomena; still in the realm of the five aggregates, and are not to be clung to.

Though the mindfulness of breathing and the meditation on loving-kindness appear to be quite different, the flavour of the *dhyana* experience is the same. The mind is firmly established with no discursive thoughts, and nothing is felt from the other five senses. The experience of *dhyana* and the various stages of the *dhyana* experience, is well described by the Buddha in the *Samannaphala Sutta* of the

214

Digha Nikaya. Regarding the entry to the first *dhyana* *(Pali: jhana)*, the Buddha says:

"And when he knows that these five hindrances have left him, gladness arises in him, from gladness comes delight, from the delight in his mind his body is tranquillised, with a tranquil body he feels joy, and with joy his mind is concentrated. Being thus detached from sense desires, detached from unwholesome states, he (the disciple) enters and remains in the first jhana, which is with thinking and pondering, born of detachment, filled with delight and joy. And ... there is no spot in his entire body that is untouched by this delight and joy born of detachment." [(67)]

To be dwelling in the *dhyanas* may be extremely delightful, and deeply calming, but we are to move on with our main task of developing the insightful wisdom that liberates. It is important not to develop a clinging to the experience of *dhyana,* and not to treat it as an attainment. We want to drop the tendency to give rise to the discriminating mind which compares attainments and seek experiences. Otherwise, this may give rise to subtle mental excitement that can hinder our access to *dhyana.*

A word of caution is due here for the beginning meditator. Sometimes a state of seeming calm, which is however dull, and which lacks clarity, may be experienced. It is as if one is stuck in a muddy pool. If so, the meditator should rouse himself (or herself) with the light of mindfulness, and with vigour, disengage from that dull state.

In the cultivation of the *dhyanas,* we develop the deep calm, which supports the development of deep insight. However, it is not necessary for us to have developed the *dhyanas* to the fullest extents, before moving on to the practice of developing insight. As long as our mind is calm and clear, we will begin to be receptive to the arising of insight. These are the transformative insights which help awaken us to "see things as they really are" and give us real release from unease and suffering.

In the practice of meditation, we will always want to be sincere with ourselves and about our practice. This has already been mentioned elsewhere. Some practitioners, who may be of a friendly disposition, may still find difficulty with the full meditation practice on loving-kindness. This may be due to past experiences which may have left some unresolved emotions in them. If this is what one is confronted with, then one can start at a pace that one feels comfortable with. One can start with just working on the first stage of the practice; that of developing loving-kindness to oneself. One has to accept that this is what one has to start with, and not try to force the practice on to oneself. When one has gained a good foothold on the first stage, one can then progressively add on the second stage and so on. Alternatively, one can instead start with practising the mindfulness of breathing first. The walking meditation practice is useful anytime, and can be used as a supplement to both the meditation on mindfulness of breathing, and the meditation on loving-kindness.

The mindfulness of breathing, and the meditation on loving-kindness can be done together or alternately, as they can supplement each other. The mindfulness of breathing practice develops our concentration and mindfulness, and the meditation on loving-kindness develops our positive feeling of the unbounded loving-kindness of *maitri*. Both practices incorporate the development of attentiveness to the object of meditation, joy and one pointed concentration. At a later stage, they can be further tuned to focus on the development of insight.

When we end a seated meditation practice, we do so with gratitude. We dedicate any merit we have gained from our practice to all beings everywhere. We thank, with humility, the cushion and the mat we sat on, for they had given us comfort and supported our practice. We give a thankful bow to the mat and cushion.

It helps that we have a good grasp of the *Dharma* when we start practising Buddhist meditation. It is the Right View or Right Understanding that ensures we will be on the right path. Otherwise, our practice may be skewed or we may be disconcerted by the experiences which may arise. It is therefore generally always better to practise with a group of like-minded practitioners or with guidance from a teacher skilled in the practice. However, having said that, there may be conditions which do not allow us to do so; we may not have access to either a practising group or a teacher. If that is the case, we can begin practising the *Dharma* and meditation by ourselves, with sincerity and honesty as our guides. When the time is ripe, a teacher will appear.

Cultivation of the Mind in Meditation

The Buddha emphasized the development and cultivation of the mind. In a teaching from the *Anguttara Nikaya*, the Buddha says:

"Luminous, bhikkus, is this mind, but it is defiled by adventitious defilements. The uninstructed worldling does not understand this as it really is; therefore I say that for the uninstructed worldling there is no development of the mind." And "Luminous, bhikkus, is this mind, and it is freed from adventitious defilements. The instructed noble disciple understands this as it really is; therefore I say that for the instructed noble disciple there is development of the mind."[68]

The Buddha here points out that the mind will manifest its true nature, or its full potential, when the veil of ignorance is lifted. One could see elements of this teaching reflected

217

in Song dynasty Ch'an Master Hongzhi's (宏智, CE 1091-1157) verses. In his "Admonishment for Seated Meditation" (坐禪箴), [69] Ch'an Master Hongzhi gives a taste of the meditative state in which the mind is brightly lucid and perfectly at ease. A translated extract from this work is given below:

"The essence of all Buddhas, The critical point of every patriarch

Without encountering things, it knows,

Not opposing conditions, it illumines.

Without encountering things, it knows,

This knowing is inherently subtle."

These verses point to the non-separateness and pervasive nature of the awakened mind. It no longer encounters phenomena in the "me versus another" context. What is it that knows? Why is this knowing subtle? What is it that is known? Ch'an Master Hongzhi goes on to tell us more in the next few verses. However, he does not want to spell it all out too clearly. The mystery is for us to delve deeply into, when we cultivate our mind in meditation.

"Not opposing conditions, it illumines,

This illumination is naturally wondrous.

This knowing is inherently subtle,

From non-discriminating thinking."

There is no more "this and other" and no more "with or against". The discriminating mind of particulars had dropped off. As the *Heart Sutra* says, "*All things are marked with emptiness.*"

"This illumination is naturally wondrous,
From not the least bit of separateness.

From non-discriminating thinking,
This knowing is remarkable, incomparable.

From not the least bit of hurriedness,
This illumination is non-grasping yet complete."

There is sameness in emptiness and there is complete interpenetration. There is also no "before" and no "after".

"Clear water penetrated to the base, fishes to appear,
Boundless wide empty sky, birds flown out of sight."

No tracks are left by the birds in the empty sky. In the full clarity of total illumination, there is no wanting, no coming and no going. Nothing more need be said, just the boundless, clear, timelessness.

Chapter 9: Reverencing the Three Treasures

Connecting to the Three Treasure

The reverencing of the Buddha, his *Dharma* and the *Sangha* (the community of his followers) should be an important part of our spiritual practice. These practices can give us a positive emotional linkage, and another avenue to express our commitment to the practice of the *Dharma*; to express our gratitude and our wish to be of benefit to others. They allow us to connect with the spiritual legacy of the Buddha, which has been passed down through his enlightened disciples and taught or communicated to us. Here, we include the transcendent *Bodhisattva*s who are the emanations of the spiritual realisations of the various aspects of the Buddha's enlightenment. By doing the reverencing, we open our heart-mind to be receptive to all these powerful positive influences. For a practitioner who has developed strong faith in the Three Treasures (the Buddha, the *Dharma* and the *Sangha*) by virtue of his practice and by the benefits he has gained, doing the reverencing will strongly gladden and inspire him.

When we really treasure something, we will want to express it in a tangible way. If we care for a good friend, we will want to get her something she will like. On "Teacher's Day", we give presents to our teachers as a show of respect and thankfulness. Even more so, when we feel enriched by, and have greatly benefitted from the *Dharma*, we will also naturally want to express that feeling of reverence and gratitude. This is why we happily bow to the Three Treasures, and gladly offer flowers, lights and incense with deep reverence.

"In the far off distance
A light shines
Unwavering, true
And bright.
Each step I tread leads me closer,
And I approach with infinite gratitude
For he who marked the straight and
Wide path
Built bridges
Across chasms
Tunnelled iron mountains and
Moved others to follow the trail
He blazed

Happy is he who leaves
His playthings behind" [70]

The more we have benefitted from the *Dharma*, the more profound will be our feelings of reverence for the Three Treasures. When we pay reverence to the Three Treasures, we are also at the same time, acknowledging the high ideals we are aspiring to. The attainment of the full and perfect enlightenment of the Buddha, as the personified ideal of perfected wisdom and compassion, is surely worthy of our reverence. So in a way, we are bowing to ourselves, to what we can be when we realise our full and true potential; our Buddha nature. The full reverencing practice is given in Appendix II. In the following pages, we look into the components of the practice.

Going for Refuge in the Three Treasures

Whether we progress or regress in our cultivation of virtue, concentration and wisdom, is all of our own doing or undoing. There is no need to appeal to any higher power or authority. It all rests on our own shoulders, and we fully bear the responsibility. We, however, do invite inspiration from all the sources available to us: from the Buddhas and the compassionate *Bodhisattva*s who sustain and guide us, from our teachers and spiritual friends, from the exemplary lives of those who have awakened, from works of art and literature which engender positive and inspired states of mind, and from the beauty of nature that is all around us.

We should not stand where we are, and try to imagine what the difficulties will be if we embark on this path of self-development. We know this path, first cleared by the Buddha, is now a well beaten, and well-trodden path. Countless beings have now walked on it, and have realised the benefits of doing so. Some of us may not know much about the Buddha's teaching at this stage, but after reading what has been presented earlier, may have found that it has struck a chord which has resonated within us. Perhaps we felt that the *Dharma* seemed to address some unease stemming from our experience of life. Some of us may have already started doing some meditation practices to help relax and to de-stress. Some may have experienced the calm states of mind from meditation practice, and wish to know what else there is to learn. Some of us may be seeking the fundamental answers on the meaning of life. Some may be just inquisitive about what Buddhism has to offer.

The *Dharma* will be many things to many people. It may be regarded as a philosophy of life, or a guide to a wholesome life. It may be revered as the path to unlimited growth. It may be taken to be a refuge from confusion and distress. It may be acknowledged as a repository of great thought, a compilation of teachings which have lasted over two thousand five hundred years. It may be thought of as an interesting approach to living; perhaps still of some relevance today. We may have one of these views.

The Buddha taught the *Dharma* as a complete system of practice which can lead one to the complete freedom from the taints of greed, hate and delusion; to the complete liberation of enlightenment and the end of all suffering. Whatever way we view it, the *Dharma* will benefit or enrich us only if we participate in it, to have it unfold from within us.

When we take the Buddha's teaching to be our guide, we are taking refuge in the Buddha, in his teaching (the *Dharma*), and in his spiritual disciples and the community of those who similarly participate in doing so (the *Sangha*). They are the Three Treasures (also known as the Three Jewels). The Three Treasures can be our refuge because we can go to them for Truth, shelter, protection, nutriment and for inspiration. They are true refuges because they can be fully relied on to provide the means to fully liberate ourselves. When that happens, we then become a true refuge for others. When we acknowledge the Buddha as our teacher, which means we accept his teachings and practise what he taught, and when we take the Three Refuges and the Precepts which signify our commitment to spiritual growth, we technically become a "Buddhist".

In his *Bodhicaryavatara* (The Way of the *Bodhisattva*), Shantideva, who was an eighth century Indian prince before he became a Buddhist monk, conveyed the spirit of taking refuge in the Three Treasures by the following verses :

"Thus from this day forward I take refuge

In the Buddhas, guardians of beings,

Who labour to protect all wanderers,

Those mighty ones who scatter fear.

And in the Dharma they have realized in their hearts,

Which drives away the terrors of samsara (the unending cycle of birth and death),

And in all the host of Bodhisattvas

Likewise I will perfectly take refuge. "[71]

The Five Precepts

Taking the precepts means we make the commitment to skilful living. There are a number of precepts the disciple can undertake. The basic five precepts for the lay disciple is a starting point, and it can be further enhanced to the eight or ten precepts for one who wishes to take on more rigorous training.

The five precepts are:

1)   I undertake to refrain from taking life.
We refrain from intentionally taking life. The positive
expression of this precept is that we do not do harm or
cause distress in others. We cultivate love and compassion,
and extend a helping hand to those in need.

2)   I undertake to refrain from taking the not given.
We refrain from stealing or misappropriating the property
of others. We respect ownership, and give due
remuneration when we trade or employ the services of
others.

3)   I undertake to refrain from sexual misconduct.
Sexual misconduct can disrupt the family unit, and bring
much suffering to those affected. We refrain from doing so.
The broader application of this precept covers the refrain
from indulgence in the five senses (sight, sound, smell,
taste and touch). We cherish and develop our relationships
based on mutual respect, caring and sincere trust.

4)   I undertake to refrain from false speech.
We refrain from resorting to slanderous speech, deceit or
telling lies. We communicate truthfully, and sow goodwill
and friendliness.

5)   I undertake to refrain from taking intoxicants.
We refrain from being intoxicated or to have our senses
dulled or distorted by alcohol or drugs. The state of
intoxication clouds our judgement, and does not allow us to
be mindful, or to act with awareness. We develop clear
mindfulness, and act to benefit all beings.

These five precepts provide a basic code of behaviour
which gives the disciple support and guidance in his
development of virtue; to help him maintain the moral
discipline he has voluntarily undertaken. These precepts are

universally valid. One does not need to be a Buddhist to understand that abiding by these five precepts will accord with the ethical code of behaviour of any lawful society which has shaken off barbarism.

The disciple undertakes these rules of training for his own good. He takes on the observance of the precepts by himself. There is no "sin" if he fails to keep the precepts. The law of karmic retribution takes care of that (or simply put, we reap what we sow). He will have to bear the full consequences of his misdeeds, but he can always start afresh. However, in breaking the precepts, besides causing pain and suffering to himself and others, he will have put more hindrances in his path; piling on more work in the way of his development. Chief among these are remorse, regret, and guilt; negative emotions he will now need to dispel as soon as he can.

As important as keeping the precepts is, it is just as important not to have our development on the path be held back when we contravene or break them. If we do break the precepts, we need to realise our foolishness; we have to accept and be remorseful of our wrongdoing, and then we move on. The past is done with, and there is no way we can change it. However, we can have a fresh start with renewed commitment and effort in the present moment. The reader may wish to refer to the section on "Letting Go of Guilt and Remorse", in the chapter on "The Freedom That Comes from Relinquishment".

Taking the Refuges and Precepts

In taking the refuges and precepts, we acknowledge the Buddha as our teacher; worthy of our devotion, respect and homage. We take refuge in the Three Treasures which are the true refuge, which we can fully depend on. Going for refuge means that we rest our heart-mind in the Buddha, the *Dharma* and the *Sangha*. It also means we rest our highest aspirations in our own awakening, in our attainment of enlightenment.

We undertake the observance of the precepts to establish ourselves in cultivating the virtues which support our development. Traditionally, a Buddhist practitioner would normally have taken his refuges and precepts from a respected member of the *Sangha* in a simple ceremony.

We can also take the refuges and the precepts as a daily practice. We first recite the traditional Salutation to the Buddha:

I revere with body, speech and mind:

The Blessed One, The Fully Awakened, The Perfectly Enlightened One.

We follow with reciting the Refuges:

To the Buddha I go for refuge

To the Dharma I go for refuge

To the Sangha I go for refuge

And the Precepts (here, the Five Precepts):

I undertake to refrain from taking life.
I undertake to refrain from taking the not given.
I undertake to refrain from sexual misconduct.
I undertake to refrain from false speech.
I undertake to refrain from intoxicants.

The taking of the refuges and precepts is incorporated into the practice of "Referencing the Three Treasures" given in Appendix II.

Prostration Practice

When we perform the prostration practice, we open ourselves up to the positive and inspiring influence of the Buddha, the *Dharma* and the *Sangha*. This practice is especially of great benefit as a purification practice which clears karmic obstructions; we leave our transgressions behind us and start anew.

We chant the Refuges and Precepts. Then, facing an image of the Buddha or a *Bodhisattva*, we clasp our palms together at our forehead with fingers extended, and do a standing bow to the Buddha, the *Dharma* and the *Sangha*. We then lower ourselves to the floor, using our hands to support our body weight. When we are down to our knees on the floor, we place both our hands palms down on the floor, on either side of where our forehead will be when we place it on the floor. We next lower our head to the floor, and touch our forehead to the floor. While doing the prostrations, we mentally take refuge in the Buddha, the *Dharma* and the *Sangha*.

We then lift ourselves up, with the support from both our hands, back to our standing position, and put our palms together at our heart in reverence. We continue with the next prostration by again raising our joined palms to our forehead. We do this as many times as we wish, and finish the series of prostrations with a dedication of our merits to all beings. This can be a daily practice, or as often as we wish. In lowering and raising ourselves from the floor, we should give adequate physical support with our hands so as not to overstrain our joints or our back.

When we do the prostrations, we keep in mind our practice:

-        *We cultivate a reverential mind of gratitude when we bow. We are thankful to the Three Treasures that are our true refuge, and worthy of our respect and salutations.*

-        *We cultivate a mind of joyfulness when we bow. We feel joy and happiness in our practice of the Dharma that benefits all beings.*

-        *We cultivate a mind of wisdom when we bow. We bow with cultivating no thought of a separate self, no thought of a permanent self. We cultivate bowing with emptiness.*

-        *We cultivate a mind of compassion when we bow. We share with all beings our good fortune of having known of the Dharma, and any merits gained from the practice.*

Some of us may feel that bowing to another is an act of submission or a lowering of our status. If we feel that way, then that is absolutely right! When we come face to face with someone (e.g. the Buddha) who has wisdom beyond words, or something (e.g. the *Dharma and the Sangha*) which gives us great inspiration and support, we may feel we cannot help but offer our utmost admiration and respect. We sincerely bow to express our feelings of reverence. If we have further greatly benefitted from them, and have cultivated a deep faith in them, we may feel we want to do more than just give a bow. We feel they are worthy of more. So we lower ourselves to the floor and do a full prostration.

We acknowledge how highly we hold that which we are reverencing. We submit ourselves to their influence; we open our hearts fully to the inspiration they give us. This is, however, not to be a showy act. We do not do this to let others see how respectful we are. We do not want to turn this profound practice into another self-serving act. There may be situations when it may not be fitting for us to even express our reverence outwardly. We can always do a reverencing of the Three Treasures in our heart-mind.

The prostration practice is an effective practice to help us lay down our feelings of inadequacy or remorse, and to start afresh. We need to let go of our habit of dwelling in, or holding on to the past. We need to let go of whatever we had done, whatever we could have done, or whatever we feel about what had been done to us. We are done with all that! We relinquish the past, for it is gone. We stay mindful in the present, which is where the opportunity for growth and development is. Doing what is right by our actions in the present means the future will then take care of itself.

Dedication of Merits

Whenever we have done a prostration practice to the Three Treasures, ended a meditation practice session or have carried out a meritorious act, we dedicate our merits so gained, to all beings everywhere. We practise the perfection of giving of the *Bodhisattva*. All our merits are given away for the benefit of all beings, without discrimination.

We recite with palms joined at our hearts:

"I dedicate all my merits to all beings everywhere.

May they always be happy, joyful and free from pain.

May all attain to the highest peace of supreme Buddhahood."

And we end with a prostration or a bow.

Introduction to The Heart Sutra

The *Heart Sutra* is the heart of the Buddha's teachings on the Perfection of Wisdom. This short Mahayana *sutra* contains the essence of Perfected Wisdom. In this *sutra*, the *Bodhisattva* Avalokitesvara; the "Hearer of the cries of the world", gives a teaching on the Perfection of Wisdom to the Venerable Sariputra. The *Bodhisattva* Avalokitesvara, as the embodiment of transcendent compassion, is also known as the *Bodhisattva* of Compassion, or in the Mahayana Chinese tradition, as Guanyin Pusa. The historical Venerable Sariputra is an *Arhat*, who had attained to the stage of no further training, on the path of emancipation. He is also the foremost of the wise among the disciples of the Buddha. As such, he is enlightened, and there is nothing more he needs to learn. If he has, the Buddha would certainly have taught him. However, in this Mahayana *sutra*, the Sariputra who is addressed is not the historical person; just as the Bodhisattva Avalokitesvara is a transcendent manifestation of the Buddha's compassion. In the *Heart Sutra*, *Bodhisattva* Avalokitesvara offers this Sariputra the teachings to supreme Buddhahood.

It is perhaps of some significance that it is *Bodhisattva* Avalokitesvara, and not *Bodhisattva* Manjusri (the *Bodhisattva* who embodies transcendent wisdom, and who is normally associated with the *Prajnaparamita* texts), who offers this teaching on the Perfection of Wisdom to Venerable Sariputra. We may recall that the Buddha, when he attained to supreme enlightenment, was moved by compassion to communicate his newfound *Dharma* to the world. In the same way, it is perhaps fitting that *Bodhisattva* Avalokitesvara communicates this *Dharma* of the *Heart Sutra*. It is compassion that consummates wisdom. When selfless compassion for the welfare of all beings becomes the guiding force for the communication of the *Dharma*, then it is truly total communication.

We can recite the *Heart Sutra* as part of our daily practice of reverencing the Three Treasures. With the material that has been presented earlier in this book as a guide, the reader can ponder over the statements which *Bodhisattva* Avalokitesvara makes in the *Heart Sutra*. The *Heart Sutra* has the highest teachings on the emptiness of the *Prajnaparamita* as realised by the transcendent *Bodhisattva* Avalokitesvara. The teachings of *anitya*, *duhkha*, and *anatman*, the Four Noble Truths, and the dependent-origination, are embedded in the *Heart Sutra*.

Initially, it is perhaps sufficient for us to have a flavour of the teachings which are interred in the words of the *Heart Sutra,* to start reciting it. When we do this, we will establish a karmic bond to *Bodhisattva* Avalokitesvara. This practice opens our heart-mind to the teachings of the Buddha. We need to bear in mind that this *sutra* is a most profound teaching given by a transcendent *Bodhisattva* to the *Arhat* Sariputra, who in fact is already enlightened.

The version of the *Heart Sutra* given below has been translated and adapted, primarily with reference to: the Xuanzang (玄奘) Chinese translation [72] of the *sutra*, the Conze English translation from the Sanskrit [73] and the beautiful version given by Roshi Philip Kapleau [74]. In his arduous and perilous journey to India to seek the Buddhist teachings and sutras, the pilgrim monk, Xuanzang, relied on the *Heart Sutra* as his protective chant, to overcome the many life-threatening ordeals he was confronted with, on his epic journey.

We recite with palms joined in reverence:

The Heart Sutra, Heart of the Perfection of Wisdom.

The Bodhisattva of Compassion,
When deeply coursing in the Prajnaparamita,
Sees the five skandhas are of the emptiness
That liberates from all suffering.

Here Sariputra,
Form is no different from emptiness
Emptiness no different from form
Form is emptiness
Emptiness is form
Feeling, thought, choice and consciousness
Are such as this.

Here Sariputra,
All things are marked with emptiness
They are not produced or destroyed
Not stained or pure
Not increasing nor reducing.

So therefore in emptiness,
No form, no feeling, thought, choice or consciousness
No eye, ear, nose, tongue, body, mind
No sight, sound, smell, taste, touch or objects of mind
No realm of sensory cognition and
No realm of mind consciousness.

No ignorance or end of ignorance and till
No aging and no death
Nor end of aging or death.

Neither is there suffering nor origination of suffering,
No cessation of suffering or path to end suffering.
There is no wisdom and no attainment.

Thus with non-attainment,
The Bodhisattva, through relying on the Prajnaparamita
Has mind that is unobstructed and free
Without any hindrances, without any fear or dread
Freed from deluded views
The sublime Nirvana manifests.

All Buddhas of the three eras,
Thus relying on the Prajnaparamita
Attain the utmost perfect enlightenment.

Know then, the Prajnaparamita
As the great dharani
The mantra of great knowing
The supreme unsurpassed mantra
That destroys all suffering
True beyond all doubt.

Proclaim thus
The mantra of the Prajnaparamita :

Gate Gate
Para gate
Para sam gate
Bodhi,
Svaha.[75]

Chapter 10: Awakening and the Realm of the Awakened

The Experience of Awakening

The Awakened Mind

There are different levels or depths of insight which unfold in us as we develop along the path of practice. The deep insights may occur suddenly like a great flood, or they may be cumulative. In any case, much preliminary preparation would have gone into conditioning a receptive mind for the liberating experience of awakening.

The Experience of Awakening

The path to awakening truly starts after the disciple has had a first glimpse into emptiness. He or she will then have experienced the arising of compassion and the mind to enlightenment. It is through the practice of meditation that we can directly purify our heart-mind, relinquish all attachments, and delve deep into understanding emptiness. The practice of meditation continues even after one is awakened; though perhaps it can no longer be called "practice".

Ch'an Master Hongzhi Zhengjue (宏智正觉禅师) has this to say about the meditative state which points to awakening:

"Your body and mind in absolute ease.

Mould grows from your mouth's edge,

grasses sprout from your tongue.

Completely letting go of learning,

cleansed clean and pure,

and polished lustrous.

As the autumn pool,

as the bright moon imprinting space,

Thus is the profound brilliant clarity." [76]

We can picture a clear, illuminating and boundless awareness, which springs from a quietened calm, with mind and body in perfect equipoise.

The Buddha's first five disciples were awakened after his first discourse on the Four Noble Truths. Following after the Buddha gave his second discourse on *anatman* (no-self), they attained to the enlightenment of the *Arhat*.

Upon hearing from the *Arhat* Assaji (one of the Buddha's first five disciples) this verse:

"The Tathagata has explained the origin of those things which arise from a cause, and their cessation too. This is the teaching of the great recluse." [77]

Sariputra, who would come to be the Buddha's chief disciple, instantly attained entry into the irreversible path to Nirvana (i.e. he attained to stream-entry).

When conditions are ripe, it can take but a few pointed words or even a sound, for the ready disciple to awaken; for

237

liberating insight to manifest. There are many instances of this happening, as documented in the Ch'an Buddhist literature.

The sixth patriarch of Ch'an Buddhism, Hui Neng (惠能, CE 638–713), was enlightened when he heard a recitation of the passage from the *Diamond Sutra* by a wandering monk:

"The Bodhisattva, the great being, should produce an unsupported thought, that is, a thought which is nowhere supported, a thought unsupported by sights, sounds, smells, tastes, touchables or mind-objects." [78]

Ch'an Master Xuyun, or Old Monk Empty Cloud (虛雲老和尚) as he is endearingly called, with reference to his longevity, lived to a hundred and nineteen years (CE 1840-1959). He was enlightened at the age of fifty six, when after a long meditation, he was being served tea. The attendant accidentally spilt hot water on to his hand. Ch'an Master Xuyun dropped his teacup, which smashed on the floor and he was enlightened! He shared this awakening experience in a verse:

"The cup dropped to the ground

A sound distinct and clear

The void was shattered

The crazy mind instantly stopped"

In the *Ambattha Sutta*, [79] the Buddha skilfully gave a graduated discourse to the Brahmin Pokkharasati who had served him and his order of monks a meal at his residence. After the meal, the Buddha delivered a discourse on generosity, morality, on the corruption of sense desires and the profit of renunciation.

"And when the Lord knew that Pokkharasati's mind was ready, pliable, free from the hindrances, joyful and calm, then he preached a sermon on Dhamma in brief: on suffering, its origin, its cessation, and the path. And just as a clean cloth from which all stains have been removed receives the dye perfectly, so in the Brahmin Pokkharasati, as he sat there, there arose the pure and spotless Dhamma-eye (i.e., Pokkharasati attained to the non-regressing awakening of the stream-enterer) *and he knew 'Whatever things have a origin must come to cessation.'"*

This *sutta* tells us that our mind can be truly receptive to insight when it is "*pliable, free from hindrances, joyful and calm*"; the very states we cultivate in meditation, and which we try to maintain through into our daily living. Pokkharasati was in this very positive state of mind. Though he was a learned Brahmin with his own followers, Pokkharasati had sought out the Buddha to learn from him. He had honoured the Buddha with the respect due to a revered teacher. We may say he has prepared himself to be highly receptive to the skilfully presented discourses by the Buddha. Pokkharasati thereby attained to stream-entry at the end of the Buddha's discourses.

This is also how we can be grateful, thankful, and show deep reverence to the Three Treasures. In our own practice, we can in this way allow ourselves to be receptive to inspiration from the Buddhas, the mighty *Bodhisattva*s, the *Dharma,* and our teachers, who are our protectors and guides on the path to awakening.

The Awakened Mind

The state of the enlightened mind cannot be conveyed in words. We had realised earlier on that words have their limitations, when we try to use them to express any experience. How can we fully convey the beauty of a piece of music which is divinely played? We cannot convey the depth of our experience fully with words. Maybe if someone sees us being moved to tears, that may convey the experience to a greater extent; more than what words can say. Imagine how difficult it would be, to try and describe the taste of salt to one who had not tasted it.

When we try to convey a spiritual "experience" of the transcendent kind, there is a complete loss for words. Poetry, as a medium of communication, may help give us an inkling of the ineffable peace in the nature of this experience. This is perhaps what the enlightened minds that are *"profound, unfathomable and beyond the comprehension of those not yet liberated"*, have sometimes tried to do; to inspire us with their profound insights.

As we practice the *Dharma*, we will gain ever deepening insights. There will likely be many little "awakenings" along our path of practice. We sincerely keep in mind the admonition from *Bodhisattva* Avalokitesvara in the words from the *Heart Sutra* that *"there is no attainment"*. Our practice of the *Dharma* therefore never ends, because we practice with the aimless mind of not having any end in sight.

In the accomplished masters, we see that the mind at ease is very aware, and very much in touch with the surroundings.

The Ch'an Master Shiwu (石屋, Stonehouse, CE 1272–1352) left this verse (among his many poetic writings):

"Sitting alone, in the still, deep and profound mind.

In its midst, not any trace of affective feeling.

The fallen leaves, braving the west wind, huddled by the gate,

Offering an empty path to the bright moon." [(80)]

When asked by the wanderer Vaccagotta, whether the Buddha exists or does not exist after death, the Buddha rejected his question as dabbling in speculative views.[(81)] The Buddha instead led Vaccagotta back to the understanding of non-attachment to all views, *anatman* (no-self), and liberation through non-clinging.

Vaccagotta then asked where the liberated being reappears after death. The Buddha answered that the terms reappear or does not reappear or both reappears and does not reappear, or neither reappears or does not reappear do not apply in the case of one who is liberated. This thoroughly confused Vaccagotta, so the Buddha resorted to a simile. The Buddha asked Vaccagotta, if there was a burning fire before him, and if it was extinguished, would he know that it was extinguished, to which Vaccagotta answered that he would know so. The Buddha next asked Vaccagotta how he would answer, if further asked which direction; whether it went east, west, north or south, did the fire go after the fire was extinguished. Vaccagotta answered this would not apply, for when the fire had consumed the fuel feeding it, it is extinguished. The fire would not exist as it did before.

The Buddha then said that similarly, the one who is liberated cannot be said, after death, to reappear or not-reappear or both reappear and not reappear or neither reappear nor does not reappear; these terms do not apply. There is no more arising of form, feeling, perception, volitional activity, or consciousness in the liberated one who had relinquished them. The one who is liberated is profound and unfathomable, and the term reappear or does not reappear, does not apply.

Chapter 11: The Unfolding of the Buddha's *Dharma*

Changing the *Dharma* to Suit Our Views?

The Practice of the *Dharma*

The *Dharma* beyond Words

We have covered the core doctrines of Buddhism in the earlier chapters. In this chapter, we step back from looking at the trees, to enjoy the panoramic view of the forest of the *Dharma*. The canopy of this forest stretches to the far-off lands beyond the horizon. On the mountain slopes with rocky soil, sparse vegetation has taken root. In some places, it is the hardier and shorter variety of shrubs that thrive.

It is to be expected that the *Dharma* will have changed, from the time it was first expounded by the Buddha, over more than two and a half millennia ago. If the way it has been communicated and practiced since then had not been adapted to the changes in the socio-cultural environment, developments in philosophical thought, or advancements in science, etc., it would have remained as a teaching fossilized in the distant past, in the India of that time. The *Dharma* has to be versatile to stay relevant, and it is so.

Changing the *Dharma* to Suit Our Views?

The *Dharma* is the teaching from a fully enlightened being; from the Buddha. It serves to communicate the full "experience" of enlightenment and the path of practice for the attainment of enlightenment. It is not the inviolable word of an absolute being to whom we have to submit. We need not be attached to the dogmatic form of the *Dharma*. In the Buddha's time, the *Dharma* would have been communicated by the Buddha through his speech, his demeanour, his gestures, and the way he conducted himself with enlightened wisdom and compassion.

We have the Buddha's legacies of the *Sangha* and the *Dharma* to guide us. Since the Buddha's time, the *Dharma* has come to be presented and taught in many different ways, to suit the dispositions of those who seek its soothing balm. It would have undergone many changes. We have to clearly distinguish between the changes in doctrine, practice, or the many expressions of the *Dharma*. For the doctrinal teachings, we will want to distinguish the "essential" doctrines, which relate directly to the process of awakening, from those doctrines which act as the "supporting" factors for awakening. A similar approach can be used to distinguish between the "essential" practices and the "supporting" practices for the realisation of the *Dharma*.

The Buddha's teachings on no-self, impermanence, the Four Noble Truths, the Noble Eightfold Path, emptiness, and dependent-origination, will be among the essential doctrines which relate directly to awakening. These are the core teachings, which are at the heart of the *Dharma*. These essential doctrines will also have been expounded and presented in different ways, in the many *sutras* (Pali: *suttas*) handed down to us.

The *Vinaya* prescribed code of discipline and the various other teachings which further elaborate on the essential doctrines, for example, the commentaries on the sutras, etc., may be broadly categorized as the supporting doctrines. We know that the Buddha had promulgated the *Vinaya* to promote ethical conduct and harmonious coexistence in the community of the monks of the *Sangha*. The Buddha continually made changes to the *Vinaya* to meet the needs of the *Sangha*. These changes served to uphold the integrity of the spiritual community of his monk disciples, and to enhance the discipline of their spiritual training.

The meditation practices which are the means for developing insight into the essential doctrines, may be categorised as essential practices. The reverencing or ritualised devotional practices may generally be considered to be supporting practices. The above distinctions between "essential" and "supporting" doctrines or practices, however, may not be clearly demarcated. For example, some devotional practices may have much of the elements of the essential doctrinal teachings embedded in them, or may involve an essential form of meditation practice.

For the practitioner, the supporting doctrines and practices may be just as important (as the essential doctrines and practices) because he relies on them to guide his practice. They may be crucial to his development.

Different schools have emerged from changes in the emphasis or approaches to understanding, or practicing the *Dharma*. They may have different representations of their ideals from which they draw inspiration. Changes in the practice of the *Dharma* may also be required for adaptation to different climes and cultures. The key question will be whether these changes remain in concordance with the

Buddha's teachings. This means they should be consistent with the essential doctrines or practices of the *Dharma,* and support the development of *sila, samadhi,* and *prajna* (ethical behaviour or morality, concentration, and wisdom), which are based on compassion for all beings.

The *Dharma* has also found expression in ritualized practice, art, poetry, scholarly commentary, or in devotional practices, which will have acquired varying degrees of cultural bias. We see this in the different formalised services of the different schools, and the various commentaries that support different approaches to interpreting the *Dharma.* The *Bodhisattva Avalokitesvara* even takes on a female form as Guanyin Pusa (*Bodhisattva* Guanyin) in the Chinese Mahayana. Changes made to these expressions of the *Dharma* will likely not detract from the intrinsic value of the essential doctrines, in the environment that engendered those changes. It would be hoped that these changes will add to the richness and the vibrant colour of a closely interwoven tapestry of the expression of the *Dharma*, and be a harmonious whole with the core teachings of the Buddha.

We should not perfunctorily dismiss segments of the doctrine or practice of the *Dharma* which we deem to be cumbersome, or which appear to be outdated. This is especially so if it is done haphazardly, just to give some measure of consistency with recent developments in the various fields of human endeavour. Changes to even the supporting doctrinal teachings or practices, need to be carefully considered. As mentioned earlier, the so called supporting doctrines or practices may be just as important as the essential doctrines or practices. A "development" is another affirmation of the teaching of *anitya* (impermanence) and there will be more developments to come in future, including perhaps some which may nullify or modify the "development" which is currently in vogue.

If we are scientifically inclined, we may be tempted to rationalise the *Dharma* in scientific terms. There is no denying that science has helped move the frontiers of human knowledge. It has contributed to our physical well-being and comfort by changing the way we live and work. Our quality of life has improved tremendously with the progress in medicine and health-care. Scientific knowledge has helped expose the falsity of many superstitious beliefs by providing clear and consistent explanations for the many natural occurences that are observed in the physical universe. Science evolves as results from more thorough studies, or new discoveries are made known. A particular scientific view remains true until a new theory, which can better explain the body of scientific evidence, supersedes it.

There will be much of the *Dharma* which may be considered scientific truths. There will, however, also be chunks of the *Dharma* and the Buddhist tradition which, however, will not fit in with a framework of understanding built on scientific reasoning. We may be tempted to purge the chunks of the *Dharma,* which we are convinced are illogical vis-à-vis scientific reasoning. And so we end up with a "Scientific *Dharma*". We will have to ask ourselves whether we trust that science or scientific methodology can provide the answers to what may be deemed transcendent truths.

Like scientific development, our insightful understanding of the *Dharma* evolves as we awaken to its profundity. Science works in the realm of the physical universe, with tools that register measurable entities. The *Dharma* is encountered in the realm of the mind and beyond mind.

Similarly, if we are perhaps appreciative of the teachings of another sage and feel that his teachings are also relevant, we may then be trying to rationalise the *Dharma* through his teachings. There may likely be bits and pieces of the *Dharma* here and there, which we may find to be not so palatable; which we may be tempted to modify or exclude.

In this case, we may end up with a somewhat amalgamated "Other Sage Plus and Minus the Buddha's *Dharma*".

There is really no necessity for the *Dharma* to be explained in scientific terms, or be made to fit any mould because the *Dharma* is a means to an end. The Buddha himself likened it to a raft, which is to be discarded when it has outlived its use. When we see the *Dharma* this way; when we see it with emptiness, we will not be embroiled in distracting views and notions.

There is no need to deeply pursue the alignment of the *Dharma* with advancements in science (or the alignment of scientific discoveries with the *Dharma*). It may be of some interest that some of the narratives in the collective *Dharma* (the prefix "collective" is used here to denote the collection of teachings which encompass the many culturally infused forms of the *Dharma*) may or may not be consistent with current scientific findings. However, it does not really matter that much. The collective *Dharma* is not cast in an immutable edifice. It does not need to be justified against views (scientific or otherwise) about the phenomenal world, which the *Dharma* is formulated to transcend.

Whether the Mount Sumeru of the traditional Buddhist cosmology does really exist or not, or how it exists, may not help us to understand the Four Noble Truths in our quest for awakening. In the simile the Buddha gave about the person wounded by a poisoned arrow [82], we are advised not to waste precious time on seeking answers to unnecessary questions. Extraordinary conditioning factors have given us a rare opportunity to know about the *Dharma,* or to have begun practising it. Let the practitioner therefore be focused on treading his path to awakening, for his own welfare and happiness, and for the benefit of all beings.

When we pick and choose what we want of the *Dharma,* based on what we now think we know is good for us, we are giving up on that which we do not yet understand. Perhaps we cannot avoid doing this to some extent. However, the danger is that we will then be constraining our access to the *Dharma*. In our quest to understand the *Dharma*, we will want to maintain an open and discerning receptivity to new insights, and yet be clear about whether we need to take on any views at all. It is rather easy to be caught up in the unending activity of assigning labels to what are essentially our self-created views, then having disputes about the contents of the different labels, developing preferences and further churning out even more views.

We may sometimes be emotional about our views, and may also like to dispense them freely. Knowing this, we should be more tolerant of the many differing views (arising from those with other preferences) which are proffered on any subject matter for discussion. For example, we may strongly hold the view that meditation is best done in the full lotus posture with eyes open. However, we need to be tolerant of other views, even though we may not subscribe to them. There may be those who have lost their limbs from an accident, or are born blind. They will have their views on what suits them better. We can learn to relinquish our views. We can learn to give all views an acknowledging nod. We then employ mindful discernment to assess the situation at hand, weigh the options and move forward with doing what is appropriate.

We may understand that there is much we can learn from the teachings of the Buddha. However, if we are to discard those parts of the *Dharma* which cannot be proven to our satisfaction now; which do not seem plausible, or which seemingly offend our sensibilities, we will have to tread carefully. We may be closing the door to new knowledge. In some instances, this may mean we do not accept that the Buddha taught anything about transcending the mundane, or that we can actually know the mind of the Buddha. Having these limiting views will be our great loss. We will then be restricting ourselves to only our own views. We may end up stagnating in the mundane. We will have shut ourselves out from experiencing the transcendent *Dharma*.

The Practice of the *Dharma*

There have been changes in the monastic discipline of the *Vinaya*, which are in the main, related to the need to adapt to the different socio-economic or climatic conditions, in the new lands that Buddhism was transplanted to. For example, the monastics in the Far East (in China, Korea and Japan) took up farming of the monastery grounds and preservation of food for sustenance through the harsh winters. Physical labour then became a *Dharma* practice, and was incorporated into the monastic training. Ch'an Master Baizhang Huaihai (百丈懷海) of the Tang dynasty, formulated the *"One day of no work, one day of no food."* discipline in response to this need.

The daily giving of alms food, as practised in the mainly Theravada countries of Burma and Thailand, could not be directly applied to the Far East, at the time that Buddhism was transplanted there. The monasteries were not close to neighbouring towns, and in many cases were located in the mountains; not easily accessible by the townsfolk. In view of the climate, locality, and the existing traditions, a daily walk through the harsh winter landscape into town for the collection of alms to support the sizeable monastic community, was not feasible.

We have views and preferences, and we will have our own structure of ideas built on our understanding of the *Dharma*. We will not have a clear understanding of the *Dharma* when we initially encounter it. We keep learning as we grow, and we grow as we learn. We may need to start with having some preliminary views about everything, but we need not be entangled in them. The Buddha taught that "our views" do not belong to us and we are not of them.

Let us therefore loosen our hold on speculative or discriminating views. It may not be necessary for us to take a stand on many of the views which arise in the course of our exploring the *Dharma*. It may not be worth our while to go too deeply into the many views, which in most cases are just ideas and theories; of limited application to our practice. As we practice the *Dharma*, we will recognize that our views continually change. We will develop the transformative insights which are of real worth because they induce growth and development in us. Perhaps we will then no longer need any views at all.

At the heart of the practice of the Buddha's *Dharma* is relinquishment. That which is to be relinquished, is the "I" ego. It is from this false "self" that all views emerge. Therefore, let us for now, take only a very light hold on to our views, leaving room to finally relinquish them altogether. We will not want to be attached to views which serve to divide and segregate. We do not need to belong to a particular view, or be subservient to it. Let us instead shift our focus back to our core practice, to be firmly grounded in the insights that we will gain by direct experience, from the sincere practice of the *Dharma*.

The Buddha's *Dharma* is "*to be comprehended by the wise*"; so it is chanted in our reverencing of the *Dharma*. It is to be personally practised and scrutinized. We therefore have to be discerning, to tread mindfully, and at the same time, be highly respectful of the *Dharma* that the Buddha had declared to be "*profound and unattainable by mere reasoning*" [83]. We do not ever want to lose sight of the purpose of the *Dharma*, which is to point us to the transcendent. If we are to carve out bits and pieces from it, or paste additional lumps and bumps on to it, we may then end up with a stub, which no longer points anywhere. How can we then even try to look for the moon, when we will have lost even the finger that at least can point us to it?

The *Dharma* beyond Words

The emotional connections with our cultural heritage can positively energize or bring about receptiveness in us. We can tap into them to support our practice. However, they may have to be modified to be used in another culture. For example, telling a child from the West that he will be rewarded with a thin crust pizza lunch may work wonders in getting him to do his homework. To instead tell him he will be rewarded with pickled plums or sweet fermented tapioca, would unlikely do the trick. It may be somewhat painful for us to realise no one else likes sweet fermented tapioca like we do, but if we are to get anywhere with getting the homework done, we have to go warm up that pizza.

What then is the yardstick for whether a teaching is in concordance with the *Dharma* of the Buddha? The Buddha has laid down very clear guidelines. Close to his passing into *Parinirvana*, the Buddha spoke thus:

"*In whatsoever Dhamma and discipline the Noble Eightfold Path is not found, no ascetic is found of the first, the second, the third or the fourth grade* (these grades refer to the stages of progression on the non-regressive path to enlightenment; the stream enterer, the once-returner, the non-returner, and the Arhat). *But such ascetics can be found, ...in a Dhamma and discipline where the Noble Eightfold Path is found...if the monks live righteously, the world would not lack for Arhats.*" [84]

The teachings of the Buddha are there to guide us. They all belong to the common treasury of the *Dharma*, which has been further developed, commented on, and disseminated by his enlightened disciples. It is to be expected that the *Dharma* will flower in different forms, in the different lands it was brought to. There is therefore none who can lay any justifiable specific claim, that theirs is the only one, or the only correct *Dharma*.

Do we think we can surmise and know what was in the Buddha's enlightened consciousness from the records of his teachings? We should perhaps just take the cue from a description by the Ch'an Buddhism School that says of the enlightenment experience,

"A transmission that is not relying on words, but a direct pointing to mind."

We can leave it at that.

The *Dharma* lives on not just because it is captured in words or doctrine. It lives on because there are those who tread the path the Buddha had pointed out, and directly awakened to the truth that the Buddha had realised. They have then continued to teach and inspire others, thereby continuing the lineage of those awakened through the *Dharma*. The different schools of Buddhism are these different expressions of enlightened experience, or enlightened transformation. The Buddha's doctrine and teachings are only useful if they can continue to be relevant and accessible. The *Dharma* will continue to thrive if it continues to convey, and most importantly, to transmit the enlightened mind.

May all beings be well and happy! May all attain to the highest peace!

Appendix I: Meditation Methods
General Guidelines

To begin the meditation practice, both mind and body should be relaxed. The practice itself should be done in a clean and tidy environment, and preferably in a quiet place. The practitioner should review the chapter on "The Practice of Meditation" before proceeding with the practice. For the serious practitioner, the need for sincerity in his practice and the need to practice with non-attainment cannot be stressed enough. Both topics are covered in the subsections of the same chapter in this book.

When you sit in meditation, it is most important to be fully relaxed, comfortable, and at ease physically. Ensure that your posture is correct: that your spine is naturally upright, that you feel as if you are hanging on a string attached to the top of your head; your neck is relaxed, with the chin slightly inwards, with eyes lightly closed, in the position of gazing slightly downwards at the ground about ten paces in front of you. Your tongue touches the top palate of your mouth to help regulate the flow of saliva. Your elbows are not tucked against your body, but held relaxed and slightly outwards, with relaxed shoulders. Your arms are held in a position that does not make you lean forward or back. Your buttocks should be on a cushion or cushions that lift your hips high enough to give a slight slope to your legs so that your knees are on the floor. The cushion you sit on should be placed on a mat or carpet so that you are insulated from the cold floor. You may need to cover your legs with a blanket or towel to keep them warm. Similarly, do not expose your body directly to cold draughts.

You can take the "open" position with both legs on the floor and the soles of both legs facing upwards and placed next to each other on the floor. Alternatively, you can be in the "half lotus" posture with one leg bent at the knee and the other leg similarly bent and placed with the sole of the leg facing upwards and on the thigh of the lower leg. There is the "full lotus" position, where both legs are bent with the soles facing upwards and placed on the thighs of the other leg.

In all these positions, you should have a three pointed support; your buttocks on the cushion and your two knees on the mat. If you are a beginner, you may not have the flexibility in the beginning, to have both knees on the floor. If so, ensure that your spine is upright by propping more cushions under your buttocks if needed, and that you are comfortable. Do not force your legs into a position that they are not yet flexible enough to maintain.

If you are sitting on a chair, you should not be leaning back. If you do so, you will tend to slump on the chair and your mind will be sluggish. You should keep your spine upright. If you feel any physical tension, mindfully relax the part of the body where the tension is felt.

In the beginning, you may feel some aching in the joints after you sit for a period of time. Ensure that this is not from an unnatural forced positioning of your legs. Otherwise, it will get better as your joints loosen with more sitting practice.

The overall guideline is to be seated in a position in which you will feel relaxed and alert: which will allow you to sit comfortably for a long while. If you are right handed, you can put your left palm above your right palm on the sole of your feet (right palm above left if you are left handed) and have the tips of both your thumbs touching, while forming an oval shape with your fingers and joined thumbs. This helps in settling the mind when we have the active hand resting below the passive hand.

In the walking meditation practice, mindfulness is maintained throughout the practice and we are fully absorbed in the walking. To start off with, we may want to walk slowly, to develop the feel for the placement and continuity of developing our awareness of the process of walking. When we are more conversant with the practice, we can walk leisurely and maintain a relaxed yet clear mindfulness. This helps us develop a meditative poise in the midst of motion and activity.

To derive benefit from the meditation practice, it should be carried out for a period of more than about twenty minutes each time that you sit or walk. Too short a period may not allow time for your body and mind to settle into the practice.

Mindfulness of Breathing

The mindful awareness of breathing [85] is the method of cultivation that is the direct legacy of the Buddha. The practice starts with the preliminaries of relaxing the body and mind in a conducive environment, as discussed in the earlier section. In that relaxed state, we settle mindfulness on the breathing. We stay mindful of the natural in-breathing (inhalation) and out-breathing (exhalation). Mindfulness on the breath is maintained on all stages of the inflowing and outflowing of the breath. We observe all the varieties and qualities of the breath, being aware of the length of the breath and the smoothness of the flow of the breath.

In this beginning phase, a useful tool is the counting (mentally) of the breaths, to help guide us to focus the mind and disengage it from wandering thoughts. It is recommended that the counting be not more than ten or less than five, to allow the mind to settle into the counting. We can start with allocating about five minutes to each of the four stages and adjust that later to suit the duration of our practice. We start with counting the end of the outbreaths and count "one" for the end of the first out-breathing, then "two" for the end of the second out-breathing and so on until we count to "ten" at the end of the tenth out-breathing. We then start again with counting "one" at the end of the next out-breathing. The Visuddhimagga (The Path of

Purification) [86] has a good simile for this phase of counting. It likens the counting to how a grain measurer would count. The grain measurer would count after he has emptied the grain (compare this to the end of the out-breathing) from his measure into the basket. If the process of counting is interrupted at any point (e.g. if the mind has strayed away from attention on the breath), we re-establish our attention on the breath, start again from counting "one" at the next outbreath, and continue with the counting sequence.

After the mind has settled somewhat, we count the beginning of the in-breathing, again counting from one to ten. By now, the breathing will be calm and the breath is distinctly felt. For this phase of the counting, the Visuddhimagga likens it to how a skilled cowherd will be sitting at the gate of the cow pen in the morning. As the cows are let out, he counts each one as it reaches the gate, dropping a pebble each time, and saying "One, two…"

Let the breathing be natural and not forced in any way. It is not the intent for the breathing to be adjusted to follow the counting. As the mind is focused on the counting of the breaths, the breathing naturally calms and becomes more subtle.

In the next stage, we stop counting and let the breathing flow naturally. We place our mindfulness on experiencing the whole breathing process, no more distinguishing between in or out breaths. We maintain an even mindfulness on the whole process of breathing, and mindfully experience the flow of our breath, absorbed in the in and out-breathing.

In the next stage, we calm the breathing further. A widely used method to achieve this is to settle our mindfulness on a point along the path of the breath and mindfully watch it there. We can focus our mindfulness on the sensation of touch at the location where the in and out breath contacts our body. This will typically be at the tip of our nostrils or at the upper lip, depending on whether we have a shorter or longer nose and the shape of our nose and mouth. This process is expressed in the simile of the saw. When a carpenter cuts timber with a saw, his attention is placed on where the teeth of the saw come into contact with the timber, at the place where the cutting occurs, not on the saw that is in motion.

We maintain this stage as long as we want, dwelling in the calm and peacefulness that the concentration brings us.

With practice and if conditions are right, we may enter into the deep meditative absorptions (*dhyana*). At this juncture, to further his practice in the development of the liberating insight into phenomenal existence, the reader is advised to seek a reputable teacher or group that practices Buddhist meditation.

Meditation on Loving-Kindness
(*Maitri*)

The loving-kindness of *maitri* (Pali: *metta*) belongs to a group of the four "divine-abidings" (loving-kindness, compassion, sympathetic joy and gladness, and equanimity or even mindedness); divine states which are said to be enjoyed by the highest gods. When loving-kindness is practised, the Buddha tells us that we will sleep well without bad dreams, will be pleasing to all, will be protected by the deities and will be reborn in the realm of the gods if we do not manage to gain enlightenment in this lifetime.

The meditation on loving-kindness can lead to the deep meditative absorptions (*dhyana*). It is done in the tone of unbounded friendliness and goodwill, as an antidote for enmity.

THE PRACTICE OF MEDITATION ON LOVING-KINDNESS

In the beginning, one develops loving-kindness to oneself. Before we start developing loving-kindness to others, we have to feel it for oneself. There has to be a wellspring of loving-kindness that one feels for oneself before one can effectively share it with others. The meditation practice on *maitri* should not be developed specifically to someone of the opposite sex or towards a dead person, as strong and complicating feelings other than loving-kindness may arise in the meditation.

So we develop feelings of being kind to oneself, and appreciation for oneself. We wish for our own self, wellbeing and happiness. While doing the practice, we can mentally review the lines below:

"May I be happy and live happily,

May I be well and be in good health,

May I have peace,

May I grow and develop."

When we do this, we can bring to our mind instances when we have felt being happy, being calmly inspired or being at ease, and get in touch with those positive feelings. We want to be absorbed into this very positive state of mind.

After we have become pervaded by the feeling of loving-kindness to ourselves, we can then begin to radiate loving-kindness to a dear friend. We wish for him the same that we have done for ourselves:

"May you be happy and live happily,

May you be well and be in good health,

May you have peace,

May you grow and develop."

When we feel comfortable with and feel that we have established this feeling of loving-kindness to this dear friend, we can then radiate loving-kindness to a neutral person; someone who we do not particularly feel love for or bear enmity towards. The next step is to develop loving-kindness to an "enemy", or someone who we perceive to be intransigent, a real pain.

Next, we develop loving-kindness equally to all these four persons, then widen the circle to include our family, community, country, the world including all its inhabitants, and then we radiate loving-kindness to all beings everywhere, into limitless space, unhindered, in all directions.

We stay fully bathed in and radiate loving-kindness as long as we want. If our practice is firmly established and conditions are right, we may enter into the deep meditative absorptions.

As with the other meditation practices, at this juncture, to further his practice, the reader is advised to seek a reputable teacher or group that practices Buddhist meditation.

Walking Meditation

Walking meditation is a practice by itself. The practice is for the development of mindfulness in the act of walking. The path for walking should be on level ground, clean and in serene surroundings, wide enough so that it does not feel cramped and long enough to allow a walk of about twenty paces in one direction. The practitioner then walks from one end to the other and makes a turn clockwise on reaching the end.

If the walking is to be done indoors, then the walking path can be next to the walls of the room in a continuous circle, without objects on the floor which can be tripping hazards. We walk in a clockwise direction.

Walking is done naturally, and can be at a relaxed or slower pace so long as mindfulness is maintained throughout. Let both arms be loosely held and relaxed naturally by the side. Alternatively, especially if walking slowly, the hands can be held together. Form a loose ball with the left hand and hold it softly in the palm of the right hand with arms bent, at a level below the heart, slightly out from the body.

When walking, the focus of attention is at the base of the foot. Let awareness be on the feel of the foot as it touches the floor or ground. As the foot is placed on the floor, feel the contact of the floor with first the heel, then the sole of the feet, then the upper ball and base of the toes. As the foot is lifted, feel the lifting of the heel then the sole, then the toes from the floor. Feel the foot moving forward and then the placing of the foot on the floor. Now the next foot, in a similar sequence, as it is lifted off the floor and placed in front of the other foot.

A mental note can be made of each stage of the foot placement. We can make a mental note; "lifting" when the foot is lifted, "moving" when the foot is moved forward and "placing" when the foot is placed down on the floor. Then repeat this for the other foot. The placing down action should be completed for the forward foot before movement on the hind foot is started with "lifting".

This is a good practice to use by itself. It is also useful when we are doing a long sitting meditation and want to stretch our legs mindfully using the walking meditation practice in between the sitting meditation sessions.

Appendix II: Reverencing the Three Treasures Practice

The reverencing can be simple or very elaborate. To start off, we can do a simplified reverencing as our first practice of the day. This can take the simple form given below, of a recitation of salutations to the Three Treasures (the Buddha, the *Dharma* and the *Sangha*) followed by the taking of refuges to the Three Treasures and the precepts, the recitation of the *Heart Sutra* and concluding with the dedication of merits.

It is best to have the reverencing done facing a picture or image of the Buddha or the *Bodhisattva*s, set in a position higher than our head when we are seated or kneeling, so that we look up to it in the manner of being respectful to our teacher. This helps to give focus to our reverencing practice.

We start our reverencing of the Three Treasures with a triple prostration or bow. Then while kneeling or sitting comfortably, with extended fingers held together, and with both palms joined in the gesture of giving respect, we recite the salutations and offerings to the Three Treasures as given below.

Salutations to the Three Treasures

I revere with body, speech and mind:

The Blessed One, the Fully Awakened, the Perfectly Enlightened One.

I pay salutations to the Buddha, the mighty Bodhisattvas and the Noble Ones of the three eras.

With deep reverence, I pay homage to the Buddha, the Dharma and the Sangha.

And I take refuge in the Three Treasures.

THE REFUGES

To the Buddha I go for refuge

To the Dharma I go for refuge

To the Sangha I go for refuge

THE PRECEPTS

I undertake to refrain from taking life.

I undertake to refrain from taking the not given.

I undertake to refrain from sexual misconduct.

I undertake to refrain from false speech.

I undertake to refrain from intoxicants.

DELIGHTING IN THE PRACTICE

We pay reverence to the Buddha
The Perfectly Enlightened One
The Highest Wisdom
The Deepest Compassion
Illuminating the worlds.

We rejoice
In the goodness of the Dharma
In the virtues of the Sangha.

With palms joined, let us celebrate
Let us delight in the practice
Let us pay reverence
With body speech and mind.

The Heart Sutra

The Heart Sutra, Heart of the Perfection of Wisdom

The Bodhisattva of Compassion
When deeply coursing in the Prajnaparamita,
Sees the five skandhas are of the emptiness
That liberates from all suffering.

Here Sariputra,
Form is no different from emptiness
Emptiness no different from form
Form is emptiness
Emptiness is form
Feeling, thought, choice and consciousness
Are such as this.

Here Sariputra,
All things are marked with emptiness
They are not produced or destroyed
Not stained or pure
Not increasing or reducing.

So therefore in emptiness,
No form, no feeling, thought, choice or consciousness
No eye, ear, nose, tongue, body, mind
No sight, sound, smell, taste, touch or objects of mind
No realm of sensory cognition and
No realm of mind consciousness.

No ignorance or end of ignorance and till
No aging and no death
Nor end of aging or death.

Neither is there suffering nor origination of suffering
No cessation of suffering or path to end suffering,
There is no wisdom and no attainment.

Thus with non-attainment,
The Bodhisattva, through relying on the Prajnaparamita
Has mind that is unobstructed and free
Without any hindrances, without any fear or dread
Freed from deluded views
The sublime Nirvana manifests.

All Buddhas of the three eras,
Thus relying on the Prajnaparamita
Attain the utmost perfect enlightenment.

Know then, the Prajnaparamita
As the great dharani
The mantra of great knowing
The supreme unsurpassed mantra
That destroys all suffering
True beyond all doubt.

Proclaim thus
The mantra of the Prajnaparamita:

Gate Gate
Para gate
Para sam gate
Bodhi,
Svaha.

Dedication of Merits

We conclude with a dedication of all our merits

I dedicate all my merits to all beings everywhere.
May they always be happy, joyful and free from pain.
May all attain to the highest peace of supreme Buddhahood.

We give a triple prostration or bow to conclude our reverencing of the Three Treasures.

Notes

The quoted translated texts from the Nikayas of the Pali Canon (i.e. from the AN, DN, MN and SN) are from the publications given in the Bibliography.

1	The Buddha's search for enlightenment is narrated in the *Ariyapariyasana Sutta* (The Noble Search) : MN 26 and *Mahasaccaka Sutta* (The Greater Discourse to Saccaka): MN 36.
2	*The Udana and the Itivuttaka, Two Classics from the Pali Canon*, Chapter 8, Section 8.5, Cunda, Translated by John D. Ireland, Buddhist Publication Society, Kandy, Sri Lanka, 1997.
3	*Mahaparinibbana Sutta (The Great Passing-The Buddha's Last Days) : DN 16: 6.7.*
4	*Kesaputti (Kalama) Sutta* :AN3:65.
5	*Culamalunkya Sutta* (The Shorter Discourse to Malunkyaputta) : MN 63.
6	*Dhammacakkappavattana Sutta* (Setting in Motion the Wheel of the *Dharma*) : SN 56: 11.
7	For a fuller presentation, the reader can refer to: *Guide through the Abhidhamma-Pitaka* by Nyanatiloka Mahathera, Buddhist Publishing Society, Kandy, 1971 or *Abhidhammattha Sangaha* – A comprehensive manual of *Abhidhamma*, Monk Bodhi, General Editor, BPS Payiyatti Editions, USA, 2000.
8	*Magga-Vibhanga Sutta* (An Analysis of the Path) : SN 45:8.
9	*Kaccanagotta Sutta* : SN 12.15.
10	*Raja Sutta , Mucalinda* , adapted from *The Udana and the Itivuttaka, Two Classics from the Pali Canon*, Translated by John D. Ireland, Buddhist Publication Society, Kandy, Sri Lanka, 1997.
11	*Anattalakkhana Sutta* (The Characteristic of Nonself) : SN 22.59.

12	*Aniccasanna Sutta* (Perception of Impermanence): SN 22:102.
13	*Culashanada sutta* (The Shorter Discourse on the Lion's Roar) :MN: 11.
14	*Tikanipata, Tikanna Sutta* (The Book of Threes, *Tikanna*) : AN 3:58.
15	*Mahasaccaka Sutta* (The Greater Discourse to *Saccaka*) : MN 36:38.
16	Refer to the *Mahanidana-Paticcasamuppada Sutta* (The Great Discourse on Origination) : DN 15:1 .
17	*Culasakuludayi Sutta* (The Shorter Discourse to Sakuludayi) : MN79:8.
18	*Acalakassapa Sutta* (The Naked Ascetic Kassapa) : SN 12:17.
19	*Alagaddupama Sutta* (The Simile of the Snake) :MN 22 :27.
20	*Dhammadinna Sutta*: SN 55:53. In this sutta, though the Buddha knows that Dhammadinna and the followers will benefit from the profound teachings (they had already attained to stream-entry) on emptiness, they were reluctant to take them on.
21	Adapted from: *The Fundamental Wisdom of the Middle Way, Nagarjuna's Mulamadhyamakakarika*, Translated and commentary by Jay L. Garfield, Oxford University Press, 1995 and *Mulamadhyamakakarika of Nagarjuna, The Philosophy of the Middle Way*, David J. Kalupahana, Motilal Banarsidass Publishers, Delhi, 1986 .
22	*Buddhist Wisdom Books, The Diamond and the Heart Sutra*, Translated and explained by Edward Conze, George Allen & Unwin, London, Second impression, 1980.
23	Refer to the *Mulapariyaya Sutta* (The Root of All Things) : MN 1.51.

| 24 | *"The Way of the Bodhisattva"* by Shantideva, Translated by Padmakara Translation Group, Shambala, Boston & London, 2006 and

"A guide to the Boddhisattva's Way of Life" by Acharya Shantideva, Translated by Stephen Batchelor, Library of Tibetan Works & Archives, Dharamsala, 1979. |
|---|---|
| 25 | See for example references to the six perfections in *The Large Sutra on Perfect Wisdom*, Translated by Edward Conze, Motilal Banarsidass, Delhi. First Indian Edn, 1979. |
| 26 | The 'Ten Stages' Chapter of the *Avatamsaka Sutra* describes the ten stages of progression of the training of the *Bodhisattva* to supreme Buddhahood. Refer to *The Flower Ornament Scripture – A translation of the Avatamsaka Sutra*, Trans. Thomas Cleary, Shambala Publications Inc., Boston & London, 1993. |
| 27 | Adapted from the *Alagaddupama Sutta* (Simile of the Raft): MN 22 : 13 & 14. |
| 28 | Refer to the *Heart Sutra* as translated and adapted by the author, CHY, in the 'Introduction to the *Heart Sutra*' section, in Chapter 9 of this book. |
| 29 | *Upanisa Sutta* (Proximate Cause) : SN 12:23. |
| 30 | *Things Wearisome* - Verses by the author, CHY, 1979. |
| 31 | Refer to the Diamond *Sutra* in *Buddhist Wisdom Books, The Diamond and the Heart Sutra*, Translated and explained by Edward Conze, George Allen & Unwin, London, Second impression, 1980. |
| 32 | *Upanisa Sutta* (Proximate Cause) : SN 12:23. |
| 33 | These are also referred to as the cankers (Skt: *Asrayas*, Pali: *asavas*); the three corruptions of desire, the corruption of becoming, and the corruption of ignorance. |
| 34 | *Tea Drinking Gatha* - Verses by the author, CHY, 2012. |
| 35 | *Feel* - Verses by the author, CHY, 1988. |
| 36 | *One Robe, One Bowl, The Zen Poetry of Ryokan*, Translated and introduced by John Stevens, John Weatherhill, Inc, New York & Tokyo, First Edn, 1977. |

37	*Angulimala Sutta* : MN 86.
38	*Mahakaccanabhaddekaratta Sutta* (Maha kaccana and A Single Excellent Night) : MN 133.
39	Untitled - Verses by the author, CHY, 1979.
40	*Mahasatipatthana Sutta* (The Greater Discourse on the Foundations of Mindfulness) : DN 22.20.
41	*Malunkyaputta Sutta* : SN 35.95.
42	Translated from: Taisho Canon Vol. 47 p557, section c, line 20.
43	Translated from: Taisho Canon Vol. 48 p376, section b, line 18 to p377, section a, line 10.
44	*Dhatuvibhanga Sutta* (The Exposition of the Elements) : MN 140:31.
45	Translated from: Taisho Canon Vol. 47 p557, section c, lines 16-19.
46	Translated from: Taisho Canon Vol. 65 p610, section c, lines 6-7.
47	Adapted from the *Metta Sutta* (Discourse on Loving-Kindness) : *Sutta Nipata* 1.8 , verses 143-52.
48	*Tears of Compassion* - Verses by the author, CHY, 2013.
49	*Sabrahmaka Sutta* (Brahma) : AN 3:31.
50	*Pathamasamvasa Sutta* (Living Together) : AN 4:53.
51	In the *Sunakkhatta Sutta* : MN 105:5, the Buddha tells Sunakkhatta that he teaches the monks who have overestimated their progress to guide them back to their training but will not suffer the insincere and underserving. The Buddha is not inclined to teach his *Dharma* to those who do not sincerely want to learn.
52	Translated from the Chinese: "知彼知己，百戰不殆；不知彼而知己，一勝一負；不知彼，不知己，每戰必殆."
53	Refer to segment 'Happily Being in the Present', in Chapter 3, for the practice of mindfully sipping tea.

54	U Thant was to later be unanimously voted in as Secretary General by the UN General Assembly in November 1962 and reappointed Secretary General in December 1966 on unanimous recommendation of the UN Security Council. He retired in Dec 1971 after ten years as Secretary General of the UN.
55	Refer to *View from the UN*, U Thant, Garden City, New York, Doubleday (1978).
56	Mangala Sutta (Discourse on Blessings), Sutta Nipata 2.4, Khuddaka Nikaya.
57	*Gamanisamyutta, Rasiya*, SN42:12 – III x.
58	Ch'an Master Xuyun's *"Prerequisites for Ch'an Practice"* , translated from the Chinese.
59	*Prajna Sword* – Verses by the author, CHY , 2011.
60	Gongan attributed to Ch'an Master Linji (临济).
61	*Kesi Sutta* : AN 4:111
62	*Who* – Verses by the author, CHY, 1988.
63	*Meditation Practice* - Verses by the author, CHY, 2013.
64	Ch'an Master Xuyun's *"Prerequisites for Ch'an Practice"*, translated from the Chinese.
65	The 37 aids to enlightenment refer to the thirty seven modes of training that includes the four foundations of mindfulness, the four right exertions, the four bases of power, the five spiritual faculties, the five spiritual powers, the seven factors of enlightenment and the Noble Eightfold Path.
66	Adapted from *"The Holy Teaching of Vimalakirti – A Mahayana Scripture"*. Translated by Robert A.F. Thurman. Pennsylvania State University Press, University Park & London, 1976.
67	*Samannaphala Sutta* (The fruits of the Homeless life) : DN 2:75. See also *Navakanipata* , (The Great Chapter): AN 9: 32.
68	*Accharasanghatavagga* (Luminous) : AN 1: 51 & AN 1:52.

69	Taisho Canon Vol. 48 p98, section a, line 28 to section b, line 5.
70	*Reverencing the Buddha* - Verses by the author, CHY, 1979.
71	*The Way of the Bodhisattva* – A translation of the *Bodhicaryavatara* by Shantideva, Revised Edn, Padmakara Translation Group, Shambala, Boston and London, 2006.
72	Taisho Canon Vol. 8 p848, section c, line 6 to line 24.
73	Refer to the *Heart Sutra* in *Buddhist Wisdom Books, The Diamond and the Heart Sutra*, Translated and explained by Edward Conze, George Allen & Unwin, London, Second impression, 1980.
74	*Zen: Dawn in the West*, by Roshi Philip Kapleau, Rider, London,1980.
75	*The Heart Sutra*, translated and adapted by the author, CHY, 2014.
76	Translated from: Taisho Canon Vol. 48 p78, section b, line 7 to line 9.
77	*Upatissa-pasine* (Sariputta's Question), from Mahavagga 1.23.1 – 10.
78	Refer to the *Diamond Sutra* in Buddhist Wisdom Books, *The Diamond and the Heart Sutra,* Translated and explained by Edward Conze, George Allen & Unwin, London, Second impression, 1980.
79	*Ambattha sutta* (About Ambattha) : DN 3-2.21.
80	Translation by the author, CHY, from the Chinese. Verse 157 in Chinese extracted from "*The Zen Works of Stonehouse*", Red pine (Bill Porter), Mercury House, San Francisco, 1999.
81	*Aggivacchagotta Sutta* (To Vacchagotta on Fire) : MN 72 .
82	Refer to the Buddha's admonition to the monk *Malunkyaputta* in the section, "The Historical Buddha and His Legacy", in Chapter 1 of this book.
83	Refer to the *Ariyapariyasana Sutta* (The Noble Search) : MN 26.
84	*Mahaparinibanna Sutta* (The Great Passing) DN: 16-5.27.

| 85 | *Anapanasati Sutta* (Mindfulness of Breathing) : MN 118. |
| 86 | Refer to *Visuddhimagga, The Path of Purification*, (VIII 191 & 192), Translated by Monk Nanamoli, Buddhist Publication Society, Fourth edn. 2010. |

ABBREVIATIONS

AN: *Anguttara Nikaya* (e.g. AN 3:65 refers to Chapter 3, *Sutta* number 65 of the *Anguttara Nikaya*, see Bibliography below)

DN: *Digha Nikaya* (e.g. DN 16-6.7 refers to the *Sutta* number 16, subsection 6.7 of the *Digha Nikaya*, see Bibliography below)

MN: *Majjima Nikaya* (e.g. MN 1:51 refers to the *Sutta* number 1, verse 51 of the *Majjima Nikaya*, see Bibliography below)

SN: *Samyutta Nikaya* (e.g. SN 12:23 refers to the *Sutta* number 12, subsection 23 of the *Samyutta Nikaya*, see Bibliography below)

SNp: *Sutta Nipata*

VM: *Vissudhi Magga*

Skt: Sanskrit

Chn: Chinese

Jpn: Japanese

BCE: Before Common Era

CE: Common Era

CHY: The author (Chee Hong Young, 杨志雄)

Bibliography

I have relied on the publications below for the quoted translated texts of the Pali Canon:

MN	*The Middle Length Discourses of the Buddha – A Translation of the Majjhima Nikaya*, Translated by Monk Nanamoli and edited and revised by Monk Bodhi, second edition, Wisdom Publications, Boston, 2001.
SN	*The Connected Discourses of the Buddha, A Translation of the Samyutta Nikaya*, by Monk Bodhi, Wisdom Publications, Boston, 2000.
AN	*The Numerical Discourses of the Buddha, A Translation of the Anguttara Nikaya*, by Monk Bodhi, Wisdom Publications, Boston, 2012.
DN	*The Long Discourses of the Buddha, A Translation of the Digha Nikaya*, by Maurice Walshe, Wisdom Publications, Boston, 1995.
VM	*Visuddhimagga, The Path of Purification*, Trans. Monk Nanamoli, Buddhist Publication Society, Fourth edn. 2010.

The following websites provide good additional reference material for the reader, in the indicated area of enquiry.

General Buddhist Teachings	www.Buddhanet.net
Theravada Teachings	http://www.accesstoinsight.org
Chinese Tripitaka	www.cbeta.org of the Chinese Buddhist Electronic Text Association (CBETA)

Glossary

Anatman (Skt) *Anatta* (Pali)	No-self. The doctrine of no inherent selfhood in phenomenal existence.
Anitya (Skt) *Anicca* (Pali)	Impermanence – the continual flux of conditioned change. One of the three marks of being: impermanence, unsatisfactoriness and no-self (anitya, duhkha, and anatman).
Arhat (Skt) *Arahant* (Pali)	A Noble One, one who is perfected and enlightened, who is freed from greed, aversion and delusion.
Bodhicitta (Skt)	The mind to enlightenment or the will to enlightenment
Bodhisattva (Skt) *Bodhisatta* (Pali)	Literally an "enlightenment being". One bent on the goal of Supreme Enlightenment, absorbed with the will to enlightenment, for the benefit of all beings. In the *Bodhisattva*, the *Bodhicitta* (the mind to enlightenment) has arisen.
Buddha (Skt and Pali)	A fully enlightened one who discovers the path to Nirvana. The Buddha is traditionally saluted as : One awakened, perfectly self-enlightened , perfected in knowledge and conduct , well gone , knower of the worlds, unsurpassed leader of men to be tamed , teacher of gods and men , the Blessed One .
Ch'an (Chn)	The Chinese transliteration of the Sanskrit word *dhyana* which means meditation. "Zen" in Japanese.

Dependent-origination	A translation of the pratitya-samutpada (Skt) or paticca-samuppada (Pali). The doctrine of dependent-coproduction and causality taught by the Buddha. Traditionally as the twelve links in the "wheel of becoming" which depict the conditioned processes of the coming-to-be and ceasing-to-be of samsaric existence.
Dharma (Skt) *Dhamma* (Pali)	The teachings of the Buddha and his enlightened disciples.
Duhkha (Skt) *Dukkha* (Pali)	Unsatisfactoriness, unease, suffering, pain or anguish.
Emptiness	Voidness or "shunyata" in Sanskrit. In the Buddhist context, it means being empty of inherent existing selfhood, empty of distinguishing marks, in the constant flux of impermanence, subject to dependent-origination.
Five Aggregates *Skandha* (Skt) *Khandha* (Pali)	Or in Sanskrit, the Five "*Skandhas*". The five constituents of the psycho-physical being that the "person" can be broken into i.e. form, feeling, perception, volitional formations and consciousness. Also applied to the constituents of phenomenal existence.
Five Hindrances	This refers to the hindrances to developing mindfulness or meditative concentration. They are: sensual craving, ill will, sloth and torpor, restless and worry, and sceptical doubt as to the correctness and efficacy of his practice.
Gongan (Chn) 公案	Literally a "public case". Refers to records of an encounter with a Ch'an master where the master gave an opportune teaching. Also used for study and meditation in the Ch'an Buddhist school

Huatou (Chn) 话头	Literally "head-of-word". Mostly a succinct single line or word derived form a *Gongan*.
Mahayana	"The Great Vehicle". A major Buddhist tradition that upholds the ideal of the *Bodhisattva* who strives for the supreme enlightenment of a Buddha and liberation for all beings. It has many sub-schools (eg. Pure Land, Ch'an, Vajrayana, etc.) and is mainly practiced in China, Tibet, Korea and Japan.
Maitri (Skt) *Metta* (Pali)	Friendliness of loving-kindness.
Mozhao (Chn) 默照	The Silent illumination meditation practice. It is an all embracing penetrative contemplation in silent stillness. The *Mozhao* method is called *shikantaza* (just sitting) in the Japanese Soto Zen School.
Mudita (Skt and Pali)	Sympathetic joy - Rejoicing in the happiness, good gains and joy of another.
Nirvana (Skt) *Nibbana* (Pali)	The enlightened state, the highest bliss, the deathless, the utter release of emancipation.
No-self *Anitya* (Skt) *Anatta* (Pali)	The doctrine of no inherent selfhood in phenomenal existence.
Paramita (Skt)	The Perfections. Refer "Perfections" below.
Perfections	The *paramita* (Skt. and Pali), as in the ten perfections that are required to be developed by the *Bodhisattva* in his quest for Buddhahood.
Prajna (Skt) *Panna* (Pali)	Transcendent wisdom. The wisdom that sees emptiness and the true nature of things.

Pratitya-samutpada (Skt) paticca-samuppada (Pali).	The Buddha's teaching of dependent-origination. Usually presented as a cycle of twelve links which characterises samsaric existence, as a continuous cycle of conditioned physical and mental processes.
Samatha (Skt and Pali)	The meditation practice of calming the mind and bringing it into a settled focus.
Samadhi (Skt & Pali)	The state of deep concentration in meditative absorption
Samsara (Skt)	The continual mundane cycle of life and death, of unsatisfactoriness and suffering, the arising of which is conditioned by ignorance and craving.
Sangha (Pali) *Samgha* (Skt)	The community of the order of monks, or more broadly the fellowship of the followers of the Buddha's teachings. The *Arya Sangha* (the Noble Assembly) refer to the Noble Ones and include the transcendent *Bodhisattva*s like Avalokitesvara and Manjusri who are enlightened or are on the irreversible path to enlightenment.
Sila (Skt & Pali)	Ethical conduct and virtuous behaviour.
Skandhas (Skt)	The aggregates as in the five aggregates. Refer to "five aggegates".
*Sutra (*Skt) *Sutta* (Pali)	Literally means a thread. A text of the Buddha's discourse or teaching of the Buddha.
Tathagata (Skt)	Literally "The thus-gone" or "one who has gone to thusness" i.e. "one who sees reality as-it-is". A term that the Buddha frequently uses when referring to himself.

Three Treasures	Or the Three Jewels: the Buddha, the *Dharma* and the *Sangha*.
Theravada	"The Doctrine of the Elders". The school of Buddhism with the Pali Canon as its doctrinal basis, widely practised in Sri Lanka and South East Asia. The path of training in the Theravada culminates in the attainment of *Arhat*-ship.
Transcendent Dependent-arising	The Buddha's teaching of the transcendence of or an arising from the mundane dependent-origination to the supramundane path. This is when the disciple develops in the Noble Eightfold Path and takes leave of being caught in the samsaric cycle that is depicted in the dependent-origination.
Vinaya	The monastic observances of the rules of training.
Vipasyana (Skt) *Vipassana* (Pali)	The meditation practice of developing insight, typically after the mind is settled and calmed with *samatha* practice.
Voidness	Refer to "Emptiness".